From Award-winning author
Denise Domning

LOST INNOCENTS

PRAISE FOR THE
SERVANT OF THE CROWN MYSTERIES

"In this Medieval mystery of stunning realism, Domning brings the English countryside alive with all the rich detail of a Bosch painting. CSI 12th century style. I can't wait to see more."
— Christina Skye, *New York Times* best-selling author of *A Highlander for Christmas*

"Pure and unapologetically Medieval ... Five solid stars."
— Kathryn LeVeque, *USA Today* best-selling author of *The Wolfe*

"Fascinating details of Medieval life"
— Catherine Kean, author of *Dance of Desire*

INTO THE WOODS

A serving girl is found in the well of a dying hamlet and the one who put her there has fled into Feckenham Forest. But the sun is setting and Sir Alain, Warwickshire's sheriff, is hunting his new Crowner. That sends Sir Faucon de Ramis and Brother Edmund, his prickly clerk, racing for a nearby abbey only to meet the man he least wishes to see at the abbey gates. Before long, Faucon finds himself riding into the dark at Sir Alain's side as they hunt for yet another lost innocent.

Other Books

Dedication

To my lost innocents, Adam and Justin.

My Apologies

My apologies to the people of Warwickshire. I have absconded with your county, added cities that don't exist and parsed your history to make it suit my needs. Outside of that, I've done my best to keep my recreation of England in the 12th Century as accurate as possible.

lost innocents

DENISE
DOMNING

LOST INNOCENTS

Copyright © Denise Domning 2016

ISBN-13: 978-1533539380
ISBN-10: 1533539383

EDITED BY: Martha Stites

COVER ART DESIGN: Denise Domning

Printed in the United States of America, First paperback edition: June, 2016

Horarium (the hours)

Matins	12:00 midnight
Lauds	3:00 A.M.
Prime	6:00 A.M.
Terce	9:00 A.M.
Sext	12:00 noon
None	3:00 P.M.
Vespers	6:00 P.M.
Compline	9:00 P.M.

St. Elizabeth's Day

The shivaree at last! Yawning, I shift in the darkened corner behind the altar where I took refuge from the rude gaiety common to this sort of event. All around this tiny church the wedding guests don cloaks or blankets as they prepare to follow the bridal couple to their bower.

Of the three dozen or so folk in attendance, everyone is drunk in celebration, if not with ale. Those who own musical instruments begin to ply them with no attempt at skill. Drums bang, pipes squeal, and bows saw across gut strings. Those lacking such noisemakers either sing at the top of their lungs or take up whatever is at hand. A metal spoon clashes on an emptied pot. Someone rattles his fingers rhythmically against a food-stained wooden platter.

The church door is flung wide as they make their exit, letting rain spatter in on a gust of cold air. Dying torches flare as they draw their first full breath in hours, leaping back into fiery life. For one brief instant the plastered walls of the sanctuary seem to writhe, alive with dancing shadows. Then out the door everyone goes, moving in a undulating line that waves like a hound's tail, taking their cacophony with them.

More's the pity for any soul in this vale who expects to sleep any longer tonight. The wedding guests will surround the couple's bower and maintain their noise for as long as they can bear the weather. They seek to distract the groom from performing his duty, which is to turn the holy words of the marriage vows into a

11

grin.

His voice echoes in me, chiding me for my doubt. Thy will, not mine, I respond to my Holy Master. Although the tender sits upright, she is sound asleep, as lost in her dreams as those she should be tending.

Still smiling, I eye the colorful gaggle of children on the floor before me. What a pretty image they make in the oily yellow light of the torches. They lie like pups, curled and piled one upon the other. From infants to those owning a half-dozen years, their limbs are relaxed and mouths open, save one little lad who sucks his thumb.

My gaze comes to rest on the one revealed to me as His, the one I was beckoned here to fetch. But of course she sleeps on the far edge of the group, closest to the door, her back to the others. Even in the uncertain and shifting light her golden-red hair gleams with that otherworldly glow I've come to recognize as His touch. As I watch, the illumination grows until it circles her whole body. Oh aye, she is beloved by Him, chosen for His special purpose.

The girl is the best dressed among the babes, her tunic made of a fine green wool, as it would be. Until recently her mother was one of the leading wives in their home village. Despite myself, compassion stirs in my heart for her daring dam. Here is one woman who will grieve mightily in her daughter's absence when she should be rejoicing that her Lord cherishes her child above so many others.

I circle around the sleeping watcher, then skirt the group to kneel beside His chosen lass. Again I hesitate, as sinful doubts once more consume me. This moment is the true test of my mission. If I am wrong, if my faith had been misplaced all these years and what I do—have done—is the most heinous of sins, then the child will surely awaken and call out in alarm.

Bracing my heart, I begin to chant the words of my prayer, doing so inwardly, praying not for myself, but for this child and all the future lasses who might be denied their heavenly home should I fail.

I ease my hand beneath the slumbering girl. She stirs, her foot moving until it touches the babe sleeping next to her. He groans sweetly in his sleep. I send a muttered blessing his way and wait until he settles.

Then closing my eyes, barely daring to fill my lungs, I gently shift my arms beneath her. She murmurs. I wait until her breathing is even once again, then lift her until she rests against my breast. With a sigh, she drapes herself bonelessly over my shoulder.

Her weight is greater than I expect. I stagger back a step as I balance her in my arms. A moment passes, then another and still she doesn't awaken. My heart takes flight. Blessed am I to be His most faithful and true servant.

Rearranging my cloak to shield the sleeping girl from the rain and sharp night air, I tread as lightly as I can to the church door. With a push of my foot, the heavy panel opens just enough to let me ease into the gap. I slip outside and carry another of His maids into the darkness. As the panel shuts behind us, it takes all my will not to sing out prayers of thanksgiving as we go.

Chapter One

"**G**awne lad, this is taking too long. Let us bring you out," the smith shouted into the well, his tone pleading.

Although the man's wild mane of fair hair and thick graying beard concealed much of his face, worry filled what could be seen of his strong features. His fists were clenched around the ropes that connected his youngest son to the world outside the watery shaft, his forge-scarred knuckles white.

He stood bare-chested under this day's weak sun, his leather apron having been converted into the sling that supported his son in the well. Still wearing their own leather gear, the smith's elder sons, dark- haired and already taller than their sire, were aligned behind him. These two, their appearance neater than that of their father, held fast to the same hempen lines as he, in case something should go awry. All three men wore their workaday attire, well-singed leather chausses to cover their legs and charred wooden sabots on their feet. Healed burns marked their burly forearms and their bare chests where their leather aprons hadn't protected them; these men chose to preserve their shirts rather than their skin.

Gathered in this clearing hewn from Feckenham Forest and separated from the deer by the pale—here, that separation being both tall wooden fencing and thick stands of holly trimmed into a wall—were the villeins of Wike. All had put aside the usual tasks they owed their lady in her fields and orchards to watch one of their own as she exited her watery grave. At their smith's call, the older folk among the watching serfs all ceased their impatient muttering to attend the doings around their well. Not so the youngsters. Wearing rough homespun dyed in shades of acorn brown, mossy green, or chestnut yellow, the children made good use of these carefree moments, chasing a few dogs around a sunbathing sow and her soon-to- be slaughtered piglets. Their play set a small flock of chickens to squawking and flapping as they escaped the activity.

Only one soul among the fifty or so families of Wike hadn't joined the watchers. Yet standing outside the kitchen shed, a structure larger than the miserable manor house beside it, was the dead girl's mistress. Wide of waist and wearing gowns the cheerful shade of beetroot, the old woman stood with her head bowed and her hands folded as if in prayer. Her white braids were uncovered, proudly naming her never married. That was an uncommon thing for any female in a place such as this, but especially for one of her age.

"Leave be, Da!" the lad in the well cried up to his sire. His words echoed hollowly into the air above the shaft. Coughing, he splashed in water that could take him as easily as it had the unfortunate lass. "I won't come up until I can bring Jes with me."

"Brave lad," murmured Sir Faucon de Ramis, the shire's new Coronarius, the man responsible for discerning the murdered from those who departed this Earthly vale due to accident or in happy answer to the Lord God's call. One thing was certain. When it came to water, that boy had more courage than his Crowner, as the commoners were coming to pronounce Faucon's title. He'd rather die an embarrassing death on the edge of the sheriff's sword than face drowning in a well.

Gawne had volunteered to do the dangerous deed of retrieving the drowned girl's body after the well proved too deep for any ladder from either the manor's barns or the nearby homes. When the smith sought to dissuade his son, the boy argued that the dead girl had been a friend and he could do no less for her. Then, with a boldness beyond his age, he pointed to the manor's overgrown fish pond and reminded all the adults within hearing that he swam better than anyone in Wike. When that still didn't convince his father, Gawne had added that he was both small enough to maneuver within the narrow shaft, and strong enough to do what must be done.

At that, all the smith's neighbors shouted for his father to agree. They wanted the use of the well, and that meant the corpse had to come out. So down the lad had gone, his father's leather apron and a web of ropes his only guarantee of returning to the bosom of his earthly family.

There was another spate of splashing in the shaft. "There's only one more knot to tighten. She's almost ready," Gawne called, wheezing again, his words punctuated with the echo of his chattering teeth.

"Almost ready," Faucon's clerk repeated sarcastically in his native French. "I doubt that."

Brother Edmund stood beside his employer, his hands braced on the waist-high stone wall that encircled the well. The clerk's black Benedictine habit wore spots of the same ruddy Warwickshire mud that spattered Faucon's surcoat and chain mail. Last night's storm had turned this morning's journey to the nearby village of Studley into a filthy plod.

It had taken longer to reach this corner of their shire than it had to resolve the death of one of Studley's wealthiest farmers. As it turned out the man had returned unexpectedly from a horse fair to discover his wife in bed with her lover and had been killed in the fight that ensued. Within an hour of Faucon's arrival, he'd called the jury so they could render the verdict of death felonious, then called for the arrest of the woman's lover.

After sharing a tasty but meager midday meal with the canons of the local priory, Faucon and Edmund then spent a pleasant hour appraising the lover's home and chattel, that being the true purpose behind the creation of his position at the Michaelmas court just past. It was now Faucon's duty to set the fee England's king received for the man's wrongdoing, based on the value of the accused's estate. What would profit King Richard left both the killer's family and Sir Alain, Warwickshire's sheriff, poorer. The arrested man's kin had offered Faucon treasure in trade for a lower appraisal only to have their new Crowner spurn what their sheriff would have accepted.

Edmund's well-made face twisted in impatience under his circle of carefully trimmed dark hair as he launched into his complaint. "More than an hour we've been here, waiting as they tried this crook or that ladder, now a boy on a rope. They shouldn't have called for us to come until after they'd gotten her out. It's not ours to retrieve the body, but theirs."

"Retrieval is their duty," Faucon agreed with a casual shrug, "but I thought the law required that they leave the body where it is until we arrive?"

The monk ignored the question—they both knew that answer well enough—and gave a disgusted shake of his head as he continued to prosecute his complaint. "This is but another child's accidental death, and only a girl child at that. Why are we wasting our time? There can be no profit for our king here, only our Church. Command me to note the servant's orphan status and that she drowned, then you can declare the well deodand. Once you've done that, we can be on our way home."

Faucon grimaced. Far too many youthful deaths had already been inscribed on his clerk's ever-lengthening parchment roll. Until Faucon stepped into his newly-created position three sennights ago, he'd taken little note of how often and easily children died. Why, in this past week alone they'd added yet two more babes to their list, three if he included this unexamined girl.

The first had been an infant who crawled into the household fire pit while his admittedly young and careless mother had stepped outside their home to visit with friends. It proved a terrible tragedy but not murder, despite the claims of the child's great-grandfather who, it turned out, despised not only his granddaughter-by-marriage but her whole family. The second was a boy who died by falling from a tree. The grieving mother had raised the hue and cry, charging murder on the part of her child's playmates. But all those who witnessed the event attested that her son had been trying to follow the older children onto the next higher branch when he'd lost his grip.

Edmund was right about this death, though. If the well became deodand, their king saw no profit. Instead, whatever priest or prior was connected to this place would collect a fee from the residents to bless the manor's water source, removing the stain of murder from it.

What was likely here in Wike hadn't proved true for the other two childish deaths this week. Just as there was a price to pay for doing rape, burglary, or killing another, fines could be levied for bringing false charges or wrongly raising the hue and cry.

"For shame, Brother Edmund," Faucon chided quietly as he glanced at the folk around the well. "If you must complain, at least lower your voice."

His rebuke only provoked a rude sound from the monk, the disrespectful reaction one Faucon had come to know too well over their brief acquaintance. Edmund was incapable of deference. Faucon suspected this character flaw was why the monk found himself banished from his convent and clerking for Warwickshire's first and only Servant of the Crown.

"Why?" Edmund shot back, although he did lower his voice. "I doubt there's anyone in this rustic place who speaks our tongue other than their bailiff, who's not here just now to overhear. And he's barely fluent." As the lad had descended into the well, the hamlet's headman had excused himself, saying he needed to feed his stock and promising to return soon.

"Nor is there any priest here who might know a word of our tongue," Edmund continued. The wave of his hand indicated the flimsy mud-and-manure homes used by those whose lives were forever chained to this place. "I saw nothing church-like as we rode past yon cottages. Nor do I see anything resembling a chapel within this demesne. Hardly a surprise, as impoverished as the place is."

This time, when the jerk of Edmund's head indicated the manor house, Faucon shrugged to concede that point. Save for its barns, outbuildings and the amount of land attached to it, the manor house looked much like the homes it ruled, save that, unlike the other dwellings, it was poorly tended. Its thatch was rotted while moss and more stained its plastered exterior. The stone foundation that raised it a little above ground level was moldy.

"Rustic this place might be, but even if you're correct that no one understands you, I say again, for shame," Faucon once more chided his clerk, still keeping his voice low. "Although these are naught but uncouth serfs and it's only an orphaned serving girl in the well, their lives and her death deserve our respect."

That sent Edmund's brows high upon his forehead

as his dark eyes widened. "You mistake me," he protested, this time matching his master's quiet tone. "I mean no disrespect to you or them. All I wish to point out is that by the time the lad manages to knot the ropes around the girl's corpse, if he manages it," the monk emphasized, "I doubt there'll be light enough for me to note even these few names when we call them to view the body." Although he gestured toward the crowd, the movement was meant to include only the men and boys over twelve years of age among the watchers.

"Let them do what they can to retrieve the child tonight while we ride for home. We can return on the morrow when the sun and I will both be fresh," he insisted.

Faucon read the longing in Edmund's tone. Over the three weeks the monk had served Faucon, they had been on the move across the shire on a daily basis. Nor was there any indication their pace of travel might change. Edmund's demotion had cost him what he prized most—the comfort of familiar walls around him as well as the regularity of a learned brother's daily routine.

However, the monk was right about the light. Faucon glanced heavenward. Day was fading, its oncoming death promising to tint the thin and ragged clouds, remnants of the previous night's storm.

But unlike his clerk, who had groaned at the thought of a second investigation in one day, Faucon couldn't have been more grateful when the bailiff of Wike sought them out just as they were departing Studley. Warwickshire wasn't like his home county, where villages and hamlets were so many that they often shared boundaries, and fought over them. Here, there could be long stretches of untended wastes between this place and that settlement. Such emptiness offered excellent opportunities for an ambush.

Five days ago, Sir Alain, who had more than mone-
tary reasons for wanting to rid himself of his new
Keeper of the Pleas, had sent men in secret to end
Faucon's life. Although the assassins had failed, their
failure wasn't their sheriff's. Now, each time Faucon
departed the stone walls of his new home in Blacklea,
he did so fully armed against the certainty of another
attempt.

The worst of it was that Sir Alain almost always
knew where to find his new Coronarius. By long custom, folk with a corpse in need of viewing reported to
their sheriff. It was Sir Alain who sent them on to
Blacklea and Faucon, just as he'd done this morning
with the soldier from Studley Keep.

As much as Faucon despised playing the rabbit to
Alain's fox, without a small army of his own there was
no way to escape that role. Unfortunately, he lacked the
coin necessary to hire either a trained knight or the four
or five common soldiers he'd like to keep at his back.
That left him looking for what his purse could tolerate—one experienced mercenary to ride with him.
Finding such a man was no easy task. Nor was entrust-
ing his life to a stranger who wasn't honor- bound to
him, one whose allegiance was guaranteed only by the
silver Faucon was able to put into his purse.

Faucon shook his head as he eyed Edmund. "Even
if the lad fails to bring the girl up before dark, we won't
be returning to our own beds this night. We're farther
from home than you think, Brother, given that beast of
yours."

Once again Faucon avoided the explanation that
was Edmund's due. Only two men knew of the sheriff's
attack, and his clerk wasn't one of them. At least there
was no need to lie. The monk's donkey was a headstrong creature who kept to his meandering pace no
matter the goad.

Edmund opened his mouth to protest. Faucon raised a forestalling hand. The monk's mouth snapped shut. It was a gratifying reaction, as it didn't often happen.

"Why should we ride all that way to Priors Holden and Blacklea only to turn around and repeat our journey come dawn?" Faucon continued. "Perhaps the bailiff is permitted to offer us the use of yon house for the night. If he cannot, I'll wager Sir Peter's steward will open the door to his keep in Studley for us," Faucon added. "Or, if taking your rest with soldiers and servants doesn't suit you, perhaps you can stay at the priory there."

That teased a second rude sound from Edmund. His clerk aimed his gaze back into the well's depths as he spoke. "Bad enough that we had to share bread with that rude bunch this day. Did you not see that house? Profligate and lacking in discipline, commoners coming and going! Nay, I'll not sleep with them," he said harshly, then huffed in irritation as he gave way.

"So be it. I can see you're set on remaining in this area for the night. Just know that I won't be resting my head with the rats or whatever other vermin surely infest this rustic place," he said in scorn. "Why should I, when I can instead take comfort and find peace within a house of my own order in Alcester? The town is just a little to the south, perhaps no more than two miles from here," the monk explained for Faucon's benefit, his employer being new to this shire. "If my brothers don't have space in their guest house for you, Alcester is a market town. The folk there are accustomed to opening their homes to strangers for a penny or two. Perhaps you can find an alewife willing to rent you her bed and feed you as well," he finished.

As the thought of food and drink stirred Faucon's stomach to wishing, he nodded at Edmund's suggestion. "Alcester it is. Not that it matters to me where we stay. Nor do I care how long it takes to complete our task. Even if the girl in the well was only an orphan without a penny to her name, I'll remain in this corner of the shire until we've done our duty to her and our king."

His comment teased a strangled sound from the monk. It took Faucon an instant to recognize the noise as a laugh, the first he'd ever heard from his clerk. When Edmund lifted his head, the narrow-eyed look he sent his employer was definitely amused. Faucon watched in astonishment as his usually humorless clerk offered him a tight-lipped smile.

"Ah, the truth will out," Edmund said. "I say your pride was piqued when the bailiff flagged us down, asking for you by name. That's why you came here even though you knew his request for your attention was premature. I think me that's why you're determined to stay. You're savoring the experience. Never mind that it was Studley's prior who told him your name and that he should seek you out instead of the sheriff."

Despite himself and his worries, Faucon gave a quiet laugh. "I'll admit that it was a pleasant surprise when we're barely known in this place."

Barely known, but becoming better recognized daily, God be praised. The sooner folk stopped going first to Sir Alain before they came to their new Servant of the Crown, the better for Faucon's health.

Edmund's mockery of amusement faded as swiftly as it had appeared, his expression flattening into its usual emotionless mold. "As you will. We stay," he said as if he were the one with the right to decide the matter. Then he gave another disgusted shake of his head. "All this for a girl child, and only a kitchen lass at that."

As if responding to the monk's final complaint, Gawne's hollow cry echoed up out of the well. "She's ready. Pull her up."

His voice broke in the middle of his call, sliding up a notch. Faucon wondered if this was a testament to his age or the effect of the cold well water.

"Nay, you must come first," his father commanded.

"Da, the ropes are wet and it's so dark down here I can't see to know if I'm knotting properly," his son countered impatiently, his voice piercing the stillness. There was a short spate of coughing, Gawne's reaction to breathing air he'd earlier remarked smelled strange. The lad continued when he caught his breath. "If she slides free, I'll only have to come back down and try again. Nay, take Jes first so I can be her guide as you raise her." This time when the lad's voice broke Faucon heard grief for his friend.

The smith's white-knuckled grip on the hempen lines relented not a whit. Still shaking his head in silent refusal, he looked across the well at the three villeins responsible for the ropes the boy had tied around the corpse. Like most of their neighbors, they wore tunics stained with dried mud. Their bare legs and feet were caked in heavy red earth. It suggested that despite the wet, the manor's gardens were being prepared for garlic, what with the day for planting it now at hand.

Although each man stood ready, his rope wrapped once around his wrist for security, his grip steady and strong, none of them moved. The man nearest the smith lifted his brows. "What say you, Ivo? If you want to raise your son first, you should do it." There was more than a hint of disapproval in his voice, no doubt born out of the smith's meek reaction to a rude retort from one of his children.

Ivo hesitated. His elder son, who stood closest to him, touched his father's back without releasing his hold on the ropes that connected him to his youngest brother. "Don't do it, Da. You've heard our Gawne this day. This is his to do and he's proud to do it. If we ignore his command, you'll but prove him right about us always making a child of him when he is child no longer," he warned quietly.

The smith's shoulders slumped in defeat. "Bring her up, Rob," he told the farmer, "but be swift and sure about it, knowing that my heart won't cease its trembling until my boy is once more safe in my arms."

Ivo let his grip relax just a little, so his youngest son could maneuver as he would around the rising corpse. There was a dull thud in the well as the boy hit the side of the shaft, followed by a quiet grunt. At that same instant, the three serfs put their backs into their work. Born from long habit and intimate knowledge, they matched each other pull for pull, doing so without word or sign.

As the watching folk saw something at last happening at the well, they dropped into an tense quiet. Even the children and dogs ceased their play. Within an instant, the only sounds in the demesne were the pleased grunting of the sunbathing hogs and the distant steady ring of a small bell. Its tone was of the sort worn by a bellwether, suggesting some villein's sheep were on the move.

A few of the youngsters pushed their way closer to the well. Following them came a gray-haired oldster who didn't stop until he stood at the forefront of the crowd. This rustic was wrinkled of face and bent of posture. Twiglets and bits of dried leaves were tangled in his white beard and the long thin strands of hair that escaped his torn hood. His tattered green tunic and faded brown chausses, even his rough hempen purse, were held together by layer upon layer of patches. Given his ragged appearance, the plain but slightly worn leather shoes upon the old man's feet were unexpected.

"Hold a moment! She's swinging," the boy called in

warning from the watery depths, his voice echoing into the new stillness around the well. "Da, pull me up a bit so I can steady her."

As the farmers and the smiths responded to Gawne's commands, Faucon leaned against the well's surround, intending to grab the girl if they were able to bring her high enough. There was yet nothing to see in the depths save inky darkness.

When the boy called that the men could again haul on their lines, Faucon watched the ropes shift and tug. Another quiet thud echoed in the shaft, again the sound of flesh contacting with stone. No reaction followed, saying that it was the one beyond all earthly complaint who hit the wall this time.

Then the corpse rose into the first reaches of this day's hazy light. The girl had already grown stiff in death, or so said the rigid way she hung in her bindings. Beneath the long dark hair that streamed across her torso, the bare skin of her back and legs gleamed a pearly white.

That brought Faucon upright with a start. He shifted swiftly from side to side, eying the area around the well. There wasn't so much as a discarded head scarf in view. What child stripped before accidentally plunging into a well with a waist-high surround, then floated in the tight space of this shaft as if she'd died abed?

None, that's what.

With that, the joy of the hunt overtook him, only to depart as swiftly as it had arrived. His trail began with the one who had directed his neighbors to look in the well for the girl, and there it ended. There was no hunting to be done here. He would ask two simple questions, both of which had equally simple answers, and then call the jury. Faucon sighed in disappointment and once more braced himself against the surrounding wall.

"What were you looking for?" Edmund asked, yet speaking their native tongue.

"Discarded clothing," he replied, stretching downward to curl a hand around the dead girl's nearest arm. As always, the strange sensation of soft, still-yielding skin over death-hardened tissue startled him, and this lass's skin was even softer than usual, what with her having spent time in the water.

"Why? You knew there was nothing around the well," Edmund said. "If there had been, we would have seen it when we first arrived, and you would have asked me to note it."

"And so I wished to reconfirm," Faucon said as he pulled the girl's cold and dripping corpse over the surround. He grunted in surprise. She was heavier than he anticipated considering her slight form.

Only then did Edmund notice the child's lack of attire. "You didn't say she was unclothed!"

As the villeins closest to the well also noticed this lurid detail, the news became a rumbling mutter in the quiet ward, passing from mouth to mouth. Faucon made his clerk no reply as he stepped back to give the smiths room to work.

Immediately, Ivo the Smith cried "Pull!" to his sons and they began to raise their kinsman.

With Edmund following, Faucon moved a little distance from the working smiths. Dropping to one knee, he laid the corpse face-down on sod warmer than she, then leaned back a little to eye her. As he'd already noted, she lay as if she'd died abed, legs outstretched but slightly bent, arms close to her. That, alone, guaranteed she'd died elsewhere and been put into the well after the fact. Her head was turned a little to the side, not quite resting on one cheek.

Clearing the lass's hair off her back to expose the

knotted ropes, he paused in pity. The half-healed crisscrossing marks of a viciously plied switch cut into her from shoulders to midsection, with bruises of about the same age laid atop them. The villeins who'd hauled her out of the well also noticed the marks. Shifting uneasily, they whispered between themselves, the one called Rob muttering that they should never have agreed to give her to someone they knew had so harsh a hand and merciless a disposition.

Edmund crouched on the opposite side of the corpse. "May our Lord have mercy on her," the monk whispered, crossing himself. "At least she's at peace now, and beyond all pain."

"Indeed," Faucon agreed, still lost in his inspection.

The girl's back had that unnatural red color that said she'd rested face-up for a time after her death. That surely hadn't been near the well or any place within this hamlet's bounds, else she'd have been discovered before she went into the well. What purpose was there in putting her into the shaft after she was dead?

Opening the last knot, he rolled the girl face up. Her dark wet hair fell like a sheet across her face. Sweeping aside the sodden mass, he breathed out in appreciation. Despite that her skin had a faint greenish tinge, a hue given to those who had been dead for more than a day, she'd been a beautiful child, with a perfect oval face, narrow nose, and a mouth that still owned a sweet curve even in death.

The shape of her torso and gentle roundness of her budding breasts said she'd been rapidly making her way into womanhood, even though Ivo had said she owned but a dozen years. Not that a woman's age or the maturity of her body had any bearing on the sort of trauma Faucon suspected this girl had suffered prior to her death. There were some men for whom a female of any age could be used and discarded after.

One eye, blue in color, was partially open. Faucon pried up its lid until he saw what he expected to find—the cloudy line that proved she hadn't drowned, but had instead lain in a dry place for some time. But also in that orb and on her face was a bloody tracery that he recognized, one that told the true tale of her last moments.

Clearing her hair from her throat, he found the marks he sought. As he stretched his hands across the slender column of her neck, he matched his fingertips to the bruises left behind by the one who had ended her life. A set of hands around the size of his own, neither overly large nor overly small, judging by the placement of his fingers.

"Holy Mother!" Edmund breathed as he understood the meaning of his employer's actions. "She did not drown." The monk looked at Faucon, his eyes wide. "My pardon. You were right to insist that we remain here instead of riding for home. What if, when she'd come to light on the morrow, these marks had been too faded for you to read? You might have missed the trail that leads to the one who did this horrible deed."

Faucon gaped at his clerk. A jest, a laugh, and an apology all on the same day! It was too much to be believed.

That ringing sheep's bell was almost upon them now. A woman shrieked from the back of the crowd. "Aaiye! Don't touch me! Look out, stand back! She's making her way to the well!"

Of a sudden, men and women scattered, crying out as they leapt this way and that. The dogs barked and snarled at the unexpected activity. Squealing, the sow and her brood fled, adding to the chaos.

Faucon came to his feet. It was no animal that came. Instead, a cloaked woman drove through the crowd, racing straight toward him, ringing the bell in her left hand while she whipped the staff in her right from side to side to clear the way.

There was no need. No one, Faucon included, wanted to make contact with a leper.

Chapter Two

"**M**ary save me! Jessimond! My baby," the leper cried as she neared the well and saw the girl's corpse.

Faucon staggered back, stumbling into the three men who'd brought no orphan, but Jessimond the Leper's Daughter out of the watery darkness. The three were also on the move, retreating from potential contagion.

With a womanish shriek, Edmund started to rise only to slip on the wet turf. He fell back to sitting as the leper dropped to her knees next to him. As the panting monk scooted crab-like away from her, the smith's older sons shifted swiftly around the well until they stood opposite the diseased woman, releasing their ropes as they went.

Those same ropes hung loosely from Ivo's fingers as he stood frozen, his gaze locked on the leper's hooded face while a dripping Gawne hung over the stone surround, half-in, half-out of the well. That was too close to drowning for Faucon's comfort. The linked metal rings of his mail tunic jingling, he darted around the leper and grabbed the lad by the back of his apron sling. Hauling Gawne with him, he retreated until he felt they were beyond any chance contact with the diseased woman.

The leper paid no heed to the desperate sidling going on around her. She dropped her staff and bell, then gathered her daughter's earthly remains into her arms. With the girl's wet body staining her swathing robes, she bowed her cloaked head to rest her brow against Jessimond's cold cheek. There the leper stayed, sobbing as she rocked her rigid child in her arms.

For that brief instant her grief was the only sound in this grassy vale. Then the startled serfs forgot their fear of contagion and closed ranks. Every one of them began to shout for her to be gone, shaking fist or finger. Within the space of a breath their cries became the steady chant of "Leave us!"

Clutching her rigid child close, her face yet concealed by her oversized hood, the woman swiveled on her knees in their direction. "You dare order me away!?" she shrieked. "You have no right, not after you betrayed me. I gave her into your care. Every one of you swore an oath to treat her as if she were one of your own. How did you repay my trust? With her death!" she shouted in accusation.

"Enough all of you, but especially you, Amelyn," bellowed the bailiff of Wike from the back of the crowd. As tall as Faucon, broad-shouldered, with powerful arms, his scalp showing through wisps of dark hair, this was the villein who ruled his peers at their lady's command.

An instant and uneasy quiet fell over the folk he ruled, one fraught with a strange tension. Men and women alike turned to watch as their headman moved toward the well. When he passed them, his neighbors shifted as far back from him as they had from the leper.

The bailiff stopped a fair distance from the well and Jessimond's grieving mother. Dressed in sober brown almost the same shade as his graying beard, his face was thin and long.

"Amelyn, by coming here this day you have broken the vow you gave us and our lady when she sent you to live at the hospital two years ago. Leave now and I will forgive your intrusion. Stay, and I'll see that you pay the full price for your disobedience," he called in warning, his voice raised so all could hear him.

Amelyn the Leper turned her hooded gaze on the bailiff. "This is my child and only I will bury her. If you want me gone, Odger, you'll have to carry me out of Wike," she retorted in warning, her voice yet thick with tears.

"Jessimond is your child no longer," Odger shot back, his tone harsh. "You gave her into our care, ceding all claim to her after our lady bought your pension. On that day you promised to never again bring your contagion here to threaten us and our children. Leave us now," he again commanded her. "We will wash and bury Jessimond in your stead, as you agreed then, and as is right and proper."

Rather than argue with him, Amelyn gently set her daughter's body on the ground. Her former neighbors watched in anxious silence as she combed her gloved fingers through Jessimond's dark hair, straightening the wet tresses around her child's still face. When the leper was satisfied with the results, she came to her feet, proving she was taller than most of those around her. Her water-stained gray cloak fell in graceful folds around her as she scanned the crowd, or so said the movement of her hooded head. The quiet stretched. When she owned the complete attention of all in the bailey, the leper made a show of lifting her staff until she held it like a cudgel.

"Never," she snarled, "not even if the lady retracts my pension and I die bereft of comfort on some distant verge. There's not one among you I would allow to touch my babe, not after this. I was a fool to give up the child I loved to folk who failed to protect me when I needed it. I, of all people, should have realized your vows to care for her would be empty. Well, I'm a fool no longer. Only I will tend my daughter, and I'll do it despite any of you!"

With that, she dashed into the crowd, her staff swinging. Folk within reach of her and her makeshift club fell back, crying out. They tumbled over each other as they sought to escape. She whirled, her cloak opening. Beneath it she wore faded gray gowns a little too short for her, revealing bare ankles above worn cloth shoes. Hidden beneath her swathing cloak, her long hair was unbound and the same deep brown color as her daughter's.

Staff held high, she menaced those in the other direction. Again, folk screamed and retreated in panic, knocking into others. All, save for the ragged rustic. The ancient in his patched attire held his place and watched the chaos around him. Beneath his wild snowy brows, his pale eyes were alight with perverse amusement.

Content that her point was made, Amelyn the Leper retreated to where Jessimond lay. She straddled her child's body and spread her arms wide. "I curse you, each and every one, for betraying your oath to care for my daughter, and for my Jessimond's death! May the Devil take you all!" she shouted.

Shrieking in fear, mothers caught their children by the hands and fled, singing out prayers and making signs with their fingers as they went. Their menfolk did the same, racing for the safety of their own homes as if woven withe walls were enough to protect them from the denizens of Hell. As they went, a few among the men dared return Amelyn's curse with their own. Empty words, so proved by how swiftly they overtook their wives along Wike's twisting pathways.

At the well, the three villeins who'd brought Jessimond back into the light abandoned their ropes, departing as swiftly as their fellows. So too, had the smith's elder sons started to flee, only to pause when they noticed their sire hadn't followed. Instead, Ivo stood as if he were rooted, his gaze locked upon Amelyn.

Now shivering in both cold and fear, Gawne threw off his Crowner's embrace to leap to his sire's side. The boy buried his head against his father's chest as if that might protect him from the leper's hex. Edmund speedily touched shoulders, forehead and heart, then unwound his beads from his waist and began to pray.

Faucon considered both their reactions unwarranted. If Gawne had been Jessimond's friend, then he was someone Amelyn wouldn't wish to harm. As for Edmund, the leper knew neither her new Crowner nor his clerk. Faucon didn't think she meant to include them in her curse.

"Cowards! Idiots! Nothing this lewd wretch says can have any power over you," Odger threw angrily after his frightened folk. "Come back, all of you!"

His tone said he expected their immediate compliance. If so, he was disappointed. No man or woman turned. The sounds of doors closing and bars dropping began to fill the air.

That brought Odger around, his angry glare focused on the leper. His arms were tense and his fists held tight. "Spew your foul nonsense as you will, Amelyn. You can't frighten me, not when I know you for who you are. Nor does any word you speak change matters. Jessimond is no less dead and you no longer have any right to be here. Be gone with you. Return to Saltisford from whence you came."

Almost as tall as he, Amelyn drew her shoulders to a proud angle. "When you banished me from Wike, Odger, you freed me from all the bonds that once imprisoned me here. I no longer bow my head to you, and you no longer have the right to command me," she retorted, then threw her challenge a second time. "You want me gone? Come lift me in your arms. Carry me to the cross and the Warwick Path. If you can do that, I'll return to Saltisford as you wish."

Faucon waited until she fell silent before speaking. "Bailiff, the leper may not yet depart," he said, using the commoner's tongue, one he'd learned at his nurse's knee and liked as well as his own, even if his command of it was less than perfect. "She must remain here until I am ready to ask my questions of her."

Aye, and there was one question Faucon needed answered more than any other. If Amelyn now resided in Saltisford, how was it she came to be in Wike at exactly the right moment to say farewell to her murdered daughter?

The rustic and the smiths gawked at him as they heard the tongue of England's commoners issue from the lips of a man whose black hair and dark eyes proclaimed that his ancestors had come with the Conqueror so long ago. Then their gazes shifted to Odger. Once again Faucon sensed that odd tension. It suggested that the bailiff wasn't well liked by those he ruled.

As for Odger, gone was any trace of the congenial, deferential servant who had humbly begged his Crowner to witness the retrieval of a drowned girl and declare her death an accident. In his place stood a haughty, defiant man who jealously guarded the power he claimed in his lady's name, and the control that gave him over his peers.

"You may not countermand me, Sir Crowner," the headman snapped. "This is not my will but my lady's. As her agent, I am sworn to do my duty by her, and so I shall despite you."

Then Odger sneered at Amelyn. "Moreover, I cannot imagine what questions you could have for this degraded creature. She knows nothing of her daughter's life since we sent her from Wike, much less anything about Jessimond's death. How could she, when she's lived far from us for the past years?"

Faucon raised his brows at the man's proud rebuke. "Refuse me on pain of royal fine, one that can be levied against you as well as every family in this place. Your lady will pay as well," he warned.

As always, Edmund couldn't resist intruding where he had no right to tread. Finger wagging, he chided Odger in his own accented English. "Fie on you, commoner. You cannot defy Sir Faucon in this. You and your lady are law- and oath-bound to assist your king's servant in this matter, doing so in whatever manner he requests. Any man or woman to whom he poses questions must reply with answers that are honest and true, else face the wrath of the royal court."

Odger glanced from clerk to knight. "My lady will have no leper here," he spat out, "especially not this one. If you wish to ask questions of this wretch, you'll do it away from Wike and the decent folk who reside here. Retreat with her to Coctune, or even as far as Studley. Or better yet," he paused to aim another narrow-eyed glance at the becloaked woman, the corner of his mouth curling. "Let her lead you to Alcester. She knows that place well enough, having whored there until she took ill. I say it was in punishment for her lewdness that our Lord afflicted her with her contagion."

Amelyn didn't respond to the bailiff's jab. Instead, she shifted toward Faucon, her hooded head bowed and her gloved hands hidden by the hems of her long sleeves. "Ask what questions you will, sir knight, and I will tell you the truth, the only truth worth knowing," she replied, her voice rising with every word even as it quavered with tears. "I will tell you that the folk who live here are murderous liars and abusers who have caused my precious child to kill herself."

Then she shifted until she faced the kitchen shed with its domed oven. "Do you hear that, Meg?" she shouted. "It's you I accuse above all others. Your cruelty toward my child killed her as surely as if you pushed her into this well."

Faucon shot a startled glance at the old woman in the cheery red garments, having forgotten her. Spurred to it by Amelyn's charge, this Meg started toward the well at a clipped and angry pace, her white braids snapping from side to side as she came. Behind her, the kitchen door opened and a youth of no more than a score of years eased through the portal to step into the yard. He looked like a beggar, what with large ears jutting through his knotted mop of dark hair and a patchy, untrimmed beard covering half of his overly-long face. There was something wrong, something womanish and weak-jointed, about the way he held himself.

"You dare to chide me, leper!" Meg snarled in reply to Amelyn's charge, as she came to a halt beside Odger, her arms akimbo. Her narrow face was tight in rage, her dark eyes bare slits. In that instant bailiff and cook looked like kin, not in their features but in their angry stances and harsh attitudes.

"Have a care with what you say, or I'll make you pay a price for your slander," Meg spat at the leper. "Odger has taken his lash to you once for fornication. If you persist, I'll see that he does it again despite your disease, to punish you for lying."

"Now Meg, have pity," Ivo said, at last bestirring himself out of his surprise over the leper's arrival. "Amelyn is distraught, as any parent would be upon losing a child."

Then Ivo looked at the leper. "As for you, Amelyn, calm yourself and think about the words you use." Unlike Odger, whose tone boldly proclaimed his dislike for the diseased woman, the smith's voice was tempered with gentle affection. "If you persist with your accusations, you may well doom Jes to be wrongly buried in unhallowed ground. We all know she didn't kill herself. Gawne told us."

Having shed his web of ropes and leather apron in the last moments, Gawne now clung to his father's side, shivering in his wet clothing. His sire pried him off, then gave his youngest a light push until the boy stood out in front of him.

"Tell Amelyn, son. Ease her heart. Tell her how you saw Jes fall into the well. Tell her how her daughter's drowning is nothing more than an terrible accident."

That brought Faucon's sharp attention onto the smith, as he wondered how any man could see an accident when he looked upon the dead girl's unclothed and bruised body.

Emotions flashed across Gawne's face as he glanced from Jessimond's bare corpse to her mother, then he shot a swift glance at his Crowner. Although their gazes met for only the space of a breath, that was long enough. The boy's cheeks flared with the color of uncomfortably held secrets, the spots vivid against his cold-whitened skin.

As Gawne looked away, he protested, "Da, I never said I saw Jes fall into the well." Again his voice slid up into the painful squeak that marked a boy's transition into manhood.

Ivo frowned at his son. "But did you not call out to us all that Jessimond was in the well?"

"And Gawne was right, she was in the well," Faucon interrupted. More than anything, he didn't want the lad spewing just now whatever it was he withheld, not here where the wrong person might overhear. But preventing that meant revealing some of what Faucon had learned thus far, doing so much earlier than he liked.

41

"Bailiff, Jessimond did not enter your well of her own volition nor did she drown. She was already with our Lord when someone placed her corpse into this shaft," he said, carefully parsing his words as he watched those around him.

There was no reading Amelyn's face, not when it was concealed beneath her oversized hood. Ivo and his older sons appeared surprised by their Crowner's revelation. Gawne and the wild-looking beggar glanced at each other, their shared look suggesting much. Odger and Meg both stared flatly back at their better.

Then something flared in the woman's dark gaze. Dropping her hands from her hips, she pointed a finger at Gawne. "If that is so, Sir Crowner, then I say it was Gawne who killed her," the old woman charged, her voice raised and harsh. "Jessimond was missing for two full days before Gawne came crying that she was in the well. Who else would have known she was in there save the one who put her there? And who else would have put her there save for the one who killed her?"

There they were, the simple questions Faucon had expected to ask, the ones that should have easily led him to the girl's murderer. But the answers were no longer obvious, and the trail the woman's accusation indicated would prove naught but a dead end. Gawne's hands were too small to have throttled the girl, and his form too slight for him to have lifted the corpse high enough to have put her into the well by himself. And despite what strength the lad claimed for himself, he couldn't have brought the girl from where she had died to Wike by himself, not without someone witnessing.

But Gawne knew naught of what his Crowner did. His eyes flew wide at the old woman's accusation. With a choked cry, he pivoted and raced away from the well.

"Nay!" Ivo howled after his youngest son, the word filled with heartbreak.

"Neighbors, come to me!" Odger's voice drowned out the smith's cry. "Stop Gawne, son of Ivo! He has done murder!" the bailiff bellowed, raising the hue and cry.

So certain was Odger that those he ruled would follow that he turned instantly to chase the boy. He should have waited. Not a single cottage door opened. Neither did the ragged oldster nor Ivo do as the law required. Instead, both stayed where they stood.

The smith's elder boys weren't so sanguine. Shooting sidelong glances at their new Crowner, they started after their brother and their bailiff, albeit moving at a half-hearted shuffle. Near the kitchen the odd-looking youth also joined the race, but his awkward gait was as strange as his appearance. Lifting his heels and raising his chin high, he tiptoed precariously after the others. As he went, he flapped his hands and matched each step he took with a clicking sound made with his tongue. All in all, it was a pathetic chase and Faucon couldn't have been more pleased.

He watched Gawne race toward the pale, aiming toward the hatch—the narrow low- hung gate that allowed men entrance into the king's forest, albeit bent in twain and one at a time. The lad threw open the gate. He was short enough that he didn't need to duck as he passed through it. Even from this distance, Faucon could hear Gawne's footfalls echo on the plank bridge that crossed the deep ditch lining the pale, meant to prevent the deer from leaping over the fence.

Odger reached the hatch, started through it, only to turn back with a shout of frustration. It seemed the lad had kicked the planking into the ditch after he was across. Still the bailiff persisted, now bearing right to a stretch that was fenced with a thick holly hedge. There was a gap where the holly had died. That the bailiff didn't return once he pushed through the sharp-edged foliage suggested that another plank bridge was located there.

Faucon sighed. Hopefully, the boy had enough of a head start to send Odger back empty-handed. The sooner the bailiff returned, the sooner his Crowner could be off to Alcester for the night. Faucon wanted to reach the safety of town and abbey before darkness fell.

Arms folded in the manner of monks, hands at his elbows and hidden inside his sleeves, Edmund came to stand beside his employer. "Why do you not aid in the chase this time, the way you did last week in Stan-rudde?" his clerk asked, retreating into their mother tongue.

Faucon laughed. Beneath his undecorated and mud-spattered linen surcoat he wore not only his chain mail tunic and leggings but the usual padded gambeson and woolen chausses of a knight. All in all, these garments added nigh on three stone to his weight.

"What? Run that race in my armor? I'd be moving even more slowly than they." He waved in the direction of what passed for the hue and cry in Wike. Across the bailey, Gawne's brothers were managing a snail's pace. The strange youth had given up the chase altogether and was making his way back toward the well at that same odd gait.

"Moreover," Faucon continued, "I'd be far more likely to get lost in yon wild wood than to find the boy."

Then, having made his jest, he offered Edmund the more serious reply the monk deserved. "Last week, I needed to introduce myself to as many of the townsfolk as I could. The hue and cry made that an easy task. But why expend such effort here? All those in Wike have already seen my face and accept, or are at least resigned to, the fact that I serve king and court in this matter."

"Ah, I hadn't considered that," his clerk said, then rocked back on his heels. "It seems I was wrong to worry over how long it will take to note the particulars of this death. While they chase the boy, I'll scribble the details of what he's done onto our roll. When the bailiff returns with the lad, we can call the jury and be finished with this. I think me that we'll yet sleep within our own walls this night."

Faucon shot a smile at his clerk. "Is that so? What say you to a wager? I'll put coin on the possibility that the only walls we see tonight will be those surrounding Alcester, if there are any. Aye, and I also say that the morrow will find us back here at dawn, ready to spend our day sniffing out the trail that leads to the one who actually ended the girl's life."

His clerk shot him a startled look, then blinked rapidly. An instant later, Edmund's arms opened. His eyes widened.

"What do you know that I do not?" he demanded. "You showed me that she was throttled, not drowned in the well. Thus, it must have been the lad who killed her. He's the one who called the others to find her. Like the old woman said, who else could have put her in the well?"

"That is the wrong question, Brother. Her placement in the well is but a curiosity," Faucon replied with a quick lift of his dark brows. This time, when a huntsman's excitement overtook him, he gave way to it in pleased anticipation. He couldn't wait to uncover the spoor that would lead him to the girl's killer.

His response teased another frustrated sound from Edmund. "Why can I not see what you do?" he cried, only to dismiss his own question with the wave of his ink- stained hand. "Ack! What does it matter how you do it? At least one of us sees it. I'll fetch my basket, then enter what little I do know. Which, it seems, is only the dead girl's name, the manner of her death and that she was put into the well after she passed," he added irritably.

With that, the monk turned and stalked away from the well, following the arrow- straight pathway that led away from the manor toward the tiny settlement. Just beyond the farthest cottage was a rich greens ward. It was in that small, grassy meadow that Faucon's big white courser and the monk's donkey grazed, waiting for their masters. The basket containing Edmund's writing implements yet hung from his donkey's saddle.

As the monk went, he called back over his shoulder, "It would be good to know when the lad announced the girl's presence in the well. Also, mayhap you can also encourage the leper or the girl's mistress to swear that the child is English? At least we'll get that much done before we must leave this place for the night."

Once again Edmund issued commands where he had no right, but against such a successful day, and the possibility of an even better day on the morrow, it didn't rankle just now. Faucon grinned and called back, "So I shall, although I doubt I can do the task as well as you."

If his clerk noted the friendly sarcasm in his employer's reply, he gave no sign of it.

Chapter Three

Still shaking his head over Edmund's impossible behavior, Faucon brought his attention back to the four living people yet near the well. Once more weeping, Amelyn now sat upon the moist sod, her daughter's corpse cradled in her arms. As for the oldster, the rustic continued to watch his new Crowner with sharp interest.

The old woman, her gaze yet afire with the satisfaction of having accused Gawne of murder, stared boldly at her better. That was rude behavior for an unmarried woman, even one as old as Meg. What sort of gentlewoman, even as an absent landlord, employed a servant with so a disrespectful a manner?

As for Ivo the Smith, he stared after his departing sons, looking as stunned as he'd seemed when Amelyn the Leper had approached the well. And stunned Ivo should be. In the space of a breath his youngest child had gone from rescuing hero to accused murderer.

Faucon touched the smith's bare arm to draw his attention. With a jerk, Ivo smith sidled away from his Crowner. Then, like a man startled out of a terrible dream, he gave a violent shake of his head.

"Gawne didn't do this," he shouted at his Crowner, his fists closing. "They were like brother and sister, those two. Just a pair of children seeking to wring a little innocent joy out of a life gone sad and sober too soon. Gawne would never, ever have hurt Jes."

"Master Smith, you protest when I have said nothing at all about your son," Faucon replied mildly. He

47

picked up the leather apron Gawne had used in the watery depths and handed it to Ivo. "Take your gear and go home. There's nothing more you or I can do for the now save wait on your bailiff's return."

Which Faucon continued to pray would be without Gawne. He also hoped that Ivo or Gawne's brothers had some inkling where their young kinsman might choose to hide. More importantly, Faucon needed to find a way to win their trust. If the bailiff didn't bring back the boy, then one of them would have to lead him to Gawne on the morrow.

While the smith blinked in surprise at his Crowner's command, Meg freed an irritable huff. "Better that you hold tight to this sorry ass until Odger finds his lad, sir knight. Ivo cares nothing for your laws or your king, only for his own flesh and blood."

She turned her disrespectful gaze on the smith. "I warned you, didn't I? Spare the rod, spoil the child, said I. But you didn't heed me. The way you let Gawne wander as he would, making whatever mischief he chose!" She made an impatient sound. "I tell you, it wouldn't surprise me to learn you've never asked so much as an hour's work out of that child. See now how you spoiled your boy until he thought he could do this horrible thing with no fear of consequence? That little smell-smock! His sin rests upon your shoulders."

"There is no sin," Ivo protested again. "He didn't kill her. Gawne is innocent."

"Innocent, indeed!" Meg retorted. "There was nothing innocent about those two when they were together."

She turned her shoulder to the smith to address her Crowner as if she were his equal. "Make note of my words, sir knight, and you'll understand why Gawne did murder. Those two were forever stealing off together, disappearing into yon woods, sometimes gone for the whole night." The wave of her hand indicated the direction in which Gawne had fled. "And her just this year coming into her courses! I told Ivo his boy was out to steal that brat's maidenhead. I warned him that if she came with child I'd see to it both his boy and Ivo paid the price. But our smith ignored me.

"I say it's because of Ivo's neglect that the worst happened. I say that the smell-smock got her with child and, not wanting his father to learn what he'd done, killed her. That boy didn't want to be forced into wedlock with a penniless pauper whose dam is a whoring leper. Who would?" she added, shooting a hateful glance at Amelyn.

Then Meg pointed at the dead girl. "As for that brat, it's no surprise to me that she spread her legs for the first man who touched her. Her mother bred lewdness into her bastard's blood and bones, and that sly little creature was never going to be other than a whore. Headstrong bitch! It didn't matter what punishment I dealt her, she kept stealing out against my will.

"And what was she doing while she was out of my sight?" Meg threw her question at Ivo, then answered it for him. "Bedding your son!"

"Gawne wouldn't have touched her that way! He didn't!" Ivo protested again at a shout. "I tell you, he loved Jessimond like a sister."

Meg ignored him, her attention coming back to Faucon. "You've heard me, sir knight, and you've heard our smith," she told him. "Now also know that I speak the truth when I say he'll do anything and everything to protect his son. If you don't hold Ivo, that little dastard will never face just punishment for the wrong he's done. Arrest the father, else you'll never get custody of the lad."

"That isn't what the law requires," Faucon replied flatly, looking away from her to hide a dislike that grew with every breath.

"Go home, Master Ivo," he once more commanded the smith. "I'll need to speak with you about this matter but our conversation must wait until the morrow. I'll seek you out when I'm ready."

Clutching his apron close, the smith gave his Crowner a startled but respectful nod. Then sending a final scathing glance at the vicious old woman, Ivo departed, moving like a man twice his age. As he went, he crossed paths with the strange youth now circling in the direction of the well.

"Go, with your tail between your legs, knowing the price you paid for ignoring me," Meg threw after him, as if needing the last word, only to hiss in annoyance as she saw the odd young man making his strange way toward them.

"What are you doing here, you dulcop?" she shouted at the youth. "I told you to stay in the kitchen. Go home!"

The youth didn't spare her a glance as he continued toward the well at his unusual gait, heels raised, hands flapping, tongue clicking.

"You imbecile!" Meg shrieked. "Dimwit you are, but I know you can hear me. Go back to the kitchen!" When he still didn't heed her words, she added, "Mary save me, but I should just slit your throat and be done with you."

That stopped the simpleton. His heels and chin lowered, his arms fell to his sides. Then, blinking as if only now coming into awareness of where he was, he scanned the few folk still gathered around the well.

Amelyn sighed, yet holding her daughter close. "I'm so sorry, Johnnie," she said sadly.

Hearing his name spoken, this Johnnie swiveled until his gaze fell upon the leper. A crease formed between his brows as he noticed Jessimond's body in her mother's lap. This time when his hands began to flap, the motion was clearly agitated. With a high-pitched squeal, he came straight toward Amelyn, moving as fast as he could given his odd bearing.

"By all the Holy Helpers, I told you to go home and you'll do as I say!" Meg screeched, flying at him, slapping and punching.

The youth squealed again at this attack. Amelyn echoed his cry and started to rise, only to have the weight of her daughter's body drive her back to sitting. She turned her hooded head toward Faucon. "Stop her! Don't let her hurt one so helpless," she begged.

Faucon had already started forward, intending to part the two. Instead, he paused. Imbecile or not, there was nothing helpless about this Johnnie's defense. The youth had lowered his head so his ears and skull were out of Meg's reach as he used his arms and shoulders to deflect the woman's blows. Then, at precisely the right instant, Johnnie gave a swift jerk. Meg tumbled off his back with a frustrated shriek. As she sprawled onto the turf behind him, the youth began again to lumber toward Amelyn.

"What's happening?" Edmund shouted out, having returned as far as the edge of the manor's demesne.

Not wanting his clerk's presence to alter what might next happen, Faucon held up a hand. It was a clear command that Edmund should stay where he was, and a wasted gesture. As always, his clerk ignored him and lifted his heels into a trot, his quiver-like basket of tools bouncing against his back from the strap slung over his shoulder.

At the well, Meg was back on her feet. She launched herself at the idiot with a raging cry and grabbed the neck of his tunic. Given her modest stature, the woman's hands were larger and stronger-looking than Faucon expected.

Twisting and writhing, the youth sought again to throw off the cook. This time, Meg held tight, beating at his head with her free hand. Unable to shuck her, Johnnie continued forward, carrying her with him until he fell to his knees next to Amelyn. Meg caught a hank of his knotted hair and pulled. Johnnie bleated. However much pain she caused him, it wasn't enough to stop him from wrapping his arms around Jessimond. Using his elbow like a lever, he tried to pry the dead girl from her mother's grasp.

"Nay, Johnnie! Leave be," Amelyn shouted.

As she fought for control of her daughter, her gloved hand brushed the sleeve of Meg's gown. The old woman yelped in panic, her fear of contagion greater than her need to punish the simpleton. Releasing Johnnie, she stumbled back and collided with the oldster. As the ragged ancient started to fall, he cried out and caught Meg at the waist in instinctive reaction. The old woman pivoted, her arms raised and fists closed. Instantly, the rustic released her and tumbled to the ground. There, he stayed head turned to the side and arms raised to protect himself from an attack. Meg ignored him, shifting to once again watch the idiot and the leper. As she did, she scrubbed her hand against her skirt.

"Johnnie, it's me," Amelyn cried as she battled the youth, now clutching Jessimond's body close to her. "I am Amelyn, and Jessimond is my daughter."

That stopped the simpleton. Without releasing the dead girl, Johnnie shifted until he could stare under the leper's hood. The crease between his brows returned.

"That's right," Amelyn said to him, her soothing tone owning a mother's lilt. "It's me, Amelyn."

That crease deepened. Releasing the corpse, the idiot sat back on his heels. Once again, he began to make that clicking sound. Then with a swift sweep of his arm, he knocked the hood off Amelyn's head. With a frantic cry, the leper grabbed for it and missed as it came to rest between her shoulder blades, exposing her face and neck.

Pity raced through Faucon. Jessimond had been her mother's image. Although Amelyn was in her middle years she remained a beautiful woman, despite the reddened, misshapen lumps that told the tale of her progressing disease.

"Lord save him, he touched the leper!" Edmund cried as he halted a little distance behind Amelyn and the well. He let his basket of tools slide off his arm. As it tumbled to the ground he folded his hands and bowed his head.

"You touched her?!" Meg shouted, echoing the monk's shocked protest.

Then the old woman laughed, the sound deep and satisfied. "God be praised, you touched her! My prayers are answered. I won't have you back now and there's no one who can force you on me, not for any reason. Starve, you dulcop, and know that I'll happily watch you die." With that, Meg whirled and started back toward her lady's kitchen at the same raging pace by which she'd left it.

Johnnie paid no heed to either clerk or cook. Instead, making a cooing sound, he lifted a hand as if intending to touch one of the angry patches on Amelyn's face. Yet seeking to retrieve her hood with one hand, the leper caught the idiot's arm with the other, trying to forestall his touch at the same time. She looked up at Faucon. Her eyes were a crystalline blue beneath the arch of her dark brows.

"Meg's wrong. I swear he didn't touch me," she vowed, then turned her gaze on the youth. "Nay, Johnnie, I will not allow this. If you touch me, you may grow ill as I have."

Johnnie relaxed and gently freed his arm from

Amelyn's grasp. The youth looked at the dead girl in the leper's lap, then drew his hand down Jessimond's cold cheek. As he did, he raised his gaze to Amelyn, his brows lifted as if in question.

"She lives no more," she told him, her voice quavering anew. A mother's grief again filled her eyes. "Like your mama, my Jessie has also gone to Heaven to dwell with the angels."

This provoked a moan from Johnnie, suggesting he wasn't as witless as Meg named him. Once more, the youth stroked Jessimond's face, tears now rolling unheeded down his cheeks. Faucon eyed the odd man's hands. They were of a size with his own.

"Who is he to you?" he asked Amelyn.

Before replying, the leper restored her oversized hood to its rightful place, concealing the disease eating her alive. When she looked up at him, all that was exposed of her face was the end of her nose, her chin and jaw, and they were cast in light shadow.

"Another unwanted child of Wike," she murmured bitterly, then continued in a stronger voice. "He is my half-brother, the son of Meg's sister Martha, who married my father when they were both widows facing their later years."

Amelyn shook her head. "She was a good woman, Martha. Too good for this hateful place, I say. Look how she welcomed our Lord's gift of a child, one who came long after she thought her womb capable of harboring life. Despite that her son was damaged by coming too early, Martha cherished him so dearly that she turned her back on our custom of leaving infants like Johnnie to die in some distant glade. Indeed, she stood fast, even when all of Wike demanded that she be shed of him.

Amelyn sighed at that. "Much to my shame, I added my voice to theirs. I warned her that keeping such a babe might lead to more sorrow than joy for both of them. Would that I hadn't been right," she added at a whisper before continuing. "Instead, Martha told us all that the Lord had given her Johnnie and she would raise him, vowing to do so at no cost to any of us."

Arms crossed, Faucon nodded to show he understood. Many a crippled or halfwit babe ended their short lives in some far-flung or hidden place, especially in communities as small as this one. Trapped in inherited bondage to this place, even the able-bodied among these villeins barely survived each year with lives and limbs intact. They could ill afford to carry the burden of an unproductive mouth. Not that it was much different in wealthier places. Even the grandest of God's holy houses were conservative about how many useless mouths they sheltered.

"It's one thing to promise that her child will cost them nothing, but another to manage it," Faucon said as Edmund made his way around the well to stand beside him. "I'm surprised more wasn't done to thwart her. What of your father? Did he have no influence over her? What did he think of bearing the cost of a damaged babe?"

"My sire died before his son was born," she told Faucon, "and Johnnie was his only surviving male heir. Because of that, no one could gainsay Martha. At least, not so early in Johnnie's life, in case we were wrong about him," she added. "But Martha kept her word. She sold every bit of my father's chattel to keep her precious son fed. When there was nothing more to sell, it fell to me to see to our daily meals.

"If only I hadn't become like this," Amelyn touched her hood to indicate her illness. "I know in my heart that Martha died of hunger, because she gave her beloved son the food from her own mouth.

"As for Johnnie, when Martha passed last year,

dealing with him was no longer as simple as taking him into some far-flung thicket and leaving him to die. Not that Meg, who is his only kin, didn't strive mightily to refuse to care for him. But to their credit, no one here allowed her that. Instead, they forced him into that kitchen of hers." The leper pointed to the shed that was Meg's domain within the demesne, then offered a harsh laugh.

"Poor Meg," she said, her voice holding no pity at all for the lady's arrogant servant. "How she must hate having to be charitable for once in her sorry life. Although it pains me to admit it, the folk in Wike were as right to force Johnnie on Meg as they were wrong when they pressed Jessimond into yon kitchen after I was banished."

That made Faucon frown. "Idiot or not, Johnnie is your daughter's uncle. If your stepmother was yet alive when you left this place, why was your daughter given to Meg rather than being left with her own blood kin?" That was especially so when it seemed that all here knew Meg had a harsh hand while, if Amelyn's tale was true, Johnnie's mother had been a kinder soul.

"Johnnie is no idiot," Amelyn protested. "Aye, he's dumb, but he hears and understands, and he can do many tasks. Can't you, sweetling?" She patted the youth's sleeve as she spoke. "You like sweeping the floor and tending the fire. You can even chop wood."

The child-man smiled, this time nodding his answer, proving that he did indeed comprehend the spoken word, at least those spoken by his sister. After giving her half-brother another pat, Amelyn glanced up at Faucon. Beneath the concealment of her hood, she offered him a brief bend of her lips and a quiet laugh.

"Not that Meg would ever admit Johnnie is capable of anything. If she did, she'd lose her excuse to complain ceaselessly about him and the burden his existence is to her," she said.

"So much is obvious." Faucon grinned in return, liking the leper despite her contagion, when he had no right to form such opinions. His only duty was to determine if his monarch could wring any value from her daughter's death.

"As to why my Jes was forced onto Meg," Amelyn started, then paused to give a sharp shake of her head. "It's not Johnnie who deserves to be named dimwit in Wike. Putting Jessimond into Meg's custody was a futile attempt by the others to stop her thievery. I don't know how anyone thought a child in that kitchen would prevent Meg from doing as she always has, especially not when the lass they chose to use was as gentle as my Jes."

"What does Meg steal?" he asked, wondering what could be taken from those who had so little.

"In Wike we pay our lady for the privilege," Amelyn gave the word harsh emphasis, "of using her oven to bake our bread and Meg is our bakestress. She rules that oven the way our king rules his realm. We give her our dough and she returns the loaves to us once they're baked. Every loaf comes back lighter than it left us, every time. She steals a goodly pinch or two from each one before she bakes them, then uses these stolen bits to make her own loaves. These she sells in Alcester, filling her purse at the expense of our hungry children. And her with no family of her own to feed! At least, not until she was forced to support both Jes and Johnnie."

That sent Faucon's gaze to the bee hive- shaped oven that stood near the kitchen. It was cold at the moment, no smoke issuing from its top opening. A theft such as Meg's wasn't uncommon among bakers, whether they lived within town walls or in a wee place like this.

His attention shifted to the spacious kitchen shed

that was Meg's domain. The sow and her grunting brood were sauntering past it, no doubt on their way back to their sty for the night. Although the door remained open, there was no sign of the old woman. That Meg had such freedom was strange indeed, particularly when Wike was ruled by one with a hard and grasping hand. Odger hardly seemed the sort to tolerate such behavior—that was, unless he profited from it somehow.

That sent Faucon's gaze to the pale and the woods beyond the fence. Just then, a flock of birds rose from the balding treetops into a sky glowing with the faintest hint of rose. The birds began to swarm as they were wont to do prior to taking their nightly rest, their dance a writhing cloud that moved with astonishing precision.

It was time to be leaving for Alcester. But if they went now, Faucon was absolutely certain he wouldn't find Amelyn here upon the morrow. Once Odger returned, the bailiff would find a way to drive the leper from his vale despite his Crowner's command.

"Your bailiff doesn't do anything to stop Meg from her theft?" he asked the leper.

Amelyn shrugged. "Odger has no choice in the matter. Meg would rule our oven even if he could prove her theft to our lady. Our old master, God rest him," she added, the shift of her head saying she glanced at the monk, "made Meg bakestress before she was twice Jessimond's age. When Wike became part of our lady's dower upon her marriage, it passed to her with the stipulation that Meg remain keeper of the oven until her death. I doubt even our lady could wrench the right to bake our bread from Meg."

"That explains much," Faucon murmured to himself.

"Idiots!" Amelyn charged again, her harsh word drowning out his muttered comment as she aimed her cloaked gaze at the kitchen once again. "I warned them, every one, on the day they sent me away from this place. I told them that forcing Jessimond into that kitchen would do nothing save expose my precious child to Meg's always angry hand. And I was right. Odger proved that when he later pressed Johnnie onto Meg after Martha died. This he did not in an attempt to control Meg, but to force her to open that weighty purse of hers." She glanced in the direction of the well and the rustic as she continued. The old man was again on his feet and now half-leaned, half- sat against the well's surround. His worn face was once more alive with that perverse amusement as he listened closely to the dead girl's mother.

"I'm guessing that's what he proposed to the others when they all met to discuss Johnnie's future. This, when I'm certain everyone else had decided that my half-brother should be taken to the abbey in Alcester where the monks could turn him into a beggar, to collect coins on their behalf."

She brought her attention back to her crippled kinsman. "That the folk here might shift furrows so abruptly surprised me to my bones. I never expected they would accept such a proposal, not when doing so meant they agreed by default that Wike would continue to support Johnnie after Meg follows her sister into the grave."

Again, she looked at the oldster. This time, her gaze remained fixed on the old man as she aimed her words at him. "Perhaps it's because you all believe Meg will give Johnnie that purse of hers upon her deathbed, Johnnie being her only kin," she offered snidely, then gave another harsh laugh. "If so, you're mistaken to a one. I say it's more likely that Meg will bury her coins rather than allow another soul to enjoy what she stole. Especially Johnnie."

Shaking her head at her own rough jest, she brought her gaze back to Faucon. "Whatever the intent or hope of my former neighbors in moving Johnnie, they achieved their aim. With everyone watching her, Meg has had to spend her ill-gotten gains to feed and clothe her nephew and my daughter. And, as angry as I am at them for forcing Jessimond into Meg's custody, I'm grateful that they now watch to see that Johnnie is cared for," she said quietly. "If they did not, I know in my heart Meg would take him to some distant place and kill him, just as she promised a few moments ago."

The leper brushed a gloved hand against the nest of her half-brother's knotted hair, then ran her fingers over his cheek at the top of his untrimmed beard. "She may feed and clothe you, but she doesn't tend you at all, does she?" she murmured.

Johnnie swabbed his nose upon his sleeve before again grinning at his kinswoman. Amelyn returned his smile with her own. It was a sweet spread of her lips and revealed a full and even row of teeth. That was unusual for one raised in the poverty of a place such as Wike.

"What will happen now?" Faucon wanted to know, his gaze still fixed on what he could see of the leper's face. "Will Meg do as she threatened and rid herself of your brother by declaring that he touched you?"

Her smile yet lingering on her lips, Amelyn looked up at her Crowner before answering him. When she realized how closely he watched her, her mouth straightened and she bowed her head as if she were a modest woman when, as a former whore, that wasn't a title she could claim.

"I think not. Now that Jessimond is—" her voice caught and she paused to clear her throat. "Now that Jes is gone, Odger won't want to give up his only control over Meg. I say he'll force her to keep Johnnie until he sees signs that my brother has contracted my disease, which he won't," she assured Faucon.

Then she reached out and patted the youth's knee. "A pity that is, despite the tragedy of this ailment. Although I pray you aren't affected, sweetling, if you did grow ill, I would claim you as my own and bring you to live with me."

Chapter Four

With her comment Faucon released any remaining concern that Amelyn might force her touch on him, seeking to infect him with her disease for spite's sake as it was said some lepers would do. The linked metal rings of his armor rattling quietly, he lowered to one knee in front of her. Just as he anticipated, the leper shifted back to prevent any accidental contact.

"What are you doing?!" Edmund's shocked whisper came from behind him.

"What my duty requires," Faucon replied to his clerk without looking at the monk.

To Jessimond's mother, he said, "I am Sir Faucon de Ramis. As you heard me say to your bailiff, I have questions for you. You've also heard me state that I speak with the king's authority in this shire. If you don't yet know, our sheriff no longer examines the bodies of the murdered or those who have died under questionable circumstances. Instead, as this shire's Coronarius and Keeper of the Pleas, and as ordered by the royal court, it's now mine to both determine if your daughter's death was murder and to discover the one who killed her."

That last bit was his personal interpretation of his new position and its duties. To his way of thinking, if he was to assess the wrongdoer's estate, then he needed to prove to himself who it was that had done the wrong.

His words set Amelyn's chin to quivering anew. She

once more stroked her daughter's cheek. "I hold her in my arms and feel that she is gone, but my heart will not accept it. I should have fled with her when I knew I was ill," she cried softly, her words springing from her broken heart.

"Of course you couldn't have taken her with you," Edmund retorted. "If you'd done so, you would have intentionally shared your disease with her, dooming her to a terrible death. That would have been a mortal sin. Who would trade the promise of eternal happiness for an equal term of pain for such a selfish reason?"

His interruption earned him a chiding look from his Crowner. Edmund blinked and frowned. Faucon gave a single negative shake of his head, the tiny movement reminding his clerk that he wasn't to intrude or interrupt unless signaled to do so. This, Edmund understood. He took a backward step as if that could retract his interjection.

"But that's not why I couldn't take her with me when I left," Amelyn spewed in bitter response. "Odger's revenge on me included wrenching my little love from my arms and putting her into Meg's kitchen, just because he knew how much I prized her!"

"Revenge for what?" Faucon wanted to know.

She bowed her head. Her shoulders began to shake as she cried in silence. Johnnie made a pained sound. Easing around to sit beside his half-sister, he leaned his head against her cloaked shoulder. Then he caught her nearest hand and drew it to his chest, pressing it to his heart. Rather than push him away, Amelyn curled her fingers around his, holding his hand tightly as if the youth were the rope supporting her in her personal well of sorrow.

When Amelyn at last raised her head, glistening tears trembled on the line of her jaw. She again turned her gaze toward the old man at the well. Faucon followed her look. Although the ancient stood still as a statue, the amusement had left his expression. There was no mistaking his intense interest in what went forward at his community's well.

"I suppose if I don't tell you all of it, there will be others here quick to spill what they know, when they only speculate," Amelyn sighed. "No one but Martha ever knew all. Odger sought revenge because I refused his unwanted advances before a witness."

Here, her voice broke. She fell silent, her mouth yet open as if there were words yet trapped in her throat that she couldn't bring onto her tongue. After a moment she cleared them loose and threw herself into her tale.

"It was before Jessimond's coming, two days after my husband was buried," she began, her voice muted. "Odger came to me as I was collecting my belongings, preparing to return to my father's home, the one that Martha had by then claimed, what with Johnnie my father's only heir. My brother-by-marriage needed my cottage for his own son, which was his right," she added in explanation.

"So you had no heir by your husband?" Faucon interrupted. The lack of a male child was the most common reason for a widow to leave the house she'd shared with her husband but not the only one.

"Nay, no lad. The only child I gave Tom was the little lass I bore before we traded vows." She sighed, the sound holding an older and more tolerable grief. "Sweet Tilly. She died a year after we were wed. After that, there was nary a stirring in my womb."

That startled Faucon. He glanced at Jessimond, then remembered that Meg had named the girl a bastard. "Then Jessimond wasn't your husband's child?" he prodded.

But Amelyn didn't answer his question or follow his suggestion that she tell her daughter's tale. Instead, she continued with her own. Content to let her speak as she would for a moment or two, Faucon shifted into an easier position as he listened.

"The harvesting had just begun and every soul save me was out reaping. I had petitioned Odger to stay behind so I might have time to collect my belongings. He agreed. I thought he was being kind. I was wrong."

When she lifted her head, her tears had dried and the line of her jaw was hard. "There I was, grieving for my husband and alone in the home that had once been mine. When Odger tapped at the door, I assumed he'd come to reclaim those tools that belonged to the lady, the ones Tom had used while he lived. Instead, when I let our bailiff inside, he drove me back against a wall, seeking to lift my skirts. As he did so, he warned me not to scream.

"But I couldn't help myself," she said, her voice ragged. "I screamed and told him nay as I fought him with all my might. I did so even though I had no hope that anyone might hear me. How could they when he'd made certain they were far from me, beyond offering any aid?

"Then, like a miracle, Martha was in the house with me, adding her screams to mine. When Odger realized he wasn't going to have his way with me unless he took me in front of Martha, making her a witness to his rape, he retreated. He said nothing as he departed, but I knew—we both knew—he would never forgive either of us for how we'd stymied him.

"We were right. Even though neither Martha nor I ever told another soul what he'd done, when the chance came to destroy me a year after Jessimond's birth, Odger did so joyfully."

"Jessimond was a bastard, then?" Faucon asked more directly this time as he sought to steer her in the direction he wanted her to go.

"She is. Was," Amelyn corrected herself sadly. "Nor was she my child by choice."

After she said that, she gave a quiet cry and covered her face with her free hand as if trying to hide from what she'd just revealed. Her distress stirred a worried sound from Johnnie. As the youth patted his half-sister's arm, seeking to comfort, Edmund shifted nervously behind Faucon, his movement so sharp that his habit rustled. Faucon tensed, ready to chide should his clerk again seek to offer commentary, but the monk said nothing.

Drawing a bracing breath, Amelyn continued. "A dozen years and more have passed since the night of Jessimond's conception and I've only told the whole tale once, the day Martha recognized I was with child. She deserved to know, for I was living in her house, dependent on her charity for a place to lay my head at night. But just now the words fight me, as if they don't wish to be spoken," she offered in soft explanation, her voice barely audible.

After a moment, she cleared her throat and began. "It happened deep in the night of our Autumn Ale, about two months after my Tom's death. Here in Wike, we always celebrate once the harvest is in. By long tradition, we do so at our lady's expense," she added, her hooded head moving briefly in Faucon's direction.

Her explanation was unnecessary. Although someone who had lived all her life in a place as isolated as Wike might not know it, such events were common across the land, not only in communities as small as this but on the larger estates, like the lands owned by his family.

Now that Amelyn had opened the floodgates on her tale, the words were flowing more easily. "Like everyone else, I was eating, drinking, and dancing to my heart's content. It felt so wonderful to be happy again, if only for that one evening. In my determination to celebrate, I drank more than I intended, so much so that I exhausted myself long before the night was done.

"Thinking to rest for just a while, I found a quiet corner, but the ale took me. When I awoke, I was still befuddled. The world spun around me and my stomach was no better. I lifted my head and found the barn as dark as pitch, and silent. That stunned me. I couldn't believe everyone had departed and left me behind, especially Martha. How could she not have roused me as she prepared to leave?"

Then Amelyn shrugged. The gesture suggested that if she'd ever placed blame on her stepmother over this she did so no longer. "Martha told me later that she'd been as befuddled as I. She thought I'd already returned home, but by the time she was barring our door, she'd forgotten me and didn't check to see if I was inside," she explained, then continued.

"Already trembling at the thought of having to make my way home alone in the Devil's darkness, I started to roll onto my side. Then he was there, forcing me face-down onto the hard dirt floor. He was on me faster than I could blink and I was helpless to stop him. He was heavy, and much stronger than I. Indeed, I could barely breathe, so forcefully did he hold me in place. He said not a word and made no sound except to breathe as he had his way with me. When he was done, I lay where I was, stunned beyond all movement as I listened to him running from the lady's barn."

Amelyn fell silent at that, her gaze aimed at her daughter's corpse in her lap.

"Was it Odger?" Faucon prodded.

That brought her head up with a snap. "Of course it was! Who else among the men in Wike would have done such a cowardly and cruel thing to me, save the one who'd already tried once and been rebuffed?" she cried in painful retort.

Faucon cocked his head, the bits and pieces of information he'd collected thus far shifting with her tale. "Yet, you saw no face and heard no voice. I think you cannot say for certain it was he," he replied quietly.

Amelyn caught her breath at that. For a long instant, she sat as if frozen. From the cast of her shoulders to the tightness of her arms, it was clear she resisted his suggestion with all her might. Faucon recognized the moment she gave way as her shoulders reluctantly sagged.

"By your reckoning, sir, I will admit that I cannot say for certain it was Odger," she conceded. "But if not him, then who?" she demanded, her voice raised to a higher, wounded pitch.

Then she shook her head and cried, "But it's not who did the deed that cuts me the deepest each time I think on what happened that night. Why did I let myself drink until my head spun? Then, when he attacked, why did I do nothing to protect myself? I should have screamed as I'd done that first time! Why, when he was finished, did I not leap up to chase after him, raising the hue and cry? That night left my life in ruins and I still don't know why I didn't move to save myself. Why, why, why?" she finished, her words dissolving into an aching silence that lasted until she gave an outraged huff.

"Do you know what I did instead? Coward that I am, when I could at last find the will to move, I crawled into the darkest corner of the barn. There I crouched, emptying my gullet as I gasped and cried like some dying fish, even though I bled not nor had any bruise. Try as I might and despite how dearly I longed to be home and safe within familiar walls, I couldn't stand, so terribly did my arms and legs tremble. I was certain he yet lurked in the dark along the way, waiting to use me again. Even when first light came, my heart pounded in terror as I raced along familiar paths in the newborn light. And, still I quaked and wept, certain that I would be taken again at every corner."

She shuddered at the memory, then turned her hooded gaze to her daughter's corpse. With a finger, she outlined the girl's brow and followed the line of Jessimond's nose to its tip. "For years there'd been no life in my womb, but on that night and in that one instance, a seed took root. If you wish me to say right now that not even his daughter's face proves that Odger did the deed, I would agree. In all ways, Jessimond was mine and mine alone, and I cherished her for that, despite the manner of her coming and what it cost me."

Once again, Edmund shifted, this time sighing as he did. The sound was unexpectedly sad. Amelyn must have heard the monk for she looked up at him as she continued.

"Odger never repeated his attack," she said, her voice firmer than necessary, as if she yet struggled with her Crowner's suggestion that it might not have been the bailiff who misused her. "If there's a cause for that, I think it most likely because he had expected me to be barren. Instead, I'd come easily with child.

"Still, taking me that night didn't sate Odger's need to destroy me for my earlier defiance. Once Jessimond passed her first saint's day, proving that she was hale and in all ways unlike Johnnie, our bailiff called everyone to that door." Amelyn indicated the front of the crumbling manor house. Entrance was by way of a small oaken door that looked heavier than the wall in which it was set. The door stood a little bit above the ground with a narrow porch in front of it, accessed by single wooden step.

"There, and in front of all my friends and neighbors, Odger did as he had done when he called Tom to claim our Tilly. He shouted for the one who had made Jessimond in me to step forward. And just as Odger had known would happen this time—" she once more shifted, turning her hooded gaze toward Faucon, then insisted "—because he was the one who had done the deed, no man took that step. Then, Odger demanded that I provide the name of Jessimond's father so that man could be forced to claim and support his child."

This time when her hooded head moved, it was clear that she addressed the oldster. "What could I say? There was no point in telling a tale of rape that had happened at an ale almost two years' prior. No woman can cry misuse so long after the deed. Odger would only have denied all, and every one of you would have believed him," she said to the rustic, now speaking only to him.

"Do you think I hadn't heard the whispers and asides you all traded about me? All of you thought I was trysting with a married man, even though none of the gossips could determine which of Wike's husbands had made me his lover. Some speculated that my paramour came from Coctune even though no stranger had tread Wike Lane in months. If I had spilled the truth, you would all have scoffed. You would have accused me of concocting a false tale to protect a man I loved but couldn't have."

The old man made no reply, but his wild brows drooped over his now-hooded eyes.

"So I said nothing," Amelyn continued, once again including her Crowner and his clerk in the audience for her tale. "I accepted my sentence for the sin of fornication. As I bared my back, I prayed that once our bailiff set aside the lash, my life would finally go on as it had—" Her words gave way to a startled sound.

Shifting sharply, she looked toward the farthest of the homes in the hamlet, the one closest to the green-sward where her Crowner's horse grazed. Without looking back at her better, she said, "But what if, as you suggest sir, it wasn't Odger who set Jessimond in my womb? Of a sudden, all certainty about who fathered Jessimond is gone. Perhaps this is because of what you said. Or mayhap it's because my tale sounds so different, now that I finally speak the words aloud. How is it that everything can change in but an instant?" Although the leper aimed her words at Faucon, there was aught in her tone that suggested she spoke only to herself.

It was another moment before she brought her gaze back to the men around the well. She shook her head as if stunned. "Only now and because of you, sir, do I finally begin to make sense of what Odger did after he set aside the lash. No longer do I see a man bent on revenging himself on me for my first refusal, but one in a rage because he thought I'd given myself freely and illicitly to another when I had resisted his attack."

One more time she turned her head to look toward the far end of the tiny settlement. "But if not Odger, then who?" she mused.

"What is this thing that your bailiff did to you?" Faucon asked, urging her on as he kept one eye on the sky.

Still gazing at that distant cottage, Amelyn said, "Although our customs gave Odger no right to it, on that day he forbade me from ever again working in the fields of Wike. When Martha asked how I was to feed myself if I couldn't work, he told all my neighbors that I'd already proved myself a lightskirt by bearing an anonymous bastard. If I wanted to eat, he said, I could earn my bread by whoring."

With a quiet, pained laugh, Amelyn once more directed her words at the oldster. "That set off a storm among the others. Not because any of you wished to protect me," she said, her words bearing harsh emphasis as she addressed the old man. "Instead, all any of you wanted to know was if Odger was freeing me from my bond to our lady and her family. You included, Hew. That's all any of you asked of him, if he was setting me free!" A small choked sound escaped her as if she remained astounded by their betrayal despite the years.

At the leper's charge, the oldster took a step closer to where she sat. When he halted, he canted to the side in his stance as if one hip ached. The old man spread his arms in a gesture of innocence.

"We didn't know he was wrong about you or what you'd done." Hew's voice was as worn and cracked as his face. "How could we have? You didn't spill your tale, not then, nor earlier when we all realized you were with child, displaying fertility too long after Tom's death for the babe to be his. Instead, you stood in silence, looking shamed. Not even Martha offered a word of explanation."

This Hew glanced at his Crowner before again addressing the leper. "You must have known we were all waiting for Martha to defend you. You two lived together, as close as mother and daughter. She saw you day and night. What could we think when she stood silently at your side, offering no word of support? She was the one who would have known if you were trysting. She should have told us how she'd witnessed Odger trying to take you against your will. Instead, in your shared silence you both left us to think what Odger said was true, that you'd taken a lover after Tom's death and that Martha had abetted you in your sin." This last was almost a plea.

Amelyn rocked back in astonishment at that. "You were waiting for Martha to challenge Odger?! You all knew how deeply he resented her for not discarding Johnnie as he had commanded! How could you believe for an instant she could confront him? It's easy to protest now that she or I could have swayed you by telling our tale, but that's a fool's defense, Hew. If she had dared to raise her voice to him in public, he'd have turned on her. He'd have taken Johnnie from her, then and there, punishing her just as he was punishing me for defying him.

"And every one of you would have let him do it," she cried out, her voice rising, "even though you knew Martha wanted her child just as much as I wanted mine!"

A frustrated sound escaped her. "Hew, you and the others said nothing as our bailiff instructed you to deny me, but not my child, shelter and support unless I paid for it in coins earned by whoring. Has that happened to any other woman before me?" she demanded.

The old man arms dropped to his sides. His head bowed. "We didn't know, Amelyn," he pleaded again. "In that instant, you looked like what he told us you were, a whore."

"That's what you let him make me!" she cried again, then bowed her head as if battling her emotions.

When she looked up again, it was to address Faucon. "On that day, Odger told the folk of Wike that I would remain bound to the manor even though I now had permission to travel to Alcester as often as I needed to ply my new trade. I was not allowed to take my baby with me as I came and went. He assured the others, and me, that he would hunt me down if I did so, or if I tried to go any farther than Alcester."

"You should have tried to run," Hew muttered. "It would have served Odger's pride rightly if you, a mere woman, escaped him after so many men have tried and failed to stay free of his grasp for the full year and a day."

"Go without my precious child?" Amelyn retorted, her tone incredulous. Then she sighed. "Do you know what I wished at that moment, Hew? I wished that I hadn't fought Odger when he came to use me after Tom's death, that I had let him take me," she said, sounding beaten.

"Nay, you do not." The old man shook his head. "I think me the outcome would have been no different. Martha still had Johnnie to protect. Without hearing your tale, none of us would have been any the wiser, would we have been? You should have told us. You should have come to us in private. You should have trusted us."

"I couldn't," she protested. "Martha couldn't."

"I suppose not," the old man agreed in resignation. "And you're right. We should have protested his sentence. No woman before you has suffered so for producing a bastard, even one with an unnamed father. Given your tale, I doubt any woman who follows you will receive that burden either."

Then Hew looked at his Crowner. There was naught to see in his expression now save shame. "We didn't know," he protested to Faucon. "Would that she could have found a way to tell us."

Edmund cleared his throat, the sound suggesting he struggled to swallow words. Faucon made the old man no reply. There was nothing to be said. Even if Amelyn hadn't willingly committed the sin of fornication, being driven from home and family to earn a living by whoring was a fate often faced by fallen women, no matter how innocent they might have been in the event that precipitated their fall.

Amelyn freed her hand from Johnnie's, then wound her arms around Jessimond's cold body. She pulled her dead child closer to her. Once again, she aimed her head at her Crowner as she continued her tale.

"Martha may have said nothing at the manor door, but after we returned home she did everything she could to keep me from the fate Odger intended for me," she said in defense of a woman she loved. "At first, she kept me with her and told everyone that I was paying my way as Odger required. And, indeed I was, doing so by selling the items in my dowry.

"Since Odger hadn't expected me to have the wherewithal to resist him, he sought to achieve his goal in other ways. Things happened, such as Martha's portion of flour spoiling at the mill, or so he informed us. Even then, we continued to thwart him and Odger became more bold in his attempts to drive me where he willed. He refused to let Martha join the other widows when it came time to glean the fields even though it was her right. As it was mine," she added softly, shaking her head. "It was a hungry winter, but we managed, foraging where and when we could."

"We shared with you," Hew offered, yet seeking to redeem himself.

"So some of you did," she agreed grudgingly and continued, gazing at her former neighbor. "But then the month for plowing arrived and Odger doubled the price Martha usually paid to use the lady's plow and oxen. Once again, he acted against custom, and once again, none of you spoke out to defend her."

This time, Hew made no response. Amelyn looked back at Faucon. "By then, I could bear it no longer. I left Jessimond with Martha and went to Alcester as Odger intended. For those next years, I whored, using the coins I earned to support us all, Martha, me, Jessimond, and Johnnie.

"Then this happened," she touched her hood, "and Odger brought me to our lady on one of her rare visits. He asked her permission to drive me from our bounds. Much to my surprise, and his too, I think, our lady instead bought me a place at the hospital in Saltisford. It was an unexpected kindness for which I will always be grateful, even if she strips it from me now for my defiance," she finished quietly.

This time when Edmund reacted to her words, it was to kneel next Faucon, coming but a hand's breadth beyond the reach of the leprous woman. Faucon stared at his clerk, beyond startled. He'd never before seen the monk come that close to any woman, much less one with a contagious and disfiguring disease.

"You must put your faith in our Lord," Edmund told Amelyn. "If your bailiff has done as you say, then it's certain our heavenly Father has taken note. Rest assured that He will see your bailiff pays dearly and for all eternity for the wrong he's done you," said a monk who was usually uncompromising in his judgment of sins and sinners.

"Many thanks, Brother," Amelyn murmured.

Edmund nodded his reply, then looked at his employer, speaking now in their native tongue. "Sir Faucon, the leper's tale of anonymous rape, and her later public sentencing by the bailiff for refusing to name the father— doing so before so many witnesses— makes public fact that no one in this place can truthfully state that the child is English," he whispered.

"Of course the lass is English," Faucon replied at the same low tone. "She has to be, even if the leper cannot be certain who did the fathering. Who save one of the men in this place could have done the deed on that night?"

"It matters naught who the girl's father might have been," Edmund said with a shake of his head, "only that his name is unknown. In this, the law is clear. If her sire cannot be named and proved English, then Englishry cannot be ascertained. We must name the child Norman and apply the murdrum fine."

Surprise and satisfaction tumbled through Faucon. Oh, but there was value in having so learned a clerk at hand, despite Edmund's oddities. This day would prove one of his most successful yet. The murdrum fine was dear, and everyone in the community would pay it, including their lady. As improbable as it had seemed an hour ago, the king would profit from the death of a bastard serving girl in a place as poor as Wike.

Aye, and Judgment Day was coming sooner than Odger expected. Those the bailiff ruled already resented him at least as much as they feared him. Faucon suspected that once their lady's purse had been lightened because her chosen headman had made so costly a misstep, she'd find it inconvenient to keep Odger as her bailiff. Just as Amelyn had fallen, so would her persecutor.

"Well done, Brother Edmund," he said to his clerk, grinning, "and know that I am grateful to have you at my side as an advisor."

Astonishment darted through the monk's dark eyes. His mouth opened as if he meant to speak, but words apparently failed him. In the next instant, he managed a nod then returned abruptly to his feet to once more step back as if promising to interrupt no more.

Amelyn lifted Jessimond's corpse from her lap and laid her daughter onto the damp and yet green sod in front of her. "Sir, if as you say, it's yours to discover who stole the life from my precious child, then I beg you to do so. Do it not only for our king, but for me. I can bear no more grief in my life. I need to not only know who killed my Jessimond, but why. Aye, and I pray you find a way to see that the one who took her life will face earthly justice for his crime as well as whatever punishment our Lord may choose to mete out."

"It shall be done," Faucon promised easily. Her goal was his. "But if I am to succeed at the task you set me, you must answer my questions honestly."

Reaching out, he traced a fist-shaped mark that discolored the area near the girl's shoulder. The color of these bruises suggested Jessimond had taken the beating a day or so before she disappeared. Odger wasn't the only one here in Wike who deserved heavenly justice for earthly wrongdoing. Meg had no right to use fists in her punishments, not when Church law stated that beatings could only to be administered with a stick no thicker than a man's thumb.

Looking up at Amelyn, he asked gently, "Who warned you to come to the well so you might say a final farewell to your daughter? Who told you that your child had thrown herself into its depths to end her life?"

Chapter Five

The leper straightened as if startled. Her head began to move toward Hew, but she caught herself. Bringing her gaze back to center, she aimed her attention at her lap.

Too little, too late. Faucon eyed the rustic as Hew moved back a step or two to once more lean against the well's surround. The old man met his Crowner's gaze, but the only thing to be read in his wrinkled face was the flat blankness that those who served adopted when confronted by their masters.

"No one, I but assumed," Amelyn began, then her words faltered into silence.

She drew herself up. Her shoulders squared. Her hands closed.

Faucon fought a smile. Here was a woman unaccustomed to dealing in falsehoods. With every line of her body Amelyn proclaimed her intention to lie. And in doing so, she would repeat what had happened at the manor door all those years ago. Once again, she courted her own pain to protect another.

"No one told me," she began again. "What else could I think when I saw Jessimond on the ground here at the well? I knew Meg, knew that she was never shy to lift a hand. I believed that her beatings had finally driven my sweet child to seek her own death." Every word rang hollowly.

Faucon cocked his head as he considered how best to drive a grieving mother into revealing the truth. "Tell me this, then. By my estimate, it's a two-day walk from

Warwick to the bounds of Feckenham Forest. Two days was your child missing, or so said your bailiff when he met me in Studley and so your bakestress repeated not long ago. Yet it was only on this day, the morning of the third day, that Gawne roused all and sundry with the call that Jessimond was in the well. Who told you to return to Wike at this precise hour?"

Then he added the most important question of all. "And how is it that you know the recent doings of your former home as if you'd never left this place?"

She gasped. Her mouth opened and closed as if she tried to speak, but no words fell from her lips. Still and silent, Faucon kept his eyes aimed at her. Shifting uncomfortably under his unflinching gaze, she turned her head away from him.

"No one sent for me," she said loudly, as if a stronger voice might convince him, or perhaps herself. Then she did what every liar does. She added a new lie to support the first. "I was traveling to Alcester and decided to pass through Wike this time, it being more or less along my way."

If her falsehood didn't move Faucon, it stirred Edmund. "What? Are the monks who care for you so casual? What reason would they have for sending you so far from them, and why to Alcester?" he demanded, sounding more like his usual judgmental self.

Still basking in his appreciation of the profit his clerk had wrung from a mere serving girl's death, Faucon didn't chide the monk for interrupting this time. Moreover, Edmund's questions were his own. Far better that they be asked by one who understood the doings of the brethren at a leper's house like Saltisford.

Amelyn pinched her shoulders as she fought to maintain her pretense of innocence. "The only benefit of my disease is that I can travel where I will, doing so in complete safety. All of us who are yet able to walk are sent out to plead for alms to help support our house. If I choose to beg in Alcester, why would the brothers care or stop me?" With every word her pretense slipped and her voice weakened.

"The house in Saltisford has no right to speak for the brethren who dwell in Alcester," Edmund retorted. "Nor can I imagine that your keepers might allow you to travel so far from them on your whim alone. They would want a guarantee that you could actually claim a place near the abbey's gate. This, when I'm certain there are already beggars aplenty who own the right to ply their trade in front of the abbey. I've dealt with such rabble. I know well enough that not a one of them would willingly move aside to make space for such as you, not without being commanded to do so by someone within the abbey walls."

Faced with his knowledgeable rebuttal, the leper's pretense collapsed. Amelyn again buried her face in her hands. When she finally lowered them, her hood had shifted back on her head, once more revealing her disfigured face. Her blue eyes glistened as she blinked back tears and met Faucon's gaze.

"I could not bear it," she cried. "When I was forced from this place, I left behind the only thing I loved and I could not let her go. It didn't matter to me that Odger would eagerly strip my pension from me were I discovered in Wike. It was better to die on the side of the road than to be denied my child."

Then she looked up at Edmund. "You are right, Brother. It was no easy matter getting my tenders at Saltisford to agree that I should be allowed to travel as far as Alcester. Aye, they wanted assurances, but those I gave readily and easily. I was well known to one from the abbey, one who could, and did guarantee me a place before the gate twice a month," she added quietly.

The monk drew a sharp breath at this. Whether it

was because her words attested to a sin committed by one of his own or the fact that Edmund caught sight of her disfigured face, there was no telling. Either way, only in that instant did Amelyn realize her hood had slipped. Echoing the monk's sound, she wrenched it back into place, once more concealing her disease.

"Nor are my keepers at the hospital casual about my comings and goings. I only won their agreement when I reminded them that while I'm away they don't need to feed me. Each journey to and from Alcester keeps me out of their house for almost a sennight. That's two sennights each month that they have one less mouth to worry over."

She made a harsh sound. "Would that I weren't such a coward, that I could find the strength to let myself starve. I think it would be a kinder death than the one I face."

"How did your daughter know when to expect you?" Faucon asked, drawing her back to the details he craved.

"That was easily done. Remember that in the first year of my banishment, Meg was yet making a trip to Alcester to sell those loaves of hers, her trips as regular as the moon. I sent one I trusted to Martha with an explanation of my plan. Then, on the appointed day, I waited at the set meeting spot.

"Once again, bless Martha. She and Johnnie came with Jessimond that first time, both of them creeping and cautious, to be certain it was no trap to steal an unwary child. After that, Jessimond and I settled into a happy habit, with Martha and Johnnie joining us as often as they could. For those precious hours I was again a mother to my daughter, and a daughter to one I thought of as a mother. Only after they crept back to our home did I make my way out of the forest, following the deer paths and hog trails to the Street and Alcester."

She touched her hood. Quiet amusement filled her voice as she added, "Then, with me hidden from prying eyes by my cloak, I made my way to my appointed place at the abbey gate. I often passed Meg between Coctune and Alcester. She never once realized it was me." With that Amelyn fell silent, as if lost to her memories.

"Then Martha died," Faucon prodded.

"Aye, Martha died almost a year ago now, two years after Amelyn's banishment," Hew replied on the leper's behalf.

Nodding, the leper glanced from the oldster to her Crowner. "And with that, everything changed. Having to feed Johnnie as well as Jessimond meant Meg no longer had as many stolen loaves to sell and her trips to Alcester became erratic. That left Jessimond and me no option but to begin meeting during the depths of the night while Meg slept. How it broke my heart not to be able to look upon her face any longer," she added quietly.

"Someone aided you," Faucon said, looking at Hew even as he asked the question of Amelyn.

The leper made no reply, only sat with her head bowed and shoulders bent.

"If I'm to discover who killed your daughter, then you must answer all my questions honestly," Faucon reminded her. "Who helped you arrange your meetings?"

With a sigh, Amelyn looked toward the well and the rustic. "Hew?" she asked of the old man. "Will you have me speak further?"

"You may speak as you will and say what you must, Amelyn," the old man replied without a hint of hesitation.

"As you will and as you say," the woman replied, nodding to him before addressing her Crowner.

"While out collecting mushrooms, Hew came upon

me as I waited for Jessimond in our chosen spot. That was the first time after Martha's death that my daughter and I were to have met. Not knowing that my step-mother was gone or that Jessimond was no longer free to leave Meg's kitchen, I was nearly out of my mind with worry by the time Hew found me. After he told me what was what, he carried my message to Jes, then returned with her reply."

"It wasn't only Hew who helped Jessimond reach her mother, was it?" Faucon said, looking at the idiot, trusting the strange man to understand him. "You helped, too. After your mother died and you joined Jessimond in the kitchen, you were the one who guard-ed the door after your niece departed and the one who let her in when she returned."

Johnnie met his Crowner's gaze. Save for his dark hair, he lacked any resemblance to his fair-faced kins-women. Just as his ears were too big for his head, his brown eyes were too small. His nose and chin were overly long, also out of proportion.

Keeping his gaze locked on Faucon's, the idiot nodded, then grasped Jessimond's cold hand as if claiming ownership. At the same time, he made that clicking sound with his tongue, its cadence almost that of speech.

"Aye," Amelyn said quietly, "it was Johnnie who lifted the bar so Jes could leave, then listened for her return to open the door again."

"I think he was less than perfect at his task," Faucon offered, returning to his feet. Thus Meg's complaints about housing a sly girl. Without speech, the idiot couldn't defend Jessimond or lie about her whereabouts when Meg noticed the girl was missing.

"And I say Johnnie was too good at the task Jessi-mond set him," Hew said. "I think he couldn't refuse his niece, and Jes used his fondness for her to her advantage."

The rustic looked at the leper, his voice gentling as he continued. "It's my turn to speak the truth as the good knight has asked of us, Amelyn. Once each month has Jessimond met with you since Martha's death. Do you know how many times during that period she's fled the kitchen to be with Gawne? Touch all your fingers twice and it won't be enough!

"Amelyn, I cannot help but think that you should never have returned here after you were banished, slinking and skulking about like some hunting fox. By your actions you taught your child to do the same when you weren't here to control her. Worse, you gave Jes a freedom that should never have been hers, given her sex. But once she'd tasted what you offered, she craved more still, until she'd have nothing else for her meat. No matter how Meg beat her, your daughter grew ever more daring. At the last, she was striding out of yon kitchen—" the lift of Hew's chin indicated Meg's realm "—as bold as the Queen of May."

"I never meant..." Amelyn started to protest.

"Of course you didn't," Hew interrupted not unkindly, then looked at his Crowner. "Today was the day set for mother and daughter to meet, and why Amelyn sits here now. There is no other reason and no one called for her to come. As to why Amelyn thought Jessimond had fallen in the well, it's because that's what Gawne insisted I tell her."

Once again, the bits Faucon had collected thus far shifted in his mind. He added to them his certainty that Jessimond had died in the same place in which she and her mother had met. So too did he now suspect where Gawne would be found. That was, if Odger didn't already know the location of that meeting place.

He again glanced toward the line of trees where Gawne had entered the woods. There was no sign of bailiff or boy. It didn't sit well on him that he had to leave this place without knowing what became of the lad, but leave he and Edmund must and soon. The shadows beginning to cloak the eastern reaches of the forest promised nightfall.

"Although I did as Gawne asked," Hew was saying, "speaking his lie yet eats at me. Hear the truth now, Amelyn. Two nights ago, your daughter once more crept out of that kitchen, doing just as you had asked of her so many times before, and what she'd chosen to do when she wished to be with Gawne. But this time she didn't leave to meet either of you. Instead, Jessimond braved all, going into the dark with no witness or protector at her side, to meet God alone knows who."

Here, the oldster pointed to the girl's unclothed corpse. "This is what became of her, for this is how Gawne found her."

Amelyn shrieked at that. She crumpled atop her daughter, his fists clenched. "Nay! I killed her. Mary save me, I killed my own child," she sobbed, then began to grieve in earnest.

Chapter Six

"She killed her own child?" Edmund cried quietly from beside Faucon, his voice held to a horrified whisper. There was something in the monk's expression that begged for assurances on the leper's behalf. It was definitely a day for surprises when it came to Edmund.

"Nay, she did not," Faucon replied even though he had no right to claim innocence for Amelyn. Although he believed she'd done no wrong, he hadn't yet proved that to himself.

At his answer his clerk released a relieved breath, but confusion yet marked the man's brow. "If so, then what purpose does she have in calling out now that she did the deed?" Edmund wanted to know.

Faucon started to laugh, only to catch back his amusement as he realized his clerk was serious. However impossible, Edmund didn't see the woman's grief-stricken protest for what it was. Again, he offered as much explanation as he had in store.

"I can only speculate," he began in preface, then paused to look at Amelyn. The idiot now knelt next to his grieving half- sister as she lay across her daughter's cold form, alternating between cooing and flapping his hands in agitation.

Faucon looked back at Edmund. "I can only speculate but I believe the leper has just realized how she is complicit in her daughter's death. By refusing to surrender to the fate our Lord set upon her, as severe and unfair as that fate might seem to her or to us, she

87

unknowingly planted an evil seed in her child. It's a different sort of wrongdoing that this mother claims for herself."

"Ah, I see," Edmund breathed again, the color and calm returning to his face. "The leper is in need of a priest so she might unburden her heart."

"That would likely serve her well," Faucon agreed. "Now gather your gear, Brother. There's no time left for scribbling. We need to be off to Alcester for the night."

Edmund glanced at the sky. "Aye, it's time to leave if we wish to arrive at the abbey before the porter closes the gates," he said, once again speaking as if he had the right to comment on his employer's decision.

Faucon only smiled. After today, he thought he could forgive Edmund any insult. Moreover, there was no point in chiding. Nothing he said affected the monk's behavior.

As his clerk slung his basket over his shoulder, Faucon looked at Hew. The old man watched him in return. With a jerk of his chin, Faucon indicated the oldster should join him. Resistance and not a little caution filled the rustic's expression. Nonetheless, Hew started for his Crowner, his gait hitched by his unbalanced hips. He stopped abreast of his better.

"Sir?" he asked, as he bowed his head. In that instant Hew looked like the one thing Faucon was certain he wasn't, a pitiful and helpless old man.

"My clerk and I leave Wike for the night," Faucon told him. "When your bailiff comes from the forest, let him know to expect our return on the morrow. Also tell him that before the morrow is done, I'll want to call the jury to view the girl's body, even if I may not yet be able to name the one who did the deed. Against that, Odger shouldn't send your menfolk too far afield."

As Hew nodded his agreement to these requests, Faucon added, "And lastly, I ask that you bear me company as my clerk and I make our way to our mounts. I have questions."

That brought the old man out of his humble posture with a start. Hew shot a glance at Amelyn before looking at his king's servant, a man with the right by birth and royal fiat to demand his compliance. The oldster's wild white brows inched up on his forehead. Nothing but caution remained in his pale eyes.

That promised little, even though the rustic answered the only way allowed for a man of his station. "As you will, sir."

They started away from the well together, Faucon moderating his stride to match the old man's slower gait. Edmund was already well ahead of them, moving at his usual clipped pace. "Is it safe to leave the child's body in the open overnight?" Faucon asked as they walked.

"If by that you mean to ask about wolves in these woods, nay we have none, not with the king wishing to keep deer within his pale," Hew replied with a negative shake of his head. "Now, if you're worrying that someone might do damage to the child's corpse," he continued, shooting a sharp- edged and sidelong glance at his Crowner, "don't. Between Amelyn's disease and that curse she spewed, I expect her poor lass will stay right where she is until her bones are dust." The old man gave a huff of disgust as he continued. "Indeed, unless Odger plies the lash, I think the only creatures who'll touch Jessimond's remains from this day forward are the ravens and the worms. Amelyn shouldn't have thrown those words of hers, empty though they were."

The possibility that the child's body would be denied a proper resting place set Faucon to considering. If he was careful how he pried, perhaps he could discover which monk Amelyn had served at the abbey. Other than Edmund, who was oblivious to the subtlety of what went forward around him, most monks were terrible gossips, or so claimed Faucon's sire. Faucon wondered if this was because most monks spent much of their day in silence. Thus, when the time came for their tongues to wag, wag they did.

More importantly, everyone, no matter their estate, liked to talk about their betters. The man Faucon sought, the one who had made Amelyn his leman, must sit high in the abbey's hierarchy. Only one so placed could have granted her the right to beg at the gate. Once Faucon found this man's name, perhaps a slight nudge might prod that sinning churchman into doing one more boon for the leper by providing a grave for her murdered child.

As they crossed the boundary between the manor's demesne and drew closer to the homes that served Wike's folk, the footpath he and Hew followed changed. Although the track remained just as deep, having been carved into the sod by generations of feet, it ceased to run in a straight line. Instead, it narrowed and began to snake, curling its way to and fro in front of the homes of the settlement. Such a meandering course suggested that no serf in Wike had ever chosen to hurry into his lord's—or lady's—fields.

No longer able to walk alongside the old man, not without climbing out of the deep rut to totter along its uneven edge, Faucon fell back and let Hew move ahead of him. "What was Gawne's purpose in lying to the leper about her daughter's death? Why put Jessimond's body in the well?" He threw his questions up to the old man.

"I cannot speak for Gawne, sir," Hew replied flatly without turning his head.

Unwilling to press the rustic for fear of losing all advantage, Faucon shifted onto another potential trail. "What can you tell me about how Jessimond's body looked when Gawne brought you to her."

"Sir, I fear you've heard all I know of this deadly matter." Once again, the old man spoke flatly and offered no more than his station and courtesy required.

Stymied, Faucon stifled his frustration. He needed to find the right key if he was to unlock the man's tongue, else he'd get no more. That sent him backtracking to safe ground, a trail that he'd already traveled and knew led nowhere.

"Was Jessimond with child by Gawne?"

That teased a quiet laugh out of Hew. The sound was a donkey's muted bray. This time he happily followed where his Crowner led.

"Meg is wrong in that." The old man turned his head to the side so he could speak to his Crowner from over his shoulder. "Despite that those two spent time alone together, it's as Ivo said. They were but children enjoying a few innocent hours. But it is true that Ivo has no place in his smithy for his youngest child. I think this isn't because he means to deny or ignore Gawne, but because he already has help enough with his older boys. That leaves nothing to offer his youngest, either to train Gawne in a skill or to keep him occupied. Against that, Ivo should have allowed his lad to be apprenticed elsewhere. Instead, he refused, insisting that someday soon he'll at last need to bring his youngest to the forge."

A few yards ahead of them the path curved sharply inward then straightened to run only an arm's length from the forefronts of a half-dozen moss-bespeckled cottages. As they drew closer to these homes, Faucon caught the sounds of a mother seeking to soothe her crying infant while in another a couple fought. Although he couldn't make out their words, there was no mistaking the rising indignation in the man's voice or the woman's pleading tone.

Hew stopped before he reached the nearest edge of

that first cottage, resting his hand on his painful hip. Faucon stopped with him, stepping out of the rutted path onto the narrow verge so he could stand alongside the old man. Hew's expression filled with the same distaste that the villeins at the well had shown when Ivo hadn't chastised Gawne for his rude response.

"Shame on Ivo," the old man said, shaking his head. "It's no good when a child has a father too busy to guide him. Nor can any good come of it when that child is left without mother, sister, or some other woman to note when and from whence he comes and goes. I don't wonder that Gawne sought out Jessimond, our only other motherless child near his age, as his playmate. He needed something to occupy his time and someone to ease his aching heart after his mother passed. That's what he found in Jes, who was much like her dam, swift to protect another while leaving herself open to hurt."

"What did Odger do when Meg complained about the two meeting?" Faucon wanted to know.

That made Hew laugh out loud. It was definitely a bray. "Meg would rather cut her fingers from her hand than give Odger so much as a crumb of information she might garner about what happens here. Those two despise each other, she because Odger has previously tried to steal her freedom from her the way he's done to the rest of us, and he because Meg is the only soul here who remains outside of his control.

"As for those of us who had an inkling about Gawne and Jes—and we are many—to a one we've held our tongues. For good reason. Because Ivo is too busy to tend to his youngest, he's left us to do what he will not, when it's not ours to do. Ivo knows that Odger doesn't tolerate idle hands. So too does he know that our bailiff has been sending his lad to do a man's work in the fields, even though Gawne is yet too small to bear such a burden. This is especially so over our autumn months. Harvesting is exhausting for the strongest among us. But because there are presently more than enough younger lads in Wike to do the easier tasks, Gawne found himself holding the scythe and reaping alongside his elders, despite that he's ill-fitted to the tool."

The old man looked at his Crowner and shrugged as he continued. "The lad does his best, but he's more hindrance than help. Frustrated by the constant chiding over his errors, corrections he's earned by no fault save that of his size, Gawne began to slip away for an hour or two when Jessimond was free and Odger was occupied elsewhere. All who saw and noted turned a blind eye, grateful for those periods without him. If Odger had known Gawne was escaping him, he'd have found a way to stop the boy, even if it meant tying the lad to one of us," Hew finished, speaking as if he'd been among the reapers when Faucon knew he wouldn't have been.

Drawing a bracing breath, the old man gave a quick nod. "I am ready to walk on," he told his Crowner.

But as he began to move forward along the path, leaving Faucon to trail behind again, Hew said no more. Just as they passed the fourth house, the weather-beaten wooden shutters on its front window creaked open. None of the homely sounds Faucon had heard from the other dwellings emanated from this one. Nor did he see an eye in the gap although the crack was wide enough to peep through.

The old man held his peace until the path had again curved outward, taking them well beyond the last home. When Hew spoke again, he picked up right where he'd left off. "Gawne won't be doing the same next year. By then, the boy will have seen twelve of his saint's days and it will be time for him to carry a man's load. Or, if he cannot," he added, "then Gawne will learn to bear his frustration as every man must."

As the oldster fell silent this time, Faucon sifted

through his bits and pieces, trying to discern where next to go. Nothing was obvious or enticing. Too much remained missing to make any sense of what he had in store. That left him with nothing to do save continue to confirm what he already knew.

"How is it you're certain it wasn't Gawne who killed Jessimond?" he asked, even though Hew had made no such assertion.

This time the rustic followed where his Crowner led. "I have my reasons just as you do, sir," he retorted, shooting a quick look at his better from over his shoulder.

"You're certain I believe him innocent, are you?" Faucon countered with a laugh.

"Indeed I am, even though I know not what reason you might have for judging the lad blameless, sir. What I do know is that if you thought Gawne at fault for Jessimond's death, you'd not only have joined the hue and cry, you'd have roused all the others to come help you find the boy."

"And you would be correct," Faucon agreed, appreciating the old man's assessment.

Again Hew stopped, this time turning in the path to face his better. "Aye, well, I may no longer have good use of these," he held up his hands, displaying fingers twisted beyond all but basic usefulness, and beyond the possibility of throttling a young girl, even one with as slender a neck as Jessimond's, "but I'm not blind. You aren't our sheriff. You want what's right, not what's convenient.

"As for me," the oldster continued, dropping his arms to his sides, "I known Gawne all his life and he's an honest boy. I trust him when he tells me he's done no wrong."

Faucon offered a swift and, he hoped, reassuring smile. "That doesn't surprise me. In you I see a man who knows everyone and everything that happens in this place, even if you don't much trust your neighbors," he said, now seeking to guide the rustic where he willed him to go. "I also believe that after Amelyn's step-mother died, you began joining the leper at her meeting spot, doing so in Martha's stead. I think it's because of you that Amelyn knows all the recent doings in Wike. Not only were you meeting Amelyn, I'd also wager you made yourself chaperone for Gawne and Jessimond when they met. That's why Gawne came to you after he found the girl."

"That's a great deal of speculation even for a knight as clever as you, sir," Hew retorted. Then he sighed. "I suppose if you suspect that much, you'll not rest until you have your explanation."

The old man once again held up his useless hands. "These are why I rarely ever sleep within Wike's bounds these days and why I am free to forage as I will outside of Odger's control. Our bailiff has named me useless and a burden, and he'd like nothing better than to drive me from Wike just as he did Amelyn."

With that, Hew freed an angry breath and turned to look at the far edge of the settlement behind them, at the same far- flung cottage toward which Amelyn had directed her attention when she spoke of her rape.

"I vow, that man values nothing save the control he exercises over us and what few coins he can wring from us. My family, bless them, cannot afford to resist him, and I cannot blame them for that. Such is the fate of a man who has lived too long and has only sons who have only sons. Were I to demand space under the roof that was once mine, we'd be four generations pressing one against the other, with yet another on the way. So many in one home makes our pot always hungry. And, how-ever unhappy I may be about being denied my full portion, I can but concede that those who work the fields must be fed first."

Then Hew brought his attention back onto his Crowner and offered the glimmer of a smile. "Yet, despite that my present state suggests I should be begging for Odger's mercy, I cannot bring myself to do it. Instead, my tongue moves when and how it wills. Given that, I suspect Odger would leap on any chance to do to me what he would have done to Johnnie all those years ago: he'd drag me to the far wastes and see to it that I died there."

The old man's pale eyes once again took fire with that perverse amusement of his. "I think the only reason Odger hasn't yet attempted my death is the fear that I'd not only survive his attack but crawl back to Wike on my belly just to spite him." It was a sarcastic aside. "So, having heard all that, sir, consider this. Although Odger isn't here to witness, we presently stand in full view of all my neighbors. Perhaps now you understand my reluctance to speak."

Faucon nodded. Indeed, given so capricious and controlling a headman, the old man had already risked much by simply walking alongside his Crowner. But in Hew's words Faucon also found the key he needed.

"Does your lady keep Odger out of fondness or habit?" he asked, certain he knew the answer. He'd heard it while listening to Amelyn's tale.

"Habit," Hew offered swiftly, with a confirming nod. "Wike is the least of her dower. I think that as long as our grain fills her granaries and our coins come to her purse from her oven, she cares little what happens here." Then, as if he feared he'd been too honest, the rustic added, "Not that she's unkind. Look what she did for Amelyn."

"So, if the murdrum fine were to be levied against all of Wike, including your lady, because of the wrong Odger did Amelyn years ago, do you think your lady might give closer attention to who rules here on her behalf?" Faucon asked, holding back nothing in a show of trust, one he hoped wasn't misplaced.

That sent Hew's wild white brows high upon his forehead. He stared directly at his Crowner as if trying to discern the truth in his better's expression. Faucon held his tongue, content to wait until the oldster was comfortable with what he'd been offered. As the silence stretched, the old man's eyes narrowed and the creases on his face deepened.

"Is this a certainty, or do you just speculate, sir?" the commoner at last dared to ask of his better, when he had no right to pose the question. Nor did he have any reason to expect an answer, not from one placed so far above him.

Faucon almost smiled as the trail he sought appeared before him. "The law is clear in this instance," he assured the old man. "As long as the name of the one who fathered Jessimond remains unknown, it must be done."

A slow and satisfied grin spread Hew's lips. "Well now, that's an unexpected turn of events, isn't it? Perhaps I've been overly cautious. Ask your questions, sir, and I'll answer them as best I can."

"Did Jessimond die in the place where she and her mother met?" Faucon asked immediately.

That set Hew to blinking in surprise. "Aye, so she did, sir. How do you know that?" he replied in astonishment.

Faucon only smiled and pressed on. "Might that be the same place where Gawne now hides from the hue and cry? More importantly, do his brothers or your bailiff know to look for him in this place?" Much rested on the answers to these questions.

"I cannot swear to where Gawne went," Hew said carefully, "but were I seeking him, that hidden place of theirs would be where I looked first."

Then the rustic cocked his head and squinted as he considered the second question. After a moment, he shook his head. "I'm not certain if Gawne shared the location of this place with his father or his brothers, but as for Odger, although I have no right to claim it, my heart is certain he knows nothing of the spot. That was Amelyn's reason for choosing it. She knew our bailiff had never been one who liked venturing too deep into our wild woods.

"More importantly, those two innocents built a nest high above. Even with the branches almost bare now, I doubt Odger will look upward to find what he seeks should he accidentally stumble across the place."

That teased a relieved breath from Faucon. "Then on the morrow I will not only want to visit this hidey-hole," he said, "I'll need to speak with Gawne. To do that, I think I must have you at my side," he added.

Resistance began again to darken the old man's pale eyes. Faucon held up a hand. "Know that if Gawne stays hidden from me until I leave Wike, he'll never be clear of the charge of Jessimond's murder, even if another ends up yoked to that verdict," he warned. "And if Gawne spies me coming without one he trusts at my side, all he'll see is the hangman reaching for him. Given a choice between you and his sire, I'd rather it be you with me. He trusts you more than he does his own father."

Once again, Hew blinked in surprise. "How can you know that?" he whispered.

When his Crowner gave him no answer, the rustic considered his better for another few breaths, scratching at his nose as he did. "Do you know that until the day I came across Amelyn in the woods," he said at last, "I'd given myself over to self-pity and bitter regrets, dwelling upon what I'd lost in my life and despising the one who had stripped all I loved from me. So tightly did the trap of hatred hold me that I awoke each day longing to either give death or receive it. That kept me blind to the truth. Aye, Odger had taken much from me, but in exchange for what I'd lost a great gift came. Didn't I now come and go as I pleased, bowing to no man? Aye, and I served my family far better than I had previously, collecting much of what we needed to feed that hungry pot of ours. More times than not, I managed to gather enough to fill it to its brim, leaving no one longing for more.

"Then I found Amelyn in the woods, waiting for her daughter. There she was, despite her disease and all Odger's evil will for her, finding a way to thwart him and get what she most desired. In that moment, hatred lifted and my heart began to beat again. That's when I saw I'd been doing the same, however unwittingly," he added. "And all I needed to do if I wished to continue thwarting Odger was to hold tight to my life, that being the one thing our bailiff wanted most from me."

The old man again looked at the cottages that housed his family and neighbors. "Shame on us in Wike! We gave that dastard the right to control us, then forgot that we could undo what was done, taking back what we'd given as easily as we'd bequeathed it."

As Hew paused to draw breath his features again took light with that amusement of his. "On that day, I ceased to harbor any ill thoughts. Nor do I now spend my every day foraging. Instead, four days each month I follow my secret ways to Alcester and the abbey gate where I might be found standing beside Amelyn, pretending to be her grandsire."

"Might you be?" Faucon laughed in reply.

The oldster gave a quick wink. "Indeed sir, I just might. Although only Amelyn is allowed to extend a hand in pleading, she always shares some of what she collects with me. That has gone a long way to aiding me and my family. Look at this!"

Here, the rustic braced the heel of his damaged leg upon the ground. Shifting his foot from side to side, he displayed one of his simple but sturdy leather shoes. "Look what a townsman gave to me last month! I didn't believe merchants knew the meaning of generosity, especially when it comes to our sort. Always thought they were like Odger, too wedded to coins and too full of themselves to care about the needs of others. I assumed they considered those of us bound to the fields and furrows as no better than the oxen that pull our plows," he added harshly.

"But the one who brought these to me spoke humbly and bowed as if I were his better. Me! He said he'd noticed me a fortnight earlier and saw I hadn't a stitch to cover my toes when winter was coming. Then he pressed these on me. He simply gave them to me, asking for nothing in return!" As Hew finished, he returned his comfortably- and warmly-shod foot to the hard earthen path, still shaking his head in remembered amazement.

Faucon gave a friendly shrug. "Kindness begets kindness, or so the priests ever tell us."

"Yours, perhaps," the old man shot back, then turned to once again in the direction of the greensward. Now that they were walking away from the cottages, the verge was less rugged and the path not as deep. Faucon stepped outside of it so he could walk alongside the old man as Hew continued.

"Our priest only ever speaks about how those of us who labor must bow to both God's will and that of our lady." Hew glanced up at the knight walking alongside him. "That is, when our holy man chooses to leave the comfort of Coctune to appear here. Most often, we must trek the Lane to him if we wish to have him hear our confessions and our prayers."

Somehow it didn't surprise Faucon that the priest

who served folk such as these, men chained by long tradition to their lords' lands, might choose to lecture about submission and obedience. It was a hard-fought and different sort of war that barons and earls waged these days, what with so many lucrative opportunities available in the burgeoning towns across this land, tempting their villeins to find a better life. The grander the town and merchant, the greater their need for men to produce what they sold. That made these merchants far more likely to bite their thumbs at the law, stealing what they wanted from their betters. Perhaps that explained why Odger used an iron hand to rule the folk of Wike, however misguided the practice. The bailiff was doing all he knew to keep those beneath him from fleeing to greener pastures.

"You know the best part about these shoes?" Hew's eyes flashed with amusement as he glanced up at Faucon. "When Odger accosted me about them, demanding to know how I came by them, I told him that one of the monks who tends the hogs in the woodlands had given them to me. You should have seen him choke at that. None of the monks will speak with Odger. He was irate when our lady's brother-by-marriage gave the monks the rights to run their hogs so near our fields. He wanted them moved and he thought he might accomplish that by lies. So he complained time and again to the abbot and the bailiff in Coctune about the brothers not minding their hogs, lying about how those poor piggies were destroying our fields. Now look at me! I've lied to him, knowing that between Odger's falsehoods and his arrogance, the brothers wouldn't say him *yea* or *nay*, even if he did ask them about my footwear!"

Hew brayed at his own jest. When his amusement died, the rustic picked up a trail his Crowner had given up any hope of following, much to Faucon's surprise.

"Sir, a moment ago you asked about why Gawne

wanted to bring Jessimond back to Wike. It's that he couldn't bear the thought of leaving his friend in the woods for the wild creatures to make a meal of. But neither could he bring himself to call the others to that place, not even to bear her home from where she died. That's why I believe he never told his kin where their spot is. To Gawne, it would be revealing a secret he didn't think was his to spill."

The old man released another breathy bray. "All I can say is God be praised that boy chose to beg my assistance in bringing her home the morning after he found her. Between his size and my age, if he'd waited until last night, I vow we'd not have reached Wike until midday on the morrow. Neither of us thought to steal a wheelbarrow to use."

"Why put her in the well?" Faucon asked.

"Because Gawne wanted Amelyn to believe her daughter's death an accident," the old man answered swiftly if sadly. "The lad feared she'd grieve all the more if she knew the truth. And now it seems he was right," Hew added, then shook his head. "But weren't all his efforts, and mine in aiding him, for naught? First, neither of us considered that if we put the lass in the well, someone would have to bring her out again. As you saw, sir, that was no easy task. Gawne had made it mine to convince Amelyn to stay away from Wike once she learned of Jessimond's death. I failed miserably, and only barely returned to Wike ahead of her, hoping to warn Gawne that she was coming. Yet again I failed, and Amelyn came racing in when she shouldn't have.

"But not all of this failure is mine to claim," the oldster offered with a twisted grin. "Instead, you'll have to own some of it, sir. The instant you revealed Jessimond hadn't drowned, you destroyed all the good Gawne intended and inadvertently turned him into the murderer."

Faucon laughed at that. "So I did, setting you both, with your intentions, onto that road to Hell of which our priests warn," he offered.

"That's God's own truth," the old man agreed.

They had reached the near edge of the greensward. The long and narrow strip of grass yet retained most of its summer color. Staked at its center, Faucon's white courser Legate offered a sharp snort of greeting to his master, then the gelding shifted in annoyance. Just beyond the horse, Edmund's donkey was doing his best to escape the monk as Edmund sought to mount. Although Legate was well-trained and patient for his breed, he wanted his master to know that so much agitated motion was making him edgy.

Faucon turned his back on his courser to address the rustic. "My clerk and I intend to seek shelter for the night at the abbey in Alcester. If we don't meet you while you beg at the gates as we depart from that place in the morning, I'm certain Brother Edmund will want to share Sext prayers and the midday meal with his brethren. I'll return with him and seek you out then. You will be there with Amelyn on the morrow, the morrow being her day at the abbey, aye?"

Hew only shrugged. "It is her day for certain, but I wouldn't put your trust in her, sir. I think she won't want to leave her child. I'm not certain it's wise of me to come to the abbey without her."

"I think she'll have no choice about leaving her daughter. From what I've seen, I believe your bailiff intends to drive her out of Wike once he returns this even, no matter what he must do to achieve that," Faucon replied with a lift of his brows. "I'm all the more convinced of this after hearing your tale. If Odger drives her away, where else will she go save to the abbey?"

Still Hew shook his head in disagreement. "That's hard to say, sir. But rather than depend on one man's cruelty or a grieving mother's woes and whereabouts, instead ask for one of the brothers to lead you to their hogscotes, and make your way into the woods at your convenience. Know that when you arrive at those hog pens, you'll find me waiting for you. Indeed, I think me that's where I'll sleep this night, once I bear your message to Meg."

Hew's eyes again took light as his lips lifted into a grin. "I think she'll pass your words onto our bailiff. There's nothing that old biddy likes better than to offer up commands to Odger. Now, good evening to you, sir. I'll see you upon the morrow." At that, the rustic shifted as if to depart, only to pause and turn his head until he looked at his Crowner from over his shoulder.

"Pity poor Amelyn. I worry that she'll not survive being driven from Wike a second time, not with nothing left in this world to connect her to it or us," he offered on a sigh.

Faucon sighed with him. Aye, there was much to pity on Amelyn's behalf. Then again, who was he to judge their Lord's plan for another? The only part he had to play in all this was to ignore any wrongdoing the leper might have committed in regards to what was written in the king's records.

"The road to Hell," Faucon repeated more gently this time. "On the morrow, Hew."

Hew touched his forehead in a gesture of respect, then started along the edge of the greensward, moving back into the bounds of a place that no longer offered him home or hearth any more than it did the leper.

Chapter Seven

Once Edmund managed to turn his little mount in the proper direction, Faucon guided Legate to the deer path that Odger had earlier named Wike Lane. Unlike the forested lands into which Gawne had fled at the far end of Wike, here the branches and brambles that lined the narrow track swiftly gave way to fallow wastes. As far as Faucon's eye could see there was naught but coppiced stumps and stands of saplings. Occasional swards, islands of yet green grass, sparkled amid this sea of brushy growth, those strips just now beginning to yellow despite that winter would soon be upon them.

While such an expanse might be tempting to ox, goat, or sheep, for the browse was rich and varied, it did little to please the eye. Nor was such a landscape unusual, especially in places that had been so long settled. Over the ages, each generation had harvested the trees they needed to feed their home fires, forges, and charcoal pits, until the oak or ash were gone. Indeed, it was a surprise to see so many full-grown trees yet standing in one place. But then, the only reason any forest remained was at a lord's command, that lord for Feckenham Forest being the king.

It wasn't long before the scrubby landscape again gave way, this time to something more settled and productive. The closer they drew to the hamlet of Coctune, the more cultivated fields unfolded around them. Some of these patches already rested for the season beneath blankets of rotting manure or trampled grasses. Others were yet bearded in golden stubble, all that remained of this year's wheat and barley. It was among the remains of these fields that the hamlet's geese grazed, moving slowly toward the cottages that promised them safety for the night.

Although the flock was a goodly distance from the riders, the fowl sensed strangers and raised their heads as one to look. Then they did as geese ever do when alarmed— they honked out an aggressive warning. Never mind that the travelers were on a distant track, the one that followed the hamlet's farthest- flung boundary.

As Faucon and Edmund made their way around the settlement, Faucon marked the tiny church that served the priest Hew had mentioned. It stood beside a manor house that was in much better repair than the one in Wike. When Odger had led them past Coctune this afternoon, the hamlet had appeared empty. No longer. Having returned from their fields or barns, brightly-dressed folk came and went along paths that wound between cottages and hovels, waving and calling out to one another as they finished their last tasks of the day.

Alerted to it by the geese, a band of reckless lads, all about Gawne's age, raced out to meet the riders. In their excitement at finding strangers on their lane, these brave boys dared to run alongside horse and donkey. As they did, they peppered a stranger— an armed knight in an unmarked surcoat no less—with their questions.

"Who are you? From whence did you come? Why are you riding out of Wike? Where are you going? Sir knight, why do you travel with a monk?"

Their boldness made Faucon laugh. He answered them in a voice as strong as their own. "I am Sir Faucon de Ramis. At our king's command, I am your shire's new Crowner and this monk is my clerk. Remember my name, for my clerk and I travel our shire in King Richard's name, seeking out those who have done murder and rape." He grinned as he offered this, liking the sound of it.

Talk of murders, rapes, and kings startled some of the lads. While those boys fell back, huddling to discuss this further, the more daring of the bunch yet trotted alongside the strangers, keeping pace for the sheer joy of it. Their continued presence stirred Edmund from his silence.

"Haven't you anything better to do than pester us? Now that you've marked Sir Faucon's name and noted that he is your new Keeper of the Pleas, be gone with you!" the monk shouted. The lads laughed at the toothless threat and continued to defy Edmund all the way to the headless cross, where Wike Lane met with the Ryknild Street.

Faucon once again looked askance at the Street. Earlier today the prior in Studley had lauded it as a grand thoroughfare. Thoroughfare, indeed! Although the path did run straight and true, as did many a truly ancient road, Ryknild Street looked like nothing more than another well-used trail cutting into Warwickshire's ruddy earth. Hardly impressive to someone who'd traveled marvelous stone-paved highways while crusading with King Richard.

"South, Sir Faucon," Edmund commanded unnecessarily from behind his employer.

With a final wave to the lads, Faucon turned Legate onto the Street, then urged his courser to a fast walk. In only moments, the edge of Feckenham Forest receded until it was but a golden-brown wave, marking the gentle rise of the land to the west. The fertile fields did the same, once more giving way to that ragged scrub. Even though the coverage wasn't dense, there was more than enough dying foliage to hide horse and rider.

That set the skin on Faucon's nape to prickling. His ears came into tune, seeking out every crack and snap. To the marrow of his bones he was certain that Sir Alain awaited him somewhere along this stretch. Bringing his heels to Legate's sides, he urged the courser into a trot, leaving Edmund to rouse his little mount as best he could. Fortunately, the donkey sensed the end of day. Like most beasts of burden, he didn't much care for the dark. The monk had only to apply his switch a time or two before the little creature was skittering along behind Legate, Edmund huffing as he jounced in his saddle.

Far sooner than Faucon expected, the stench of Alcester reached out to envelop him, although he couldn't yet see anything of the town. So it was with any settlement larger than a few hundred souls. That was, if any of those souls wished to eat meat. Turning livestock into food required a shambles, and there was no escaping the stink that accompanied slaughtering. Since tanners often lived cheek-by-jowl with the butchers, the foul odor of turning skin into leather mingled with that of butchery. But twining 'round and 'round all that reek was the rich, sweet aroma of malting barley.

Just as that enticing smell set Faucon's stomach to wishing, the church bells began to ring. There were three distinct voices, each marking a different religious house, all of them inviting their parishioners to celebrate the Vespers service. The one with a clear tenor tone rose from ahead of them, marking a church within Alcester proper, while a more distant baritone voice echoed from an establishment a good ways to the east.

The closest invitation came from a deep bass bell that rang out across the resting field to Faucon's left. Startled that there might be a church located so close to Alcester but not within the security of the town and whatever walls it had, he glanced in that direction.

There was nothing to see except a line of trees, the same water-loving willow, alder, and birch that grew along the bank of any waterway. In this instance, yon trees marked the course of the river that moved in a far more meandering fashion alongside the arrow-straight route of Ryknild Street.

The peal of those bells only increased Faucon's concern. At Vespers in the winter and Compline in the summer, not only did these bells announce the time for prayers; they also warned all who heard them that the moment had come to close and bar their doors, be those doors a simple panel in a hovel or the gates in a town wall.

Praying that Alcester's watch was in no hurry to bid the world goodnight, he rose in his stirrups, seeking to judge the distance between him and the security he craved. The roofs of the houses within the town's enclosing wooden wall rose just high enough for him to see the pall of smoke snaking and swirling over a sea of gentle thatch. No gate was readily visible, at least not from this angle. As for distance, the span between him and the town walls was no more than a quarter mile by his eye.

Not that he and Edmund would reach those walls or any gate that could give them access to Alcester.

Coming toward him at a walk on this Street were three mounted men. All of them wore leather hauberks while two sported metal helmets, the sort usually worn by foot soldiers. The lead rider was barrel-chested and broad-shouldered. He rode bare-headed, revealing sandy-colored hair and a full beard that gleamed reddish even in the dimming light.

Sir Alain.

In that instant, Faucon did as he'd been taught by the man who had forged him into a warrior. He sent a prayer for his continued life winging heavenward, then released his fate into his Lord's hands. As he breathed out worry, he drew in resolve. It would be three pitted against one, and that one had a monk to protect. Beneath him, Legate sensed the change in his master and reacted, snorting and lifting his head.

"This way, sir," Edmund called from behind his employer just as that nearby deep-toned bell pealed its last.

Faucon shot a startled glance back at his clerk. Edmund had left the Street to guide his little mount across the field beside them, heading directly toward that fading bass echo. Again Faucon peered at the screen of trees. This time he saw what he'd first missed. Barely visible through the tangled branches was a wooden wall.

The abbey wasn't inside Alcester.

He grinned in wicked pleasure and not a little relief. Not only was that holy house close at hand, but he'd reach the place well ahead of the sheriff. More importantly to his pride, he'd do it at a pace no faster than an easy walk.

God save them, he and the sheriff were a pair. Neither of them could bear to give another the satisfaction of a reaction. Just as Faucon would rather die than send Legate galloping for safety, he was certain Sir Alain wouldn't wield his spurs to chase down his new Crowner, not even if it meant losing his prey to holy ground, where no man dared shed blood.

In only moments, Faucon followed Edmund through the gap in the trees. It wasn't the river that fed them. Instead they lined the far side of the man- made moat that coursed in front of the monastery's weathered wooden walls. That meant the river ran behind the abbey and put this house on its own little island, explaining why it didn't need the safety of town walls.

Although Edmund had drawn his mount to a halt

before the foot of the drawbridge that led onto the artificial island, the monk had yet to dismount. Faucon glanced beyond his clerk and breathed out in satisfaction and not a little relief. The thick wooden doors that guarded this place yet stood wide in the arched entranceway. That was likely because the monk whose chore it was to close them had left his post. Instead, Brother Porter stood at the center of the bridge, his hands tucked into his sleeves. Both he and Edmund stared off to the left, their faces alive in avid and unguarded interest.

With his safety in hand, Faucon released the warrior's focus. Only then did he hear the on-going argument, three male voices, all speaking at once and in English, two native speakers while the other was clearly more comfortable in French. Each man kept raising his voice as he sought to talk over the other two. As expected, it was to the French speaker that the first two were making insistent pleas for aid, only to receive consistently negative answers from the high-born man.

Dismounting, Faucon shifted to glance in the direction of the argument. There were six, not three men, and four horses gathered a little way from the drawbridge. Two of the men faced him, one tall and powerfully built with his face buried in his hands, the other a short, balding priest with a bulbous nose and ears that stuck out from his head. Dark rings hung beneath this holy shepherd's eyes, exhaustion cutting deep lines onto his face. Despite that, the arrangement of his features suggested he was easy-going, not the sort that Faucon would have expected to raise his voice to his betters.

Both men wore wrinkled and water -stained garments, as if they'd swum in the moat then allowed their clothing to dry upon their bodies. That was an oddness indeed, for the priest wore his ritual attire, garments that generally never left the church. As for the taller man, his garment was also fine, a dark green tunic decorated with an expensive line of embroidery along its hem. Again, hardly the sort of garment a man risked to the wet.

The other four men had their backs to Faucon. Three of them were knights in full armor beneath their white surcoats and arranged in a protective half-circle behind their cloaked and hooded master. Even without knights to guard him, Faucon would have recognized their master as a wealthy magnate by the quality of his red cloak alone.

Dismissing the arguers, Faucon shifted to look at the track behind him. Just as he expected, Alain and his men were on the path leading to the abbey, about halfway across the field. And, just as he expected, the three of them moved as if they had no haste. That made Faucon grin. This time it would be the sheriff's pride rather than his Crowner's skill that cost Sir Alain what he wanted.

Just then, the on-going argument to his left escalated. "She's only a child! How can you refuse to help an innocent?!" the man with the deeper voice shouted.

Faucon shot another quick glance at the group, only to discover one of the knights now watched him from over his shoulder. The man was young, surely no more than Faucon's own score-and-four years. Although the knight's features were unremarkable, there was something in his face that sparked recognition.

That recognition was returned. The knight's eyes widened, then he smiled and raised a hand as if in greeting. Yet scrambling to place him, Faucon started to return the gesture, but the other knight had already leaned forward to speak into the cloaked magnate's ear.

Instantly, the well-dressed man pivoted. Oswald de Vere, nephew to Bishop William of Hereford and

Faucon's cousin, stared at Faucon in stark surprise. Like Faucon, Oswald had the de Vere look, long nose, lean cheeks, black of hair, and dark eyed. So too did they both affect the latest fashion of a carefully-trimmed beard, shaved back to a narrow line that followed the jaw. In Faucon's case, his beard served to hide what he considered a too-pointed chin.

"Oswald! What are you doing here?" Faucon called in astonished and grateful greeting. The sheriff could now come as he may. His new Crowner was well and truly beyond his reach.

"Stopping for the night on our way home to Hereford, Pery," Oswald replied, using Faucon's pet name. Pery was short for Peregrine, a play on the meaning of Faucon. Then Oswald laughed. "Look at us! We meet for a second time in less than a fortnight after not seeing each other for—what? Five years?"

At this greeting, the tall, fair-haired commoner shifted, catching Faucon's attention. Dark rings hung beneath his blue eyes, and the man's face was haggard. And familiar!

"God be praised! Can that really be you, Sir Faucon?" cried Alf, the new miller of Priors Holden.

Faucon's head spun at the impossibility of two such unexpected meetings at once. He called back to the former soldier in English, "Alf, what are you doing so far from home?" Then he shifted into French to address his cousin. "Why aren't you already back in Hereford, Oswald? I thought you left Stanrudde last week on the same day I did."

Speaking two tongues at once only made that spinning worsen, especially atop so many coincidences. As Faucon held up a hand hoping to forestall either man from responding, Edmund drew his little mount beside Faucon, the donkey's nose to Legate's tail.

"This is your cousin, the one you met at Stanrudde's

abbey last week? The one who is Bishop William's secretary?" Faucon's clerk demanded, staring at Oswald as he spoke.

The longing in Edmund's voice was a reflection of his overweening ambition to reclaim his previous life. Faucon suspected that the monk saw in Oswald an unexplored avenue that might lead him to that destination, or at least return to him a bishop's favor. Also implicit in Edmund's query was the request to be presented to Bishop William's secretary. That was something Faucon had been able to avoid when he'd met Oswald a week ago in the town of Stanrudde.

Edmund couldn't know—nor would he ever believe—how little such an introduction might serve him. Aye, Oswald was the bishop's right hand. But that position guaranteed Faucon's cousin knew exactly what Edmund had done to earn his demotion. And that assured Edmund would ever own Oswald's eternal disregard.

Sidestepping both his clerk's questions and his ambitions, Faucon leaned closer to the monk. "If my cousin is here, it's a given that there'll be no space for me in the guest house," he said in a low voice. "Brother, I need you to go within and beg shelter on my behalf, even if the only place Brother Hosteller can offer me is a stall in their stables. Under no circumstances can you let the hosteller refuse me. The sheriff is at our back. Against that, I cannot afford to be turned away from these walls."

"Holy Mother save us," Edmund gasped quietly as he craned his neck to look at the gap in the trees. He was in time to watch Sir Alain and his men ride through the branches.

Although Faucon's clerk might not know of their sheriff's recent attempt to end his employer's life, Edmund did know, or rather suspected he knew, why

Sir Alain wanted his new Crowner dead. Edmund's jaw firmed and his eyes narrowed. With his whole being, he radiated his intention to shield his employer, a man he'd met only three weeks ago and had initially considered a burdensome penance.

"It shall be done," the monk assured Faucon, then turned his donkey's head and rode onto the drawbridge without so much as a glance at the influential man he'd hoped to use only a moment ago. Faucon watched his clerk go, startled. As grateful as he was for Edmund's loyalty, he wasn't certain what he'd done to earn it.

Sir Alain brought his horse to a halt near Legate. "Why, if it isn't our shire's new Keeper of the Pleas," the sheriff said by way of greeting to his Crowner. As always, no expression shifted the weathered creases of the older man's face, nor did any emotion color his tone as he continued. It was the look that many an old soldier wore, the one earned by a man who'd dealt out so much hurt in his live that his heart had turned to stone. "What a surprise to find you here at the abbey when I thought you'd yet be in Studley. Have you already completed your task there, sir?"

"Indeed I have, my lord sheriff," Faucon replied, offering Alain a brief and respectful nod, the sort shared between equals. "The man who committed the foul act is presently being held in Sir Peter's keep by his steward. There he'll remain until his family raises the funds to purchase his freedom. What of you? I thought you were in Killingworth at the moment. What brings you to this end of our shire?" It was a subtle challenge, one meant to warn the sheriff that the man he wished to kill wouldn't die easily.

"Why, assessing taxes for our king, of course. There's a salt road nearby," Sir Alain replied quickly.

"Good eventide to you, my lord sheriff," Oswald said as he strode forward to stop beside Faucon. Being

Oswald, a man whose ambitions surpassed tenfold any Edmund might cherish, Faucon's cousin offered the most influential royal servant in this shire a deep bow. When he straightened, Oswald's lips had spread into a smile that didn't warm his dark eyes.

"It has been a good while since we last met, sir," he told Alain. "If you do not recall, I am Oswald de Vere, secretary to and nephew of Bishop William of Hereford. For these past weeks, I've been in your shire on my lord bishop's business, as well as tending to some personal details. Before Lord William departed for London a fortnight ago, he bid me convey to you his happiest greetings should our paths cross whilst I was here. With this my last night in your county, I'd given up all hope of doing so. But how now! I shall be able to tell my lord that I have done as he requested, albeit at the last moment."

Alain waited until Oswald fell silent before shifting his flat gaze from Faucon to his cousin. "Ah, then it must have been you who passed through Alcester a little while earlier and drew the attention of the townsmen. As I arrived, one of the aldermen mentioned seeing Bishop William's knights riding through. Thus did I come to the abbey. William has stayed here on other occasions, and I thought it would be he I caught here this night," he said.

"I beg pardon for disappointing you," Oswald replied, still displaying his empty smile. Then he startled his cousin by adding, "By your greeting to him, I take it that you're already acquainted with my kinsman, Sir Faucon de Ramis?"

Never once in all the years of Faucon's life had he heard Oswald so boldly claim a connection to any of his far less prominent—thus less useful—relations. More to the point, that Oswald made his claim so publicly suggested that both he and their uncle knew just how much illicit profit Sir Alain had lost when the royal court forced a new Keeper of the Pleas on him. That also explained Oswald's strange introduction. It was their uncle speaking through his secretary. Bishop William was doing what he could to protect the lowly and unknown relation he'd recruited to become the first of Warwickshire's new Coronarii.

What neither of Faucon's kinsmen knew was that the reason Alain wanted his new Crowner dead went far deeper than his purse. Rarely did either of Faucon's prominent relatives make a misstep, but this time they couldn't have erred more greatly. Rather than protection, all Oswald's words did was warn the sheriff he'd best be very covert about how he rid himself of his new Crowner. And that only complicated matters for the man they meant to protect.

The sheriff stared down from his saddle at the well-born coxcomb who served his erstwhile friend and former traveling companion. Alain's grizzled brows shifted, the movement minuscule, then he glanced at Faucon. "Aye, Sir Faucon and I are acquainted. Indeed, we grow ever more familiar with the other as the weeks pass."

It was both a careful dodge and a hidden promise of a future confrontation. Sour amusement tugged at Faucon's lips. Oh aye, the two of them were a pair, indeed. The time for hiring the single soldier he could afford had been yesterday.

There was a touch on Faucon's arm. He shifted in sharp surprise, his hand instinctively dropping to his sword hilt. Alf the Miller didn't so much as flinch at the aggressive reaction.

"What are you doing here so far from home, Alf?" Faucon demanded swiftly, his hand falling back to his side.

Alf scrubbed at his brow as if to wipe away his

exhaustion. His bloodshot eyes were filled with concern. "A second cousin of 'Wina was married yesterday
in a hamlet not far from here. I came with her as her
escort, for her sisters had traveled ahead of her, and
Haselor is farther than she was comfortable traveling
alone with a child," the former soldier said in explanation, then hurried on. "Sir Faucon, I know you have no
cause to grant me a boon, but I beg you—"

"I know you," Alain interrupted in English, dismounting as he spoke to the taller man. "You hail from
Priors Holden. You're Halbert the Miller's workman."

The former soldier offered his sheriff a quick and
respectful bow but when he straightened his expression
was carefully blank. Alf had his own reasons for being
wary of Sir Alain. "Aye, I was Halbert's workman, sir.
But as you well know, I no longer serve him. His son's
widow and her aunt now run the mill," the tall man lied.

Faucon blinked at that. Why lie when Alf knew the
sheriff was aware of who he was and to what Alf was
entitled by right of birth? Alain's only reaction to the
commoner's reply was another of those brief quirks of
his brows.

Alf didn't wait for Sir Alain's response. Instead, he
directed the same urgency he'd displayed toward
Oswald onto both his Crowner and his sheriff. "Sir
Faucon, my lord sheriff, I beg your aid," he began anew.
"Last night, Halbert Miller's granddaughter Cissy
wandered away from the church in Haselor where a
wedding was being celebrated. We don't know how long
she was gone before we returned from the shivaree to
discover her missing, but we've been searching for her
since that moment, scouring the fields and wastes. To
no avail. Night is almost upon us and we have yet many
furlongs left to walk if we wish to complete the task
before dark cloaks all."

He glanced across the faces of his betters. "Sirs,

she's but a wee thing, and she's already been lost out there for too long. Please, we need to find her and we need more men to help us if we're to complete our task. Help us convince the monks to assist us in our search."

"You I told! The monks not depart their abbey to seek a child," Oswald replied sharply in his clumsy English. He waved a hand, dismissing the commoner and the lost child, then glanced eagerly toward the abbey's gateway as if ready to be shed of all life outside of the comfortable walls of this house.

"The bishop's secretary is correct, Alf," Faucon seconded, as reluctant as Oswald to let anything distract him from entering the abbey, albeit for different reasons. "You're better off asking in Alcester. The townsmen are far freer to do what you need."

"We have asked them," retorted the common -born priest who accompanied Alf as he pressed his way through Oswald's armed escort to once more stand next to the tall miller. When he continued, he aimed his gaze in the direction of the nearby town, although it couldn't be seen through the trees.

"There is not a charitable heart to be found in that greed-infested place. The alderman we spoke to not only refused us, he threatened to drive us from their walls when we persisted in our pleas. That's why we came here." The priest's tone was resentful.

Again, Alain's brows shifted a little. The sheriff glanced from Oswald to Faucon. His gaze caught and lingered on his new Crowner as he replied to the priest. "Why, if you have no other who will help you in this, Father," he said, "then it must be your sheriff and your keeper who come to your aid. Is that not right, Keeper? We are both free to accompany these men on their quest, are we not? Mounted men will make short work of such a search."

As Alain paused, the corners of his mouth lifted ever

so slightly even as he kept his gaze on his Crowner. It was the mockery of a smile. "Aye, it's only right that we go together, do you not think? I and mine will seek the living child, as we must, now that our king has commanded that my only purview be the living. Meanwhile you, Sir Faucon, will ride as the court demands of you, seeking out a dead lass against the possibility that she has already passed." The faintest trace of humor and satisfaction filled his voice.

Before Faucon could form a response, Oswald took a half-step forward almost as if he meant to put himself between his cousin and the sheriff. "But you are right, Sir Alain. We must all go," the bishop's secretary said, that empty smile once more bending his mouth as he returned to his native tongue. "What man can leave an innocent child to perish in the night? If it's men on horseback these commoners require, then I and my knights must also come along. That's four more mounted men, bringing as many more sets of eyes to the task."

Alain made no reply to this, only stared flatly at the well-dressed clerk.

"Pery, tell this man," Oswald continued, speaking to Faucon as he indicated Alf, "that he has won what he needs. Tell him that Bishop William of Hereford has agreed to come to his aid and will find the missing child."

If not for Faucon's certainty that Oswald made his offer to protect him—or rather, to drive home to Sir Alain that Warwickshire's new Coronarius had a bishop's protection—Oswald's pretensions would have had Faucon grinning. Instead, the smile he sent his kinsman was one of gratitude.

"So I shall do, cousin. And I offer you and Bishop William thanks on this man's behalf. I'm acquainted with him and I know that he's grateful to the depths of his soul for what you've given him this day. But having said that, I think we mustn't delay a moment longer, not if we're to accomplish what he requires."

Faucon cast a quick glance at the sky above. "Sunset will soon be upon us."

He didn't wait for Oswald's response. Instead, he mounted Legate and turned his courser's head away from the abbey. The sooner the girl was found, the sooner he could put a wall of monks, as well as Oswald and three knights, between him and Sir Alain. That would go far to extending the span of his life. At least for today.

Chapter Eight

Oswald's youngest knight took Alf up behind him while one of Alain's men shared his horse with the priest. That made swift work of the short distance between the abbey and nearest fields around Haselor. As the impromptu rescue party made their way across the furrows and stubble, the priest called out to the searchers, telling them to return to their church. By the time they reached the churchyard, nearly a hundred followed. That so many had participated in this search spoke well of this place. It wasn't everywhere that folk would spend precious time, or have risked even more precious garments to the rain, to seek a child who was a stranger to them, albeit one related by blood to a neighbor.

The church of Saint Mary's and All Saints sat at the center of several wide- spread hamlets including Haselor. Built of stone and small in size, its style suggested an origin more ancient than the arrival of Faucon's ancestors with the Conqueror. The original builders had chosen to set their holy house on a knoll that gave its shepherd a good view of both the area and his flock.

Strewn around the sanctuary were several small cottages, one of which was no doubt this priest's home. There were also a number of sheds and barns, the sort that any rural peasant might have to serve his needs. Sheep baaed from a fold behind one shed, testifying that this priest was a shepherd in more ways than one.

There was no need to command the attention of the

foot-bound folk who gathered around the mounted newcomers. It wasn't every day that their sheriff appeared with four armed knights and an expensively-dressed coxcomb. Nor was it every day that they could boldly watch as their sheriff lost an argument to his better. After haggling briefly with Oswald over who would command the venture, Alain gave way to the bishop's secretary.

Thus it was at Oswald's command that each rider took a local behind him to act as a guide while they rode the unexamined furlongs. That was, all save Oswald. Faucon's cousin insisted that someone needed to stay behind to coordinate the effort. Faucon knew his cousin better. Oswald no more wanted to share his horse, a spirited and expensive gray palfrey, with a commoner than he wanted to be in this rustic place, searching for a commoner's lost child, especially a girl child.

Off the knights and soldiers had gone, along with the crowd of commoners to walk the last furrows with them. However reasonable the plan, it proved as ineffective as the earlier search. Just as no amount of beating the brush or peering into thickets over the course of the previous night and day had produced Cissy, neither did calling her name while riding up and down the edges of the fields at sunset. By the time the sky had shifted from orange to pewter and the first star had appeared low in the east, all the riders had returned to the church. Faucon and the youth assigned to guide him were the last to arrive, making their entry to the yard on the piercing shriek of the owl perched atop one of the sheds.

"Did you find her?" Oswald called out to him. Shouting sent his high-strung mount into another fretful dance. That set the milling commoners in the churchyard into a backward wave of motion as they gave space to the iron-shod creature.

Faucon shook his head, then drew Legate to halt not far from Oswald, as the lad behind him slid off the courser's rump. "We did not."

"May God have mercy on the child's soul," his cousin replied with a relieved sigh. "Tell them, Pery. Explain to them that they must have faith. They must believe that this child is now in their Lord's hands. If our heavenly Father wishes her to be found, she will be. But that moment will come only at a time of our Lord's choosing."

Before Faucon could do as Oswald requested, Alain raised his voice and spoke for the bishop's secretary. He translated Oswald's words, then added his own instructions. "Go home, all of you. There's nothing more to be done here."

"Nay!" came a woman's shriek from near the church door.

Cissy's mother, who had been forced by her kin to stay behind at the church on this last search, now thrust her way through the folk standing between her and Oswald. Her sisters followed, both of them holding their arms at the ready as if they expected their sibling to topple at any moment. All three women were pretty, tall, and golden-haired, although at the moment 'Wina looked ancient, beyond spent. Her blond hair was torn from her plaits as if she already mourned her child as dead. Her eyes were red-rimmed from crying.

"You cannot leave when my precious babe is still out there! We have to find her. You have to help!" 'Wina shouted as she reached the forefront of the crowd.

Then she tried to push past a bulky man, as if she intended to confront Oswald more directly. Her sisters wisely caught her by the arms, holding her in place. Lunging against their control, the grieving mother pleaded, her voice still disrespectfully raised, "You cannot go! You cannot leave her out there."

Although she directed her cries at Oswald, who watched her in disgust, it was the heavy-set man next to 'Wina who responded. "But we've looked everywhere in Haselor, goodwife. We've done it from dark to dark again, and that's as long as we can bear it," he said tiredly. All across the crowd, folk nodded and muttered in agreement.

Another man added, "Even if we wanted to search longer, we cannot. Nothing can be found in the night. You cannot ask us to squander more of our time and effort, not when we've already given you a full day. Doing so happily, mind you. Don't we all have children who are precious to us? But you cannot ask us for more, not when it would be a useless effort."

A woman pointed at Oswald. "The priest and our sheriff are right," she called, mistaking the high-born clerk for a well-heeled clergyman. "Your daughter is in our Lord's hands, just as are our own babes."

As the woman's friends and neighbors called out to confirm her words, Alain turned his horse and signaled to his men to join him. "I bid you a good night, Oswald de Vere," the sheriff said to the bishop's secretary. "Godspeed as you make your way back to Hereford. When you next see your bishop, remind Lord William that I will always be his faithful friend and servant."

Then Alain's gaze came to rest on his new Coronarius. "So, Keeper, it seems you'll be the next to see the missing lass, if they ever find her. Perhaps when we meet again you'll share the tale of your success or failure here. Oh, by the bye, I'll be in your area for a time. Aldersby," he said, referring to his wife's dower house that was only a few miles from Faucon's new home, "is in need of a new roof. I'll be residing there for the next month while the workmen do the task."

With that, the sheriff and his men departed, heading west toward Alcester and moving more swiftly than they had since Faucon first spied them. Their departure had the commoners considering taking their own leave. The folk in the yard began to mingle, some saying their goodbyes and goodnights as they walked off, others lingering to chat with friends and neighbors.

"Nay! You cannot go. How can you leave me when she's out there, lost and alone?" 'Wina pleaded once more, yet trapped in her sisters' arms. Then, recognizing her pleas were in vain, she collapsed to the ground, sobs wracking her. Her sisters sat beside her, wrapping their arms around her as they offered what comfort they could.

Pitying the woman, who'd lost both husband and child in less than a month's time, Faucon started to turn Legate away from the church. Instead, and for no reason he could name, 'Wina's final cry—that Cissy was lost and alone—conjured the memory of the dead child he'd viewed on his first day as Crowner. She'd been a lass only a little older than Cissy, found wearing a circlet of flowers and a slashed throat. That child had also been lost and alone in an empty, far-flung field.

Of a sudden, the hair on the back of his neck rose. *What if*, a niggling voice whispered. The words repeated until they were like the pulse of his heart.

That first child might have been alone in her resting place, but she hadn't been the only one. According to Brother Colin, the healing monk from Stanrudde who had become a friend, there had been many such lasses discovered over a period of years, all of them murdered in the same fashion.

What if, the huntsman in him took up the phrase, eager to be on the trail for no other reason than the love of the hunt.

Instantly, questions arose, demanding answers. The most important of them was how far a wee lass might go on her own in the dead of night through a foul storm.

It had an easy answer. Not so far that she couldn't be found by those who lived in this place. Haselor's folk knew every stone and tree within their bounds. Moreover, according to Faucon's youthful guide, these folk had searched thoroughly over the course of the day.

With that Faucon knew he was lost. He couldn't leave this place until he had answers that satisfied him, not even if it meant staying here after Oswald left. Not even if it meant riding back to the abbey alone in the depths of night.

"It's time we were on our way, Pery," Oswald said from beside him, sounding pleased with himself.

"A moment, cousin. I must have a moment longer, if you please," he replied to Oswald, and startled himself. However polite, this hadn't been a request. Instead, he had spoken to Oswald as Warwickshire's Crowner.

Before his cousin could reply, Faucon called out, "Alf? Alf the Miller?"

Across the yard the tall Englishman held up his hand so Faucon could place him. "Here, Sir Crowner."

"I have questions that must be answered. Where is that priest? Tell him his king's servant in this shire needs him to hold his flock here for a little longer," Faucon told the man, trusting Alf, who had been the first Englishman to be interrogated by his new Crowner, to not only understand Faucon's intention, but to also do what was best for Cissy.

As Alf gave a quick nod and strode for the tiny church, Oswald looked at his cousin. "What questions? And what is a Crowner?"

Faucon smiled at him. "I am. On my first day, Brother Edmund kept referring to me as the shire's new Coronarius. There was one among the listeners who knew enough Latin to translate the word for the others, and he translated it as *Crowner*. By the end of the day, all the folk in that vale were calling me by that name. I liked the sound of it so I didn't correct them."

"Huh, it's a strange word, but then is strange in the commoners' tongue," Oswald said as Alf reappeared with Haselor's priest.

"Father," Faucon called out to the balding man, when he was in fact addressing everyone yet in the yard. "I am Sir Faucon de Ramis, appointed by the royal court to act as your shire's new Keeper of the Pleas. At the command of our king, I, not Sir Alain, now have the right to investigate the murders and rapes that occur in your vale. It is also my right to call the inquest jury to confirm the manner of death of those who expired under questionable circumstances. Remember me and my name, and send to me at Blacklea when you have need."

As Faucon made his introduction, the noise in the yard ebbed into a restless, curious silence. Every eye was on him. He hoped these folk were startled enough by his introduction that they'd answer his next questions without considering they had nothing to do with rape, murder, or burglary. Then again, with the possible exception of the Archbishop of Canterbury, there wasn't anyone in England who knew exactly what a Coronarius was expected to do. The royal court had yet to clearly define his duties.

Scanning the crowd, Faucon continued. "Can any of you tell me when the lass was last seen within the church, and who it was that saw her?"

It was one of 'Wina's sisters who replied from where she sat on the ground, cradling her weeping sibling's head in her lap. "It was just before the bedding and shivaree. I watched 'Wina kiss her sleeping girl before we all danced out of the church," she called out, her voice raised so all could hear.

Faucon nodded at that. "Anyone else?" he demanded of the crowd.

"What of little Mary? She was tending the babes," a woman shouted.

"She saw nothing, for she had fallen asleep," the priest replied, then shook his head. "Poor child is distraught over the result of her inattention."

Faucon scanned the crowd again as he asked the most important question of all, one it seemed no one before him had thought to pose. "If you were all gone from the church and the girl tending the babes slept, how is it you're certain that Cissy wandered out on her own?"

Now that provoked an explosion of responses from all who heard him. "Quiet!" Their priest cried out, stepping out in front of them and raising his hands in command. But even before his flock settled, he pivoted to look at his new Crowner. "Of course she left on her own. We were all—" he began, sounding as if he thought his Crowner's question frivolous.

"Father," Alf interrupted, his tone urgent, his expression saying he grasped what his better was suggesting, "what became of the nun who was in the church last night?"

"The nun?" the priest repeated tiredly. "What has she to do with any of this?"

"What nun?" asked a man standing nearby. His question was echoed by a good number of his neighbors.

Once more the priest held up his hands, driving the muttering back into silence. "Many of you may not have seen her. We were all dancing as she came in, just after the storm burst. I invited her to join our festivities but she begged off, saying she was a stranger and didn't wish to intrude. Instead, she asked for a blanket and a quiet place to lay her head within the church. I let her stay behind the altar since she said she needed to be on the road again before dawn."

"She was traveling by herself?" Faucon asked in surprise.

"She was," the priest replied with a quick nod. "I was as startled about this as you, sir. I even asked if her abbess knew she made her way alone along the roads. The sister only reminded me that none of us are ever alone, that our Lord ever walks beside us."

The holy man shrugged. "Then again, she was big for a woman. Perhaps that makes her less likely to be assaulted whilst journeying. At any rate, she stayed behind the altar for the whole night, sir. She was yet sleeping when we left for the bedding and shivaree."

"And when you returned? Where was she then?"

The priest blinked and shrugged again. "I can't say. Alf and 'Wina arrived here ahead of me, to discover her child missing. I never returned inside the sanctuary but went directly into the fields to begin searching."

As little as Faucon thought it possible a nun would take a child, the huntsman in him insisted this was the trail to follow. "Do you remember from whence this nun came and to where she was traveling? Why she was in your vale?"

The priest tugged at his ear as he thought, then yawned. "I can't be certain what I know at the moment. I vow I'm so worn that I can't remember my own name."

"It's Otto," some prankster shouted, and won a brief spate of laughter for his effort.

"I know your voice, Dickon," Father Otto retorted, proving that the amiable arrangement of his features did reflect his character.

Then the priest glanced between Faucon and Oswald, his eyes shifting across their faces, as if he couldn't decide which of his betters he needed to address. "I think the sister mentioned she had been at Henwick. Beyond that, all I'm certain of is that she told me she'd be leaving before first light. She said she had a goodly distance to travel."

Then his eyes widened as he drew a sharp breath. Tapping a forefinger against his temple as if to shake loose his words, he grinned and announced, "North! She said she was traveling north."

"North," Faucon repeated, looking at the sky above him to gauge directions. "Father, how far did your search this day stretch to the north?"

The holy man opened his mouth to reply, then caught himself and frowned at his better. "You cannot think! Not a nun!"

Faucon agreed. Not a nun. The one he tracked had a heart black enough to slit the throats of many innocent lasses. Such a being couldn't live within daily sight of their Lord and survive. But the huntsman in him refused to listen. This was the trail to follow.

"Father, all I think is that one so small cannot have gone far on her own in last night's rain and wind, especially when she is a stranger to this place. Yet you searched and searched well, and didn't find her dead or alive." As Faucon continued, he looked from face to face, meeting the gazes of each man or woman so they would know him if he came here again. "Because of this, we must consider other possibilities. As I see it, there is only one other in this instance. If the child didn't walk out on her own, then someone must have taken her. And look how, when that possibility is explored, there proves to have been a stranger in your midst, capable of doing such a deed."

Again, everyone in the yard save for Alf and Father Otto raised their voices at this. To a one, both commoners and knights rejected the idea of a nun taking a child. Oswald was no different.

"Have a care," his cousin warned. "Accusing a nun of stealing a child might well be blasphemy."

Then Oswald's eyes narrowed. "Enough! Your duty is to assess estates and calculate what our king can collect from wrongdoers. There's no profit to king or court from a missing child."

"True enough, Oswald. Alive or dead, this particular child offers the king's treasure chests nothing," Faucon agreed with a shrug. "But consider, Cousin, how there might be more than coins to be gained here. Remember, I'm unknown to most folk in this shire, having been in this county for only a short while. So too is my position new and strange to all who hear of it. I do here what I have had to do time and again over these past weeks. I confirm my right to command these folk with the same authority given to Sir Alain. It's what I must do," he added, "if I'm to hold tight to my new position and do as my king requires."

Once again, he spoke to his cousin as an equal. It wasn't something he would have done three weeks ago. Until then he'd been but a second son with little in the way of inheritance and no expectation of advancement.

Confirming authority was something Oswald understood well, indeed. But even as his cousin nodded, he sighed in reluctance. "Do as you must, then. But how do you intend to accomplish this?"

That made Faucon smile. Not only had the reins of his new position come a little more firmly into his hand, but he could now indulge his need to hunt the child without insulting his more powerful relative. "We'll search a little longer, going farther to the north than they've looked previously."

"But that makes no sense," Oswald complained. "You've just suggested that the nun stole this child. Why would they search for you when, *if* the lass was stolen—" here, he paused to shoot a narrow-eyed look at his cousin. "Mind you, I'm not saying that she has been. But if the child was stolen, it's hardly likely that the one who took her would abandon her only a little distance from where she was taken."

If he were looking for a child that the thief intended to keep alive, that would be true. Instead, in his mind's eye he again saw the image of that lost and lonely lass. It wasn't a living child he expected to find, whether he found Cissy tonight or at some future time and in a more distant place. But if he told Oswald he was seeking a dead child, Oswald would insist on leaving for the night.

"It's not about the child," Faucon replied. "It's about the command."

Oswald groaned at that, trapped into agreement by his own arrogance. "Is there no other way?"

"You need not stay," Faucon started to offer.

"Of course I must stay," his cousin shot back. "Were you not watching? Sir Alain has no liking for you. I know how fond Lord William is of that man, but in this one instance I fear my lord's trust is sorely misplaced. You and I will remain together and search a bit longer, but only until the light is no more."

"The light is gone," Oswald grumbled. It wasn't the first time he'd suggested this.

"Not quite. When Father Otto walks past again, we'll be finished," Faucon replied.

This time and at Faucon's command, the searchers had arranged themselves in a long line, each man or woman, or mounted knight, spaced at twice the distance of their arms from their neighbors. The priest was walking up and down the line of searchers, carrying messages as they made their way at a steady slow walk along the path that led north toward a settlement the locals named Aston. With more than four dozen of

Haselor's folk participating, it made for a long line.

A moment later, Oswald stirred himself again. "Why wait for the priest? The light is gone for certain now."

That brought Faucon's gaze up from the ground as he eyed midnight blue heavens above them. He stifled a sigh. That first lass's corpse had been so degraded that there hadn't been much to see and little to gain from examining her. He'd hoped for better this time.

"I think you're right, Oswald," he agreed. "Ah well. Haselor can be along my route back to Blacklea. I'll stop here to search again after I complete the inquest at Wike."

"Wike? I thought the sheriff said you were in Studley," came Oswald's startled reply.

Faucon sent a quick smile in Oswald's direction. "I was in Studley earlier this day, much to our king's profit," he added, winning a return grin from his cousin. "As I left the place the bailiff from the hamlet of Wike met me, saying they'd found their leper's daughter in a well."

"Bah," Oswald replied in scorn at that. "Another girl child, drowned and the daughter of a leper? What profit can there be for our king in such a death?"

That made Faucon laugh. "More than you'd think, cousin. Not only did the girl prove to have been murdered, but her mother attests that her child was conceived in rape and the father's name remains unknown. That, Oswald, means our sovereign will collect the murdrum fine from the community, or so Brother Edmund informs me."

Oswald's smile fair glowed in the dimness. "There was no proof of Englishry?"

"Nay. Nor can there be, not unless the man who did the rape comes forward to claim his child posthumously," Faucon replied. Then, although he thought his effort wasted, he did what he knew would please

Edmund. "You must let our uncle know that I'm grateful to have such a learned monk at my side to guide me."

Just then, shouts rose from the left. The repetitive sound suggested a message being passed mouth-to-mouth up the line. Concentrating, Faucon caught the echo of a miracle. The girl was found. Instantly, he turned his horse, leaving Oswald without a backward glance. He didn't want anyone disturbing the body or the place where she was found, not until he could examine it.

Ahead of him, a woman appeared out of the dimness, walking swiftly toward him, bearing a small form in her arms. Faucon cursed himself for not warning the searchers to leave the child's corpse where they found it. Then the *corpse* coughed and moaned hoarsely in her bearer's arms.

That provoked a sour but amused laugh from him. Such was the hazard of dealing with death and murder on a daily basis. Look at him, starting to believe that anyone, even a nun, was capable of murder, and a heinous one at that.

Chapter Nine

It was full dark by the time Oswald and Faucon stepped out of the cottage where the child had been reunited with her overjoyed mother. The lass was fevered and barely conscious, and clots of blood marked the back of her head. Perhaps because of her head wound, she'd resisted being touched by any man, even Alf. When the Englishman had tried to take her, she'd thrashed in hysterical fear, kicking and crawling back in her female rescuer's arms. To Faucon that suggested that—if she'd been taken—it had been a man who'd done the deed.

"You should have insisted," his cousin chided. "Mother or not, that woman had no right to keep the girl from you nor refuse to let you pose your questions to her."

Faucon closed the door behind him. The same impatience gnawing at Oswald also ate at him. But unlike his cousin, who knew nothing of common folk and traded in arrogance the way others traded in silver, Faucon knew better than to press a mother in regard to her child.

"Perhaps," he agreed as they crossed the yard to where the knights and horses waited. "But I think my effort would have been wasted. Until her fever breaks, nothing the lass says can be trusted. Nay, I'll wait until she's improved before I ask for her tale, even if it means waiting until mother and daughter make their way back to Priors Holden."

Behind him the cottage door opened again, spilling warm and uncertain yellow light into the silvered darkness. Faucon glanced over his shoulder. By size alone did he recognize Alf. Leaving Oswald to mount his palfrey, Faucon retreated a few steps to meet the Englishman.

"'Wina sent me," the miller told him, offering a respectful nod. "She asks me to both beg your forgiveness for sending you away and offer you her everlasting gratitude. I think her head at last begins to clear now that her babe is once more safely in her arms."

Faucon smiled at that. "'Wina is well come to my efforts on Cissy's behalf. God be praised that we found her daughter alive. Good night, Alf."

Rather than return his *adieu*, the taller man reached out to touch Faucon's mail sleeve. "You rode without armor when we first met. Dare I ask from whom you now seek to protect yourself?" he challenged with a quiet smile.

That made Faucon grin. "You of all people know who chases me, and why. Now, if by mentioning this you're offering to stand at my back, I'd be interested in hearing what you have to say."

That won a moment's silence from the former soldier. When Alf at last spoke, disappointment colored his tone. "I may very well be."

"What?!" Faucon retorted in surprise. "But you just came into the milling life. I hear it's a fine one. And didn't you tell me only three weeks ago that you found it suited you?"

Alf sighed. "Aye, so I did. But since that time I've discovered that the one thing I want most from that life I can never have."

"Ah," Faucon murmured. Although now widowed, 'Wina had been married to Alf's half-brother. No priest would ever allow a union between her and Alf, not as

137

long as the prior of St. Radegund's wished to reclaim ownership of that mill.

"Against that," Alf continued, "I find my taste for milling has flagged. But I thought I was trapped until I saw you standing next to our sheriff at the abbey. I feared if I left the mill, the prior would find a way to reclaim it, cheating 'Wina of the lifestyle she expected to own when she wed. Now, of a sudden I see how I can hire others to do the daily tasks, with 'Wina to manage them, while I go no farther from Priors Holden than Blacklea. As long as I remain close at hand and visit the mill regularly, the prior cannot argue that I've abandoned my birthright. Instead, I'll be no different than any other landowner who holds a distant property."

Alf's smile gleamed in the dark. "What do you think, sir? Will you make room for me at your back? I could be available as early as the morrow, should that suit your purposes. I won't need much of a salary, not with the profits from the mill yet coming to me after 'Wina's taken what she needs. I do have two requests, though, should you agree. First, if I join you on the morrow, you'll need to buy me a horse. I've no coin with me at present, and I sold my nag before I came to Priors Holden. And I'll want to escort 'Wina home when she's ready to leave this place."

Faucon threw back his head and laughed. Miracle after miracle on one enchanted day. "I'll wait for you at the abbey on the morrow," was his reply.

"Where did you go and why did you leave without me?" Edmund complained from the doorway of the small tool shed that would be Faucon's chamber for the night. The monk held a large oil lamp before him. The jigging flame spilled a shifting dance of light and shadow across his features, making a grotesque of his face.

Edmund yet stood in the doorway because there wasn't room for three men inside the shed. The monk responsible for tending to the abbey's guests had sent a servant with Faucon to help him disarm. At the moment, the man was loosening the laces on Faucon's chain mail tunic.

"At our sheriff's request, my cousin, his men, and I rode to a nearby hamlet to look for a missing lass. Once the child was found, we returned," Faucon replied, again glancing around the shed as he spoke.

Brother Hosteller, had been flustered and apologetic over offering his new Crowner such lowly housing. Faucon had assured the monk that he'd made his bed in stranger places, and as such places went, there was nothing offensive about this tiny space. The tools had been removed and the dirt floor swept clean. A straw-filled pallet topped with a woolen blanket now filled the back half of the shed while a milking stool near the door would serve for a chair. In between the stool and the pallet was a makeshift table—a plank of wood resting atop two more milking stools—pushed against the wall beneath the empty tool pegs.

Awaiting him on that plank was his evening repast, the food and drink of startling quality and quantity. The ewer, and now the cup as well, held ale made by the monks, or so Faucon had been told. It was tasty, indeed. On the tray was a good-sized round loaf of fine bread—white, not the usual brown. Several wedges of fragrant cheese, made in the town, not at the abbey, according to the brother who brought the tray, sat next to a small bowl of nuts and dried fruit. Faucon's eating knife lay at the ready near a length of smoked sausage.

After opening the laces, the serving man stepped in front of his new Crowner. Faucon bent at the waist and extended his arms in front of him. The servant reached over him and grabbed the tails of his metal tunic. As he tugged toward him, Faucon yanked and pulled his body in the opposite direction. He came free of the tunic with a grunt and a gasp, then straightened, rolling his shoulders to release them. Once the servant stored the folded steel garment in its sack, leaving it at the foot of Faucon's bed, he returned to open the cross garters that held the shafts of Faucon's boots to his calves.

As the man knelt before him, Faucon reached for the ties that closed his padded gambeson, only to hesitate. As much as he longed to sleep in the comfort of just his shirt, this shed stood in the open air at the edge of the garden. If the night grew as cold as the last, he'd be grateful for these garments come midnight. Once Faucon was free of his footwear and the servant had bid them both a good night, Edmund stepped inside, closing the door behind him.

"Holy Mother preserve us," the monk said in harsh complaint. "I was wrong to think the canons at the priory this afternoon were profligate! This place is much, much worse."

"In what way?" Faucon asked idly as he removed one of his metal leggings.

"In all ways," Edmund retorted. "The meal after Vespers was an embarrassment. Can you not see what's on your tray? The food here is excessive and rich to the point of sin. And there was no reading! When I asked about it, I was met with blank stares, as if none of these brothers had ever heard of such a thing."

Faucon glanced at his clerk. Edmund's nose fair quivered with his outrage. In that instant the jigging shadows cast by the lamp he held turned the monk's expression into the Devil's own.

Stripping off his second metal stocking, Faucon managed an "Is that so?" comment as he went to store them in the sack that held his mail tunic.

Edmund wasn't finished. "As if that's not bad enough, you should have heard them chatter through the meal. Indeed, when they asked why you and I were in their area, I mentioned the death of a leper's daughter in Wike. Not one but two brothers hurried to tell me that their sub-abbot had kept our leper as his mistress," his clerk pronounced angrily.

Easing around Edmund, Faucon brought the free stool to his little table. Once aseat, he shifted to look up at his clerk. "Where is their sub-abbot now?"

"Not at a leper's hospital where he belongs," his clerk shot back. "The abbot allowed him to become an anchorite and walled him into his cellar, as if that might shield the others from his disease. Insanity!"

Faucon caught back his laugh. Apparently the sub-abbot hadn't wished to give up his fine lifestyle to become a beggar like his mistress. "Ah, then I think we can say with certainty who it was that gave Amelyn the right to beg here. Although I think now this wasn't much of a gift, not with the abbey fair hidden from the road. Who comes here to give alms to beggars?"

That provoked a scornful snort from Edmund. "More folk than you might think. The abbot supports his lavish lifestyle by selling his monks and their quills to the local merchants. These aren't holy brothers. This is a den of scribes pretending to be monks. You must insist your cousin report the misbehavior of this abbot and the excesses of this house to the bishop of Worcester. If something isn't done about this place, our Lord will take his vengeance. This house will cease to exist, I know it, aye."

That provoked another ambiguous sound from Faucon. Interfering in the matters of monks and abbots wasn't anything he ever intended to do. "Do you think I can speak with the sub-abbot come the morrow?" he asked instead, now shifting to eye his meal.

"Here?!" Edmund retorted in disgust. "Here you can speak to anyone you wish at any time you like. They've no respect for the Rule. I wager they chatter as they will throughout the day."

Good. Then, come dawn, he wouldn't need Edmund to ask after the monks and their hogs. Disappointment followed. Even if he recruited a brother to lead him into the forest, it appeared he might be making the trip with Edmund. With his clerk so disgusted at this place, he doubted the monk would want to return here for lunch or the Sext service.

"Is it so irksome here that you'd prefer to sleep in the shed rather than mingle with these brothers?" Faucon offered, taking a handful of the nuts as he glanced up at the monk.

That startled the outrage from Edmund's face. He blinked. "Your offer is appreciated, but nay. I don't wish to be locked out of reach of the chapel. I," he said, giving the word harsh emphasis, "intend to celebrate Compline and Matins services even though I suspect I will be the only soul in attendance."

"As you will," Faucon replied, relieved at his clerk's refusal. They'd had to share accommodations more than once in the past weeks. Edmund snored, the sound as loud as the size of his nose.

The nuts were freshly shelled, rich and oily. Chewing, Faucon added more ale to his cup, then sliced off a bit of sausage. The smoked meat was overly salted and only adequate, at least in comparison to the nuts, but still edible. For that he was grateful. More often than not he went hungry overnight while out and about on his duties.

"By the bye," Faucon said to Edmund as he tried a bit of cheese; it proved better than adequate, "this evening I hired a soldier to ride with us."

"You did?" Edmund replied, his brows raising in surprise. Then he nodded in approval. "As you should. It's good to have protection as we travel. Is it one of your kinsman's knights?"

"Nay, a common soldier." Faucon cut another bit of sausage to follow the cheese.

"You hired some ruffian?" Edmund almost chided as he leaned forward to set the lamp on the corner of his master's plank table. "Well, I hope you'll remind the oaf to keep his place and spare us his low opinions."

Keep his place? Spare us? What, so Edmund's opinions could be the only ones heard?

Laughter tried to escape Faucon's throat at the same time he swallowed. Choking, he grabbed up his cup and took a goodly sip of ale. He was still fighting for breath as his clerk gave an irritable huff and turned toward the doorway.

"On the morrow then, Sir Faucon," Brother Edmund offered as he retreated.

"On the morrow, Brother," Faucon managed when he cleared his throat.

Chapter Ten

Later than Faucon had wanted, he and Edmund departed from the abbey. They'd been delayed while he waited to meet with the former sub-abbot. It had been well after Prime when the anchorite at last sent a reply through a novice, saying he was too ill this day to entertain a conversation.

With geese and swans flocking noisily overhead, departing for the season, Edmund rode from the abbey ahead of Faucon. Faucon let the monk precede him only because he knew they wouldn't encounter the sheriff or his men on this day, nor any day before Faucon's return to Blacklea. Sir Alain had made his point. Their confrontation would wait until Oswald was far from Warwickshire's borders. Against that, Faucon had stored his metal armor and his surcoat in his saddle bags in favor of his more comfortable underarmor, with his sword belted over his padded gambeson.

Under the drawbridge the flowing water sparkled in mid-morning's cold clear light as he crossed, leading a workhorse. It had been donated to the monks by the son of the abbey's patron, the lord of Kinwarton. The piebald gelding was old, but of the size and with the hooves of a warhorse. According to the abbot, who proved to be as congenial and expansive as the food that came from his kitchen, the horse had been ridden in the past but now powered the abbey's apple press. With their fruit already processed for the season, the churchman had been happy to lend the nag to his new Crowner for a few pennies. When Faucon promised to return the gelding in a day or so, the abbot only laughed. He reminded the shire's new Crowner that as long as the horse wasn't here, he wasn't eating their hay.

At this late hour, the abbey's contingent of beggars was already well into their day. They didn't stand near the drawbridge as Faucon expected, but in the field in front of the trees that stood between the Street and the island abbey. No doubt this was so they could be seen by travelers. There were two elderly men, neither of them Hew, and a younger man using a crutch in place of his missing left foot.

As the rustic had suggested last even, Amelyn wasn't among them. However, Alf stood a little beyond the clutch of beggars, leaning against a tree, one foot braced upon its trunk, as he watched Ryknild Street. The miller had set aside his finer attire, and wore instead a short yellow tunic and green chausses. Or they would have been green and yellow had the garments not been so completely embedded with flour that their colors were naught but dusty memories of the original hues. Instead of a cloak, the commoner wore an aged but well-tended leather hauberk. A short, serviceable sword hung at his side.

As Edmund rode past the tall man without a sideways glance, Faucon drew Legate close enough to toss the gelding's reins to the soldier. Alf caught the leather straps, then lifted himself into what passed for a saddle on the creature's back. The old workhorse gave no sign that he found it strange or uncomfortable to again have a man sitting upon him.

"Purchased?" the soldier asked with a grin.

Faucon shook his head, smiling back. "Borrowed. He'll do for the now."

"He will," Alf agreed pleasantly.

Hearing voices, Edmund yanked his donkey to a

halt and shifted on the little creature's back to look behind him. His eyes flew wide when he saw Alf. "This is whom you hired? He's not a soldier! He's a miller's workman," Edmund protested in French.

Alf glanced from his Crowner to the monk, his expression flat. "I am the miller now, Brother. But for the next little while I've chosen to return to my original profession." If Alf's French was heavily accented, that he spoke it at all said he'd been more than a simple foot soldier in his time.

Edmund's eyes flew wide at being corrected by a commoner in his own tongue. His mouth moved as if to speak. But knowing he'd be understood by one he didn't wish to overhear him stopped the words.

Then the monk's eyes narrowed and his jaw firmed. "*Quod non servierit*," he said in Latin to Faucon.

This will not serve, Faucon translated but he shook his head. "Brother, I hope you don't expect me to understand what you just said. As I told you in our first days together, it's been years since I've had to think in the tongue of the Church. I fear I've forgotten most of what I learned all those years ago."

As a second son, Faucon had been intended for the clergy. He'd spent his early years in a monastery school until his elder brother had suffered an injury to his head, one that left Will with erratic, unpredictable and ofttimes dangerous behavior. To ensure his line, Faucon's father had chosen to make his second son a knight instead of a priest.

With an exasperated huff, Edmund once more jerked around to face his little mount's ears. His back stiff, he beat his heels against the stubborn creature's side. That teased a sound from the donkey so like Edmund's huff that Faucon almost laughed.

As the monk continued toward the Street, keeping his mount at a fast pace, Alf drew his horse up next to

Legate. "He does not approve of me?"

This time Faucon did laugh. "My clerk doesn't approve of anyone," he replied. In afterthought he added, "Although he does seem to tolerate me. I know not why."

With but a few short miles between them and Wike, it wasn't long before they were guiding their mounts into the greensward at the far edge of the settlement. Before dismounting, Faucon scanned what he could see of the hamlet. Not a soul moved along the paths that wound between the cottages and traced across the manor's bailey. Nor was there anyone in the fields that stretched from the manor house to the pale. All he could hear was the crow of cocks, the homely nasal chatter of grazing ducks, the honk of wild waterfowl as they departed these realms for the winter, and the more distant ring of hammers from Ivo's forge. Judging from the metallic sound, the smithy was located behind the decaying house in the demesne.

Save for the smiths, it seemed Odger had taken all his folk out of Wike in defiance of his Crowner's command. Then Faucon's gaze came to rest on the dome-shaped oven near the kitchen shed. A narrow stream of smoke made its lazy way heavenward out of the oven's vent at its apex. And the bakestress. The thought of having to speak with Meg made Faucon's mood sour even more.

He and Alf dismounted, Alf tying their horses with the ropes and stakes from the previous day. That these items had remained where they'd been left last night suggested Amelyn's curse kept all of Wike behind barred doors after their Crowner departed. As Legate and the piebald began to graze, Edmund yet watched his employer from atop his little donkey.

"Your soldier should stay with our mounts," the monk said. It wasn't a suggestion.

Faucon glanced at Alf. The big man said nothing nor did he look at Edmund. He but stood where he was, awaiting a command from his new master.

"Nay, Alf stays with us for the now," Faucon told Edmund. "That way he can learn what it is we do. The more he knows, the better prepared he'll be, should he need to come to our aid."

In that instant Edmund looked as sour as Faucon felt. Dismounting, leaving his donkey to graze freely alongside the larger beasts, the monk removed his basket of writing tools from the saddle. His expression hadn't improved by the time he'd hoisted its strap over his shoulder and was once again facing his employer.

"By my reckoning, we've completed but one of the duties the law requires of us. We've determined that the dead girl was murdered, something I have yet to note," the monk said flatly. "As for where she was found, I think you know better than I, sir. Should I add to our record that she was put in the well after her death? The only reason I need to do so is if it has any bearing on the estate we will ultimately assess."

Faucon shook his head. "Then do not add it. Her placement in the well was a misguided act of kindness."

"As you will," Edmund replied, then his eyes narrowed in consideration. "Also, for all intents, the old man from yesterday confirmed the leper's story that her child's father is unknown and unnamed, no matter what guesses the leper makes regarding who did the deed. However, we failed to have that man swear to the fact that all the folk here agree that no one knows the name of who fathered her child. Should we come across the old man again today, I suggest we request a more formal oath from him. That said, since we both witnessed what he said, if we don't meet with him, our word should suffice. That leaves us needing three more men who can confirm by oath that the girl's sire is unknown. Only then can we state that she isn't proved English."

Alf made a startled sound. "You intend the murdrum fine?" he asked Faucon.

"That is none of your concern," Edmund snapped.

Faucon shook his head at Alf, the motion bidding him to save that question for a later time. The soldier replied with a single nod and held his peace.

"Lastly," Edmund continued, stepping into the rutted path that led around the hamlet to the manor's demesne, "when I finally put quill to parchment, I must ascribe that the hue and cry was raised against Gawne, son of Ivo, who fled into the forest to evade capture."

"Must we note that?" Faucon called up to him as he followed. "The lad didn't do the deed, of that I'm certain."

"How is it you know this boy is innocent, sir?" Alf asked, as he trailed a few paces behind his Crowner.

"It's not yours to question—" Edmund started again to chide.

Faucon spoke over his clerk, "His hands are too small. They won't match the bruises that were left on the lass's neck by the one who throttled her. Can the inclusion that the boy was initially accused have any effect on him after the fact?" he asked of Edmund.

The monk cleared his throat as he glanced back at Faucon. "The hue and cry was raised against him, and so it must be noted. When the time comes that you name the true wrongdoer, and the inquest jury confirms you, I will note then that the boy was wrongly accused at the body's discovery. Thus is he exonerated."

Having spoken his piece, the monk reclaimed his usual no-nonsense gait and swiftly outpaced both knight and soldier. When he reached the well, Edmund circled it, then looked back at his employer. "They've moved the body. The girl is gone!"

Even though Faucon had expected no less, his dislike of Wike's bailiff flared even hotter. Dishonorable men of Odger's ilk would do anything and everything to avoid the fines and fees they earned by their actions. If Odger had moved the girl because he'd torn from Hew the confidence his Crowner had entrusted to the old man, Faucon had no doubt Jessimond's body was now deep within Feckenham Forest, lost for all time. With the girl's corpse went the murdrum fine.

That had Faucon shifting out of the rutted path to cross the manor's grassy bailey in the direction of the oven and Meg's kitchen. As he went, he signaled for Edmund to join him. The monk lifted his heels, his basket bouncing against his back, until he could position himself in front of Alf when he came into line behind Faucon.

Ahead of them, the door to the kitchen shed opened. Johnnie stood in the opening. The instant his gaze found his Crowner the idiot rose onto his toes and started toward Faucon as if he intended to meet him. As the idiot walked, his hands flapped, their movement decidedly agitated, and he began to make that clicking with his tongue. Once again, Faucon heard the cadence of words in those sounds.

As Johnnie realized he had his Crowner's attention, he held the knight's gaze, then shifted his eyes to the edge of the forest, only to swiftly bring his gaze back onto Faucon. Once again, he offered the staccato sounds that passed for words with him.

Surprise shot through Faucon. Amelyn's mute half-brother was trying to tell him something, speaking to his Crowner the only way he could.

Just then, Meg stepped outside the kitchen. "Come back here, you dulcop," she shouted at her nephew.

Johnnie didn't spare a glance for his aunt. Instead, he kept his persistent gaze on his Crowner. Meg followed his look. When she saw who came, her eyes narrowed and she crossed her arms over her chest. There was something in her movement that reminded Faucon of a warrior raising his shield just before engaging the enemy.

Today, an apron covered the old woman's red gowns. It was a ragged, well-used garment, too oft bleached, or so said the many frayed spots. To extend its life she'd added patches where the fabric had raveled. The newest repair had been done recently. A large square of fresh undyed linen was sewn to the apron above the woman's right breast. The natural tan color of the fabric was almost the same hue as the flour that coated the front of Meg's apron. She'd rolled her sleeves above her elbows. Flour coated her forearms, not quite hiding the four scabbed scratches that marked the underside of her left arm. They started near her elbow and descended almost to her wrist.

"The brat's body is gone. It was taken in the night," the cook said harshly as her Crowner stopped in front of her. "Good riddance, I say. I also say it was Gawne who crept back within our bounds to steal it in the dark. I say he'll do anything, even drag off a corpse, to escape the consequences of his wrongdoing."

So, Odger hadn't found the lad last night. "You're certain it was Gawne who took her, and not your bailiff or another man?" Faucon asked calmly although anger yet rode him hard, now aimed at both Meg and the bailiff.

"Did I not just say it happened in the night?" the cook shot back. "It was dark and I slept while the deed was done. I saw no one and heard nothing. I only speculate. Who in Wike save for Gawne had any reason to steal that corpse?"

Edmund gasped in shock as the common woman offered this rude reply to a knight. "Mind your tongue," the monk chided, "else I'll speak to your priest. I'll see to it he punishes you for your disrespect."

Meg's hard gaze slid to the clerk. She eyed Edmund for a moment, then freed a harsh, disbelieving breath. "Speak to him as you will," was all she said.

"Where is everyone this morning?" Faucon asked.

"That dastard who believes he's king of Wike took the others into the forest to collect wood. They left at dawn," the cook replied in the same disrespectful tone, "despite your command to the contrary, which I received from Hew," she added. The rustic was wrong. Meg hadn't much appreciated being used as a message bearer between her Crowner and her bailiff.

"Now doesn't that just make Odger as great a dulcop as that one?" she sneered, the jerk of her head indicating Johnnie.

Faucon glanced at the simpleton who wasn't quite a simpleton, only mute. Johnnie yet stood where he'd stopped despite Meg's command to return to the kitchen. The instant he caught Faucon's eye, his hands began again to move. This time the motion was less agitated but just as insistent, as if he begged his Crowner for a sign that the message he'd tried to send had been understood. To prove to himself he read the youth aright, Faucon raised a hand and offered a single nod of his head. Johnnie's arms immediately dropped to his sides. His shoulders relaxed as his stance eased.

"Sir Faucon, if the bailiff has removed the girl's body or sent his folk away from their homes to avoid the duty he owes his king through his Coronarius," Edmund was saying, "you may note these infractions. When the Justices in Eyre arrive, they will impose a fine on him for his disregard."

"They will try," Alf offered from where he stood at Faucon's back, "but I suspect this bailiff will but argue, as others have before him, that he had no choice about sending his folk into the forest. Most often, the day for collecting wood is set by tradition and cannot be negotiated."

Edmund's brows flew high on his forehead at being corrected by the soldier. His mouth tightened. He sent a raging glance at the tall Englishman, then bent his narrow -eyed gaze on his employer.

"I thought you were going to warn him to keep his opinions to himself," the monk snarled.

Faucon shifted until he stood between the two. "Is this true, Meg? Is your day to enter the woodlands set?"

Vicious amusement filled the old woman's dark eyes as she glanced from monk to soldier. "Aye, we have a traditional day," was all she said.

"Is it this day?" Faucon prodded, now speaking through clenched teeth. The sooner he put this miserable place behind him, the better.

Triumph filled her gaze. That was all it took. Faucon breathed out all emotions. This was a battle like any other he'd fought, save that this field was one of words instead of soil. She was finding joy in using him, even as she formed her responses with care so she could claim that she'd been pressed into revealing the truth, should Odger ask.

"It is not. With no lord or lady here to tell Odger yea or nay, our bailiff does as he pleases whether God or the Devil wills it," she replied.

"Do you know where in the forest Odger has taken Wike's folk?" Faucon asked.

She shrugged. "I can only guess where they might be."

It was the answer he expected. "What of Amelyn? Where did she go last night?"

"Where any leprous whore should go. To hell," the vicious old woman replied with harsh laugh. "Who cares?"

Faucon kept his gaze on her. "Tell me this, then. When did you discover that Jessimond was leaving the kitchen and your control to meet with Gawne?"

That startled the old woman. Meg blinked and frowned as she replied. "What does that matter? The boy killed the little whore. Find Gawne and hold your inquest so we in Wike can put this deadly matter behind us."

He heard Edmund's quick draw of breath as the monk readied another chide on fines and fees. Faucon spoke more swiftly. "Refuse to answer me on pain of fine, one that I understand you can well afford. It's quite the enterprise you've had over the years, what with your oven and your baking." He paused for a breath to be certain the bakestress understood him. Then keeping his gaze locked on hers, he added, "You may not know this, but one of my duties as your new Keeper of the Pleas includes assessing the estates of both wrongdoers and those who abet wrongdoers. When you resist my questions, you abet the one who killed Jessimond. Of course, it helps greatly when I know what assets I should seek out to value, as I do in regard to you."

That blow set the old woman's shield to rattling. She gave a sharp gasp. For an instant, surprise drove that ancient well-stoked rage from her gaze. Then her mouth tightened.

"That little whore. She started sneaking out over the course of this summer past. Don't think I didn't try to stop her every time I caught her at it, but she didn't care how I beat her. Instead, she grew ever more bold in her defiance. If I was gone to Alcester, she was gone from the kitchen, that's for certain. But I know that over these last months there were times when she spent the whole of the night with that nasty little smell-smock. I couldn't winkle out how she was escaping without my knowledge and while I slept, until I finally caught him—" she pointed to Johnnie, who now calmly watched what went forward around him "—lifting the bar to let her back in. That was almost a week ago.

"I took after them both with the switch for it, but she wouldn't let me hit the dulcop. Kept flailing at me when I tried. So I gave her both their beatings." There was nothing subtle about Meg's satisfaction as she recalled how she'd punished one she was supposed to protect.

"When I was finished, she still dared to rage at me. She said she was leaving and that she'd take the idiot with her when she went. I knew then that no matter how I hard I sought to beat the strumpet out of her, she'd never be anything but a whore like her dam. You know what she said to me when I named her a light-skirt? She said she was going to find her father and live with him!"

Meg sneered at that. "What a stupid twit, dreaming of eating the sugarplums that no bastard has the right to taste. Even if she knew who her sire was, what man in his right mind takes in the child of the whore who serviced him?"

Once again Faucon heard Edmund catch a swift breath from behind him. He glanced over his shoulder at his clerk, expecting to forestall another tirade. Instead, Edmund's eyes were closed and his head bowed. In front of him, Meg also seemed to have gone inward with her comment, her gaze aimed at her feet. Faucon made use of that quiet moment to sift through his bits and pieces, connecting those that fit while setting aside the ones that as yet meant nothing to him.

"After you punished her, how did you intend to keep Jessimond from again leaving the kitchen?" he asked a moment later.

Meg shook herself back to awareness. There was no

expression, not even anger, in her gaze. "There was nothing I could do. I knew the little whore would leave no matter what I did, even if I beat her to bloody."

Faucon eyed her closely. "So you let her leave unchallenged that last time she fled from here?"

The cook blinked at that, her mouth pulling downward into its usual scowl. "I did no such thing," she retorted, sounding more like herself this time. "I wasn't even here the last time she left these walls. I was on the Street, making my way back from Alcester. I had been delayed in town that day by a friend who asked me to visit before I left. It was full dark when I finally returned. By then she'd been gone since before the sun began its descent."

That had Faucon frowning at her in surprise. "How can you be so precise?"

She narrowed her eyes in scorn, as if she adjudged him as great an idiot as Johnnie. "The fire in the oven, of course. I always keep embers glowing, so the interior stays warm. That way the clay isn't shocked when I bring the heat up to do my baking. Those embers must be fed throughout the day. They're the last thing I check before I leave and the first things I look at when I return. And when I returned home that night, my embers were lifeless which means they hadn't been fed since before twilight, more likely longer as cold as they were."

"Who among your neighbors noticed you as you returned?" he asked.

She stared at him for a moment as if confused by his question. Then understanding flashed through her gaze. Her mouth opened as if to speak. Her gaze shifted toward Johnnie.

"Ah, so the only one about that night as you arrived was a mute dulcop," Faucon commented dryly.

Then he reached out as if to touch the healing

wounds on her forearm. "What happened here? They look nasty."

She drew a hasty step back from him. Her arms opened and she pressed them to the sides of her body, hiding them in the folds of her skirt. "The mouser I keep in the kitchen is a vicious creature when she has kits. She set on me with claws bared when I tried to move her and her new litter out of the sack of nuts where she bore them."

"Sir, if I may?" Alf asked.

Startled, Faucon looked at the soldier. Alf's brows were raised, his blue eyes alive with the intelligence Faucon had recognized when first they met at the mill. "As you will," his Crowner replied, curious what his new man intended.

Alf looked at Meg. "My mother has need of a new cat as a fox took hers last month. Is there a tri-colored one among these kits? My dam is especially fond of those."

Again, Meg's mouth opened as if to speak and, again, no word dropped from her tongue. Her gaze shifted between Faucon and Alf. Almost imperceptibly, her head began to shake.

Edmund released an infuriated sound. "Sir Faucon, I insist you put this commoner in his place and do it this instant. You and I serve our king here. He has no right to interfere in matters of the royal court," the monk demanded in French.

"My apologies if I have misstepped or misspoken, Brother, Sir Faucon. I will leave you to your business," Alf replied swiftly, then retreated until he stood a bit farther behind them.

Faucon fought his smile. Oh, there was going to be more value than a sword in having this particular commoner at his back. "What of it, Meg? Is there a tri-colored cat in the litter that my man can have?" he asked.

The old woman blinked. She started to cross her arms only to catch herself, once more lowering them to her sides. "The kits are too young to leave their mother."

"My man has to come back this way to escort a relative home in the near future. Let's have a look at them. If he sees one he likes, he can fetch it then. That will spare at least one of them from drowning," Faucon pressed, taking great pleasure in hammering at her with the weapon Alf had tossed to him.

"I'll want a quarter penny for the cat he chooses," Meg offered in paltry defense.

Faucon turned to look at Alf. "Will you pay for a cat?"

"I will," the soldier called back from where he stood. "The mill does well for my dam and she's generous to me."

"It seems a farthing isn't too much for him to pay," Faucon said to Meg. "Let him have a look at them."

That drove the cook back another step. Her gaze shifted between commoner and knight. "I don't know where they are just now. She didn't like the new spot I gave her, and took her babes elsewhere. I haven't yet discovered where she now hides."

Again, Faucon turned toward Alf, this time to hide his face as he fought a grin. "I fear you'll find no cat here, Alf, at least not this day," he told the tall Englishman.

"A shame that," the commoner replied, "but just as well, I suppose. It's a long ride home, one made easier without a kitten in a sack."

"True enough," his Crowner agreed.

To Meg, he said, "It seems I've no choice but to waste my day looking for your bailiff and Jessimond's body. What say you? May I take Johnnie with me as I make this search? Yesterday, I noticed how fond he is of his half-sister. I'm thinking he might know where Amelyn has gone, and, grieving mother that she is, she may well know the location of her daughter's corpse."

Scorn twisted Meg's face, driving all else from her expression. "You're a greater idiot than that pathetic creature if you think he can lead you anywhere. Please yourself. For all I care, you can keep the dulcop with you for all time to come."

With that, she turned on her heel and strode into the kitchen shed. The door slammed after her. Faucon heard the bar drop.

Chapter Eleven

"**W**here is the priest who tends to this folk? That woman needs to have her tongue torn from her mouth," Edmund said angrily. Then he bent a disbelieving look on his employer. "I don't understand why you let that commoner distract you from hunting the one who murdered a child with questions about cats!"

Faucon only smiled at his clerk. "Tit for tat, Edmund," was all he said, then signaled to Johnnie.

The youth came to him, once again walking on his toes. Although his hands flapped, the motion was calmer now. Amelyn's brother stopped before him, his posture alert and eager. Johnnie's gaze shifted from his Crowner to the edge of the forest behind the kitchen.

"I will follow you into the woods," Faucon told the youth, "but before we can leave Wike, I must see the smith. Can you lead me to the smithy?" This he asked to prove to himself that Johnnie understood him, not because he needed help finding Ivo and his sons. Doing that was as easy as following the din that accompanied metal being formed into tools.

Instantly, Johnnie shifted toward the rhythmic clang of hammers. Rising to his toes, he started away from the kitchen without looking behind him to see if his Crowner followed.

"I hardly think you need the simpleton to lead you to the forge," Edmund said in irritable disbelief from behind him.

"You're correct, I don't need him for that," Faucon agreed, sending a swift smile over his shoulder at his clerk. "But if he can find the smithy, I dare hope that he may also lead us to Amelyn."

"Misplaced faith, I think," Edmund grumbled.

The path Johnnie walked took them past the front of the manor house. The present lady of Wike hadn't been the first to ignore this hamlet. The house looked long ago abandoned and was even more decayed than Faucon had first thought. Birds, mice, and rats had all taken to nesting in its thatch, leaving gaping holes in the rotting reeds. More than moss clung to the walls. Wild vines, naught but browning flesh and twisted bones this late in the season, had taken root along its stone foundation, then made their unfettered way to the roof. Someone had attempted to remove a few and failed spectacularly. As the plants departed, they'd taken chunks of the exterior plaster with them, exposing the withe panels that filled the spaces between the house's ribs. The small porch that stood in front of the door, the one on which Amelyn had taken her punishment more than a decade ago, wore a speckled coat of black rot. The lower step had half-collapsed.

Faucon glanced from the house to the forest's edge beyond the pale. If the family who owned this place had lost the right to hunt in the king's woods, that would explain their lack of interest in the settlement. It also guaranteed that Wike was in its death throes, whether its demise came this year, the next, or twenty years hence. If Odger believed he could forestall that fate by way of an iron hand, he was sorely mistaken. Odger was the wrong man, and the hamlet was too small to rise above being abandoned by its masters.

At the far corner of the house, Johnnie turned again, still moving toward the sound of hammers. The smithy proved a three- sided shed, built all of stone with a wooden roof, although the ceiling stood high above the hard earthen floor, well out of reach of errant sparks. That hadn't prevented it and the walls supporting it from being blackened by soot from the forge fire. On the shed's long wall, metal tools of all sizes— hammers, pincers, chisels, and rasps—hung from pegs driven into the stones. Beneath the tools stood a narrow wooden workbench. Strewn atop it were gauges for pulling wire and wooden clamps. Two stools, to allow for ease while doing close work, were pushed beneath the bench.

The left wall supported a stone smoke channel, its narrow top guiding smoke out through the roof while its wide base hung a little above a stone fire box. Even without the bellows to feed them, the coals burning in the box were so hot that air in the gap between the box and the channel glowed a sultry red. The heat flowed out of the shed to wrap its chary arms around Faucon, drawing sweat from his brow as he stopped next to Johnnie in the open front.

Inside, Ivo and his sons were arranged in a circle around their anvil, which stood atop an ancient, blackened stump. As they had yesterday, the three wore their leather chausses and scarred sabots, and only bare skin beneath their leather aprons. The mingling of dirt, soot, rivulets of sweat and pink burn scars created a crazy pattern on their exposed flesh.

Focused on their task, they hammered at their newborn tool in a well-timed pattern, each hammer singing out in its own voice. Between that and the precision of their strikes, the clangs sounded like a fuller's chant.

Then, as if sensing them, the elder of Ivo's sons glanced up between his strokes. The dark-haired youth, who already owned the heavy muscles of a full-grown man despite that he wasn't yet a score of years, gave a welcoming lift of his chin. When he missed his next stroke, Ivo and his younger son, a youth of perhaps six-and-ten, paused in their task to follow their kinsman's look.

"Sir," Ivo called out in friendly greeting as he recognized Faucon.

Setting his hammer on the workbench, he came forward to greet his Crowner. His elder lad did the same, while the younger boy returned the length of metal they'd been working to the fire box before joining them. As they came, each man stripped off his heavy leather gloves, tucked them into his apron straps, then used his bare fingers to push back hair and wipe away sweat. The sequence was so similar, the gestures and their timing so alike, that Faucon wanted to grin. Indeed, the sons were like the father here.

"So you've had no word from Gawne?" Faucon asked.

Concern darkened Ivo's eyes as he scrubbed a hand across his brow. What had looked like filth around his right wrist proved instead a circlet of small bruises. "He did not return last night and I can only pray—" the smith began.

"Da, there's no need to pray," his older son interrupted, putting an arm around his father's shoulders. "Our Gawne knows those woods and wastes better than Rauf or I, or even you, and we all know them well indeed, don't we, Da? Rauf and I are both certain that Gawne's hunkered, safe and warm, in some hidden spot. Isn't that right, Rauf?" He looked for support from his younger brother.

Rauf nodded shyly as his elder sibling turned his attention back on his Crowner. "You told Da you didn't believe Gawne had killed Jessimond, didn't you, sir?" the older boy asked.

"I did," Faucon replied, "and so I remain convinced."

"Then, we'll see him again and soon, Da," the son assured the sire.

Ivo shook his head as if reluctant to accept comfort from his child. "Then I'll pray that you're right, Dob," he told his elder boy. To Faucon he said, "I think it's not knowing where he's gone or what's become of him that makes my heart ache most."

"I imagine that's so," his Crowner agreed. "I told you yesterday that I'd have questions for you, and so I have. You all know that Jessimond was bastard born, aye?"

"She was," Ivo replied without hesitation. "All of Wike knows this. Amelyn did not name the one who sired her lass when she was called by Odger to face us after Jessimond's birth."

"Do the two of you also know and accept that the name of Jessimond's sire has always been unknown?" Faucon asked of Ivo's sons.

"We do," Dob replied for both of them, for once again Rauf only nodded.

"By chance, were all three of you there on the day that Amelyn received her punishment for fornication?" Faucon wanted to know.

An unexpected question about Wike's past startled them all. Frowning, Dob spoke first. "I was there that day and I do remember it. But sir, I wasn't yet of age then. I'm not certain I can acknowledge or swear to something I witnessed before my twelfth year."

That brought Edmund forward to stand next to his employer. The monk lowered his basket from his shoulder as he spoke. "The law requires us to take your oaths in regard to the girl's parentage. You're not swearing to what you remember, but to the fact that all of Wike is in agreement that the girl was bastard born. We ask you to swear that you have never heard Amelyn name her child's father, not from that long ago day until this one. Nor, in that same time, has any man or woman stepped forward to accuse a man of being the one who made Jessimond on her mother," the monk said, nodding to the younger men.

"Well, that much is true," Rauf offered, his voice as shy as his nod.

"Aye," Dob agreed. "Not even Jessimond knows who her father is. Gawne once told me that Jes believes even her mother doesn't know the name of her sire, although how that can be I can't imagine," he added.

"Then all three of you will swear that the name of the man who fathered Jessimond, daughter of Amelyn, was unknown at the time of her birth and remains unknown to this day," Edmund restated for them.

"We so swear," both of Ivo's sons replied at once.

Their father only turned his head to the side. "Poor child," he whispered, then said no more.

Faucon watched what he could see of Ivo's face between the man's wild, thick hair and overgrown beard. Something akin to pain filled the smith's expression.

"Ivo the Smith, do you also swear that you know not who fathered Jessimond the Leper's Daughter?" he prodded, crafting his question with care.

That brought the smith's sad gaze back to him. "I swear that I have never heard Amelyn speak the name of the man who fathered Jessimond, not when she was at the manor door all those years ago, nor to this day. Nor have I heard any other man or woman utter that man's name."

Again, the smith sighed. "Speaking of the past leaves me awash in shame over how I did nothing when Odger so cruelly and unfairly punished Amelyn. Where was my courage? Why didn't I raise my voice in defense of my friend on that misbegotten day? Even if she had sinned, and even if she bore fruit because of that sin, Amelyn didn't deserve what Odger laid upon her."

Next to Faucon, Edmund removed the lid from his basket, setting it onto the ground. "If we can find the girl's corpse, all is now within our grasp, sir," he said quietly to his employer in French. "Four men have spoken. Englishry is not proved. I would like a few moments to note the names of the smith and his sons before we move on, if I may."

A few moments? It took longer than that for Edmund to arrange his writing implements, never mind the time it took for his scribbling. But with the murdrum fine even more firmly in hand and nothing but a long tramp in the woods ahead of him, Faucon could afford to be generous.

He smiled. "So you must, and as you do, know that I remain grateful to have you at my side."

The monk blinked rapidly at that. "My thanks, sir," he muttered, then stepped into the smithy, going to the workbench.

Faucon looked back at Ivo. "When did you first learn that Gawne and Jessimond were meeting?"

"Months ago. I shouldn't have given up chasing him when he escaped me that first time, racing into the woods. I should have persisted and brought him home. But I thought if he had some time to himself, he'd find his peace with his mother's death," Gawne's father replied in chagrin. "Instead, he found Jes."

"Your bakestress remains convinced that Jessimond was with child by your son. How is it you're certain that the two remained but innocent friends?" Faucon wanted to know.

Ivo looked startled at the question. "Because I know my son," he replied at last, then looked at his other boys. "What say you, lads? Do you think Gawne made Jessimond into more than a playmate?"

Rauf instantly shook his head as, once again, Dob answered for them both. "Not Gawne, not when he knew—" the youth started to reply.

But his father spoke over him. "All of this is my fault. After Mille died, I was so aggrieved that I think I lost my mind. I should have brought Gawne into the smithy that very next day, if only to work the bellows," the elder smith said.

"So you should have. We would have happily let him stack coal in the box," Dob offered in friendly jibe from his father's side. Rauf's expression suggested this wasn't a favored job.

"Aye, but you know Gawne. That wouldn't have been enough for him," Ivo protested. "He wants to know everything right away and his questions never cease. Just then, I couldn't bear to listen to him."

"Do any of you know who took Jessimond's corpse last night and where she might now be?" Faucon asked.

All three men looked at him in blank surprise. Dob frowned. "Why would someone take Jes's body?"

Then Ivo drew a swift breath. "Where is Amelyn?"

Faucon shrugged. "Gone as well."

"Ah," the smith replied, almost smiling. "Then it's certain that she took her daughter with her, fleeing Wike before Odger could return from the woods and drive her off as he promised. Amelyn loved that girl with all her heart, and more. From what I saw yesterday, I think no one could have wrested Jes from her arms, no matter what weapon Odger might have plied."

"You are certain of that?" Faucon demanded.

"Absolutely," Ivo assured him. "What Jes was to Gawne, Amelyn is—or was—to me, before she gave up all her childish things, including me, to have her Tom. Our parents were bound to each other in dear and deep friendship, and we two were their only surviving children, born but months apart. We became like brother and sister, and I knew her better than any."

He paused, his expression hesitant as if he fought with himself about whether he should speak further. When he did, his voice was low and quiet. "Jessimond was wrong to think that her mother didn't know the name of the man who sired her. I'm certain the opposite is true. I saw that on the day Odger took his whip to Amelyn. She withheld what Odger wanted, doing so for some reason of her own. But to this day I cannot understand what that purpose might have been. This is especially so, given what it cost her to still her tongue."

Here he shook his head. "What I don't understand is why she committed the sin of fornication in the first place. As beautiful as she is, there were a dozen men here and in Coctune, men who already had children who could inherit, who would have taken her to wife after Tom's death despite that she had proved barren."

"Only she wasn't barren," Faucon offered flatly.

"So it seems," Ivo agreed, nodding. "Nor was she ever a lightskirt, at least not until Odger turned her into one. Do you know she nearly starved to death before she bent and began trading her body to save her family?"

Falling silent, the smith threw back his head. He again dragged his fingers through his wild hair, leaving it wilder still. "Why didn't I aid her?" he whispered. "What sort of coward allows a friend to suffer so?"

Faucon gave him a moment to collect himself before he asked, "When did you know that Jessimond was missing from Wike?"

It was Dob who replied. "The morning after Meg said Jes had run into the woods."

"How long did the folk of Wike search before giving up?" Faucon asked.

All three of them shook their heads at that. Ivo made a bitter sound. "Odger wouldn't let us search, not after Meg told everyone that Jessimond had said she was leaving to become a whore like her mother. Instead, Odger said 'good riddance' and told us all that Jes wasn't worth forfeiting a day's work. That ended any discussion on the matter."

"And once again you didn't speak to defend a neighbor, this time a child?" The accusation leapt unbidden from Faucon's lips, driven from him by the difference between Haselor and Wike.

"But I didn't have to say or do anything," Ivo protested, brows high and arms spread wide. "The moment Gawne heard Odger's edict, he whispered to me that Jes wasn't lost. Once our bailiff was out of earshot, Gawne told us—" the movement of his hand indicated his sons and himself "—and those of our neighbors who knew the two of them had been meeting that he thought she'd fled to heal from Meg's last beating. My son was certain he could bring her back as soon as she was ready to come. We all were content to leave the matter of Jes in Gawne's hands. But as of that morning, I think we were also decided that once Jes returned she wouldn't go back into that kitchen, not after witnessing Meg's cruelty."

"If that's so, then I'm glad they finally came to that decision," Dob said. "A month is long enough to come to such a conclusion." He looked at his Crowner. "A good number of our neighbors came here then, urging us to find some way to keep Gawne in Wike. That's when we discussed removing Jes and Johnnie from Meg's custody?" He glanced at his brother and father, seeking their confirmation to this. Rauf nodded. Ivo sighed.

Dob continued. "Moreover, when Gawne left that morning he assured me he'd have Jes back in Wike by day's end."

"And I told Gawne that when he found her, he

should bring her home to us," Ivo added.

That brought both Dob and Rauf around to stare in surprise at their sire.

"What? Did you not hear me say that to him?" their father replied to their wordless question. Then he gave a quiet laugh. "Of course you didn't. You weren't there. Nor did I say it that first day. Instead, that's what I told Gawne on the second day, as I walked with him to the pale."

"Da, I thought—" Dob started to say.

"I changed my mind," the elder smith replied, cutting off his son as he looked at Faucon. "After Gawne returned without Jes that first day, he was adamant about searching again on the second. He was so distraught over his initial failure to find her that I did what I could to ease his mind. Offering Jes a kinder place to live seemed to soothe him."

He glanced at his sons, then looked back at his Crowner. "I admit it. When my neighbors came here, I resisted their efforts to part Jes and Gawne, and Dob's insistence that we needed a woman in our house again, one to care for us the way their mother had. My wise son had suggested that we take Jes and let her fill that role for us. On that morning as I walked with Gawne, I realized that once I brought him to the anvil, the smithy would more than provide enough to care for us as well as Jes and Johnnie. That was my intention, to make a place for both of them, had Gawne found the girl alive."

It was Dob's turn to sigh. "Would that you'd come to this before Meg drove Jes from Wike," he said.

"Spilt milk," Rauf added, his voice still no more than a whisper.

Faucon studied the faces of the three smiths. Where the smith's sons heard regret, all he heard in Ivo's words was confirmation of the elder smith's cowardice. Ivo's offer to Gawne had been empty, naught but a sugar tit meant to placate his more honorable son. If Hew knew that Odger had put Jessimond and Johnnie into Meg's custody for his own reasons and intended them to stay there, so did Ivo. Given Odger's nearly absolute control of this place, it seemed unlikely that the bailiff would have allowed either of Meg's wards to leave that kitchen, not if it meant losing what little control he had over the bakestress.

"So, do you say that after Gawne hadn't found Jes on his first day of searching, your bailiff let him try again for a second day?" Faucon asked in another carefully crafted question. "That seems out of character for Odger, at least from what I've seen of him."

The smith looked at Faucon. "Odger knew none of what Gawne was doing. Our bailiff had left Wike the day before Jes disappeared. His wife is from Coctune and her mother lingers in her final ailment. Odger only returned to Wike the morning after Jes went missing because Meg sent for him. He issued his orders to us, then returned to his wife's family where he stayed until yestermorn, when we again sent for him after Gawne told us Jes was in the well.

"And you weren't concerned when your son didn't return from the woods after his second day of searching?" his Crowner asked.

"He did return," Ivo replied, looking startled by this.

"If that's so, then he returned to the forest once you slept," Faucon said, unwilling to offer more, not when doing so meant revealing Gawne's relationship with Hew.

"You're wrong," Ivo insisted, then shifted to look at his older boys. "He was home all night before he woke us with cries about Jes being in the well. Right, lads?"

Dob looked uncertain. "As far as I know, aye."

Rauf offered a guilty shrug. "He wasn't home, Da," he said quietly.

"Rauf! You knew Gawne was outside our walls at night and you didn't tell me?" Ivo cried, sounding more shocked than angry that his son hadn't been honest with him.

"He said it was important and that he wouldn't be alone," Rauf protested. "I only vowed that I'd say nothing to you as long as you didn't notice he was gone. I warned him, Da, that if you asked after him, I'd tell all."

"You should have told me, no matter what," Ivo retorted. Again, his chide was no more than gentle words, one that would have once again earned him his neighbors' scorn.

"What can you tell me about the night that Jessimond fled the kitchen?" Faucon asked, leading them in a new direction. "Can you recall anything unusual happening anywhere in Wike on that night?"

Yet frowning over the misbehavior of his sons, Ivo shook his head. "It was a night like any other," he replied.

Dob laughed at that. He was a handsome lad when he smiled. "What say you, brother? Was it a night like any other?"

That drove the guilt from Rauf's face. He grinned. "Too much wine," was all he said.

"Da, it isn't often that you lose yourself in your cup," Dob said, wagging his finger like a scold. Then he sent a wink in his Crowner's direction. "Da's plum wine had finished fermenting and he had a sip or two more than he should have. How he groaned about his aching head the next morning!"

Ivo gave his elder son a friendly cuff to the back of his head that sent the boy's brown hair flying forward around his face. "Have a care with my secrets, son. I can't help it that I have a fondness for plums."

"And I thank our Lord for that," Rauf offered with

another quiet grin. "You should drink it more often even if you end up sleeping in our doorway when you do. Your slumber was so sound that night that you didn't snore for hours."

"What of your neighbors? Did anything unusual occur when you might have expected them all to be within doors?" Faucon pressed, now looking at the younger smiths.

But it was Ivo who replied. "We wouldn't know. Once we bank coals in the box and leave the smithy for the night, we've all of Mille's—" his voice caught on his dead wife's name "—tasks to do. It falls to me to make certain we eat while the boys care for our stock and tend our garden as they can. Once we're inside our door, we see nothing more of the outside world until the sun rises again."

"I am ready, Sir Faucon," Edmund announced from where he now sat on one of the stools taken from beneath the workbench. The length of wood he used as a traveling desk was in his lap, a span of parchment stretched across its wooden top. He held the skin flat with one hand while in the other was an ink-stained quill. Behind him, arranged in a precise line along the edge of the workbench, were his tools, knife, inkhorn, extra quills, and a bag of sand.

Without waiting for his Crowner's permission, Edmund looked at the smiths. "State your names so I may note them," he commanded.

Chapter Twelve

By the time Edmund had restored his tools and parchment to his basket, Ivo and his sons were back at their anvil, hammering at their half-formed tool. Just outside the shed, Johnnie paced, every jerk of his body transmitting his impatience. Each time he passed Faucon his gaze would move from his Crowner to the forest's edge.

"As you will," Faucon said to the mute once Edmund had his basket on his back. "Lead us to your sister."

Johnnie immediately swiveled toward the pale. Again, as he walked he threw no backward look to see that he was followed. Faucon wondered if this was because the simpleton trusted his Crowner to come along, or if Johnnie lacked the capacity to doubt. Across the stubbled and furrowed fields they went, Johnnie leading the way at his awkward pace until he reached the hatch Gawne had used yesterday when he escaped Odger. The gate in the wooden pale was foreshortened and narrow to prevent deer from fleeing the forest for Wike's fields. As such any man wanting to enter the king's woodlands had to do so one at a time, with his head lowered and his back bent.

With an ease that said he'd done this often enough, the half-wit opened the little gate and ducked through it. Once on the other side, he tiptoed without hesitation across the narrow plank bridge, the one Gawne must have yesterday kicked off the embankment as he made his escape. That it again spanned the deep ditch said Wike's folk had come this way to enter the woods.

As Faucon watched through the narrow opening, Johnnie turned to the west, again moving off without a backward look. Alf followed Johnnie, almost folding himself in half to pass through the hatch. The soldier paused on the opposite side of the ditch as if he meant to wait for his master and the monk. His view framed by the opening, Faucon waved Alf to move on as he waited for Edmund to pass through the pale ahead of him.

A moment passed, then another. Still, Edmund didn't move.

Faucon came to stand alongside his clerk. The monk stared through the hatch, his gaze locked onto the three lashed planks that bridged the deep gap. His hands were wrapped so tightly around the strap of his basket that his knuckles were white. There was aught in his expression that suggested the monk liked that make-shift passageway as much as his employer liked the water in the well.

"Will you cross?" Faucon prodded gently.

His clerk made a strangled sound. "I—" Edmund started. He looked at his employer and almost pleaded, "Is there no other way?"

Faucon nodded. "There is, but you'll like it no better than what is before you. Yesterday, the bailiff went through the holly." He gestured toward the hedge Odger had pierced and that had surely pierced him in return as he exited. "I speculate, but I suspect that yon shrubbery hides yet another bridge such as this," he offered with a shrug. Then before Edmund could reply, Faucon continued. "There's third option, one that might please you better than the first two. Now that you've taken oaths from the smiths and made note of what we've learned thus far, there's no need for you to be here in Wike or the forest, not until the jury is called. As of the now, I don't expect to do that until late this evening or perhaps even the morrow."

"But we've yet to find that old man," Edmund started.

Faucon held up a hand to forestall his clerk's protest. "I agreed last even to meet Hew sometime over the course of this day. When I do, I can take his oath. You can note that he's given it at the same time you record the names of the jurors at the inquest. Why not return to Alcester and spend your day in the abbey's chapel?"

Much to his surprise, his offer didn't win him the gratitude he expected from the monk. Instead, Edmund shot him a hurt look, dragged in a deep breath and hurtled through the open gate. He clattered across the planks at top speed. With nothing holding the ends of the bridge in place, it bounced precariously on either bank as the monk ran. An instant later Edmund was beyond Faucon's view.

Faucon followed, albeit at a more moderate pace. As he crossed, he glanced into the ditch. A ladder leaned against the slope, suggesting that retrieving the planks from the ditch was a frequent chore.

Edmund had stopped well beyond the gateway. His basket lay on the ground while the monk had his hands braced on his thighs. He was bent in half, gasping for breath as Alf and Johnnie continued on ahead of him, already a good distance into the king's lands.

Coming to a stop beside the monk, Faucon looked around him, grinning in delight. The air that filled his lungs was lush with that particular spice that was autumn, one that held hints of dying leaves and an earth made richer by their passing. The foresters who served their monarch had laid a heavy hand on these lands, or at least in this area. He saw it in the unnatural spacing of the mature trees and the flexible withe panels—protection from ravaging deer— wrapped around the saplings chosen to one day take the places of their parents once their elders were harvested.

Not far from where he and Edmund stood, this grassy meadow gave way to something a little more shaded and tangled. There holly, elderberry, and blackthorn had been allowed to grow as they would, their feet buried deep in bracken and felled trees. These natural hedges and thick barriers were intended to supply hiding places and dens for those creatures that both Man and Beast loved to hunt.

When Edmund realized his employer was waiting for him he waved for Faucon move on. "Go," he gasped. "I'll follow in a moment."

"If you're certain," Faucon replied. His comment only won him another wave of Edmund's hand.

Setting out at a trot after the two men ahead of him, Faucon's pleasure grew as he moved deeper into this place. His footfalls startled sleeping hedgehogs and sent mice skittering into the fallen leaves. Overhead, squirrels chided as the last of the season's birds darted among the almost barren branches.

If Faucon needed proof that Odger had brought Wike's folk this way, he found it in the shoe- and footprints left in the moist soil of the path and in the wide swath of trampled grasses along its verge. But human spoor wasn't all he saw. Badger, fox, and weasel had all come this way since the rain. Although he found no mark of deer, Faucon knew as well as any man that these woods were stocked with both red and roe. And boar. Oh, to have a bow in his hands and a day of his own to spend as he wished!

Still reveling in both his longing and the joy that accompanied it, Faucon came abreast of Alf. Ahead of them, Johnnie moved steadily forward at his strange pace, looking neither right nor left as he went.

"You won't get it," Alf said, shooting his Crowner a swift glance as Faucon matched his stride.

Faucon blinked, startled out of his pleasure. "Won't get what?" he asked, looking at the soldier.

"The murdrum fine," Alf replied, this time without turning his head to meet his Crowner's gaze.

That brought Faucon up short. Alf stopped with him, watching his better in unguarded amusement. For the briefest of instants, Faucon considered challenging the commoner's assertion with the king's name, then thought the better of it.

"Why not?" he demanded instead.

Alf cocked his head, yet wearing his amusement openly. "Because the moment their bailiff realizes that's what you're after, he'll force some man to claim he fathered the girl. If I were that headman, I'd claim her myself and take my punishment to avoid what you want to press on him," the tall commoner replied. His tone suggested that this was so plain he was surprised his new master hadn't considered it.

And of course it was that plain. Faucon grimaced and released a frustrated breath. He'd let himself be carried away by Edmund's rigid and uncompromising honesty, when Wike was an underhanded and sly place, a den of lies and liars.

As Alf read his employer's expression, he grinned. It was a snaggle-toothed smile. "Well then, if you're set on collecting that fine, you'd best be very circumspect," he warned. "It's in your favor that the smiths don't seem to have realized what you won from them with their oaths. More importantly, even if they do suspect, they won't have an opportunity to speak to their bailiff until he returns with his folk. Which, if it were me," Alf added, narrowing one eye as if calculating, "won't be until dark has fallen, after you've retreated and the smiths have retired behind their own walls. That is, if this bailiff is doing his best to avoid you."

Faucon laughed at that. That was one sign he hadn't misread. But murdrum fine or no, he'd see that Odger's ploy cost him. Given what he now understood of Jessimond's murder, that price would still be far more than the bailiff expected to pay. "Avoiding me he most surely is, much to his detriment."

"Just know that he'll defend himself by saying the corpse had gone missing, then rightly claim that without a body no jury could be called," Alf warned. "He'll offer the same ploy on the morrow, taking his folk away, if he can."

"That's only if my corpse remains missing," Faucon replied, smiling as he again started after Johnnie. "My thanks, and know that I've taken your advice to heart."

That made Alf laugh as he strode alongside his new Crowner, then he indicated the youth ahead of them with a jerk of his chin. "So, you're certain this odd creature can lead us to the girl's body?"

It was Faucon's turn to destroy assumptions. He grinned at the commoner. "I not only think he can, but I believe he leads us to the dead lass's mother because she asked him to do so. You heard the smith. And now, thanks to you, I know to keep the body of Jessimond the Leper's Daughter a secret until I call that jury. Odger won't have time to recruit any other man to assume the role of Jessimond's father."

Disbelief and confusion flashed across Alf's face. "Tell me this. How is it a leper can come from a place as isolated as this one?"

That made Faucon offer his new man a sour smile. "It's a complicated tale, one that includes a headman who misuses his power over those beneath him, a child of anonymous rape and a woman wrongly driven from her home, forced to whore to care for those she loved. Worst of all, it was from one who had taken vows of chastity that she acquired her disease."

Alf freed a breath and gave a shake of his head. "That's the sorry way of our world, isn't it? Only by my uncle's goodness did my mother avoid a whore's fate after my father abandoned us. So, do you know yet who throttled this child?"

Once again, the pieces Faucon held in store shuffled and rearranged themselves as he pondered how to answer Alf's question. There was no pattern that satisfied him. At last, he gave a frustrated shake of his head.

"That I cannot settle on anyone to accuse surprises me. There's been only one other death since Halbert's that's had me confounded this way." Then Faucon shot an amused sidelong glance at the Englishman. "I know who I hope did the deed, but hoping is not the same as confirming."

As he spoke, he caught a sound from behind them and threw a look over his shoulder. Edmund jogged steadily toward them, his basket bouncing on his back, the hem of his black habit flying. As Alf saw the monk, he stepped off the trail, only returning to it once Faucon and his clerk had walked ahead of him.

That was how they proceeded, moving single file behind Johnnie. Faucon marked the fork where Odger had led his folk to the right, while the simpleton bore to the left. As Johnnie tiptoed steadily on, the landscape around them shifted from wooded grove to grassy meadow and back again. But once they crossed a streamlet the hand of Man became less evident. Holly and brambles grew to the edge of the path, their leaves and branches reaching out like claws to catch sleeve or hem when they passed too close. Overhead, autumn-thinned tree limbs tangled to cast dense shadows that were only occasionally pierced by narrow shafts of light.

Then Johnnie left the path, turning abruptly onto

the weaving thread of a game trail. Within a few yards, they were passing between two thick walls of vegetation —blackthorn, elderberry, and laurel. Again turning sharply, the mute pushed his way through one of those leafy barriers. Faucon followed, only to catch his breath in appreciation as he entered a fairy glade.

An uneven circle of trees—oak, ash, and slender beech—enclosed a small parcel of cleared ground, their thick canopy shattering day's light, sending golden droplets raining down to dapple all that lay below. At his feet what remained of former trees thrust up here and there from the thick carpet of fallen leaves. These rotted stumps were studded with mushrooms and coated in brilliant green moss. Water trickled somewhere nearby.

In that instant, Faucon knew this was the place where Amelyn and Jessimond had met, the same place that Jessimond and Gawne had made their own, and where Jessimond had died. And now it was the girl's sepulcher. The lass's corpse lay at the center of the glade. Amelyn had done as she'd warned her former neighbors; she'd prepared her child for burial. Faucon wondered if Hew had found her the rough hempen fabric she'd used for a winding sheet. Gawne sprawled crossways at Jessimond's feet, his head pillowed on one arm while he'd crooked the other over his head as if to block light. The lad was so deep in slumber that he didn't stir at the crunch of Johnnie's footsteps when the half-wit walked past him.

Faucon scanned the glade again, this time seeking the nest Hew mentioned. The children had used the single rowan, one with low hanging branches. About a third of the way up the tree, they'd erected a short wall woven from osier and other thin branches. It looked much like the blinds that foresters and huntsmen employed when they wished to observe their prey in secret. Had the tree been in full leaf, the wall would have been invisible. But even with its limbs barren, the rough construct looked more like a tangle than a man-made shield.

Rather than stop near Jessimond, Johnnie continued across the glade, yet moving at his peculiar pace. Faucon glanced past him to see what drew the mute. Only then did he notice Amelyn. The leper also slept, curled in slumber. She'd made her bed at the base of a tree, a thick stand of tall fern serving as her bed curtains.

Just then, Edmund pushed through the leafy barrier behind him. Faucon twisted, his hand rising to warn the monk to silence. But his clerk's gaze was fastened on Jessimond's corpse.

"I cannot believe it! He really did bring us to the girl!" the monk cried out.

Before Edmund's last word was out, Faucon was leaping for Gawne. Yet half- asleep, the lad shot up to sitting. The boy's unfocused eyes latched onto the man coming at him. With a frantic yelp, he wrenched around, scrabbling on hands and feet as he sought to escape his Crowner.

Faucon lunged forward. Just as his fingers brushed the back of the lad's tunic, his foot caught on a trunk. He rolled as he dropped, shoving himself back to standing in one smooth move. He wasn't fast enough. The lad now had half the length of the glade on him.

Yet panting in fear, Gawne lurched up into a crouch, his hands still moving as if he crawled. Faucon's feet slid and slipped as he strove for purchase in the deep litter. Then Alf bounded past him.

The big man grabbed the boy by the back of his tunic. Gawne thrashed as he was lifted from the earth and drove a foot into his captor's mid-section. The commoner gagged and bent, all the air driven from him.

Using his foot for leverage, Gawne tore free from Alf's stunned grasp.

Too late. Faucon threw himself at the boy, wrapping his arms around the lad's hips. They went down together, rolling, crashing into stumps and logs as Gawne writhed and shifted, fighting to escape.

They came to rest face-to-face. Wrestling the lad to the ground beneath him, Faucon lay atop Gawne's legs, pinning him in place with the weight of his body. Ivo's son screamed, still trying to kick as he rose to sitting. His fists flew. Small the lad was, but having two older brothers had taught him well. One blow set Faucon's left ear to ringing. The next connected powerfully enough with Faucon's right temple to threaten stars.

"Cease!" he bellowed, ducking his head into the breast of Gawne's tunic as he sought to protect himself.

The blows stopped as Gawne crashed back to the earth. The lad howled in desperation, wrenching with all his might. Alf gasped from almost atop his Crowner. Faucon raised his head. The Englishman had Gawne's arms pressed to the ground under his knees. The soldier's face was pale as he yet strove to fill his lungs.

Even with two men on him, the boy still refused to yield, gasping and grunting as he fought. Alf traded his hands for his knees and slid back to sitting. Faucon, his ear aching and ringing at the same time, followed suit, his hands yet gripping Gawne's legs.

"Cease, Gawne," he commanded, shaking his dislodged senses back into place. "I don't come for you. You didn't kill Jessimond, of this I'm certain."

The lad instantly relaxed. Then to Faucon's complete astonishment, Gawne gave breath to a great heart-rending sob. Releasing the lad, then waving to Alf to do the same, Faucon sat back on his heels. The moment Gawne was free, he rolled onto his stomach, buried his head in his arms and began to weep.

Alf coughed. He drew in a full but ragged breath. "Are you sure I shouldn't keep a hand on him?" he gasped out.

Faucon rubbed at his temple. He'd wear the mark of Gawne's fist for at least a week. "He's yielded. I think."

Edmund dropped onto one knee next to him. "Sir! The idiot is touching the leper!" the monk shouted into his employer's ringing ear.

Wincing, Faucon looked past Alf. Johnnie now cradled his sister in his lap, making pained, mewling sounds. The leper lay stiffly in his arms, yet retaining the curl of her final slumber.

Only then did Faucon realize what he should have known the instant Johnnie approached him to bring him into the woods. Amelyn had committed the most grievous of all sins. She had chosen to join her daughter in death.

Chapter Thirteen

"Holy Mother, she knew what she was after and made certain she got what she wanted," Alf said in cautious respect as he looked at the woman's wrists.

Amelyn had removed her gloves so she could do the task she'd set herself, and used her eating knife to do the deed. That hadn't been the right knife for the chore. She'd had to saw at her own flesh with the little blade to achieve her aim.

But achieve it she had. Blood had more poured than throbbed from her, saturating the hems of her sleeves and coating her palms and fingers. As it dried, it had crusted and cracked, now flaking away as the idiot held her.

Hew's warning about a grieving mother once again echoed in Faucon. *If only*, he sang to himself. But that was a refrain he couldn't afford to repeat, nor did wishing for a different outcome change what lay before him. Instead, all Faucon wanted was to depart this beautiful place, leaving mother and daughter here, joined for all eternity, forgotten even by God Himself. Let England's king wring his coins from some other death.

"How could she do that? How could she damn herself to hell when her daughter will be with our Lord? She abandoned her child," Edmund whispered, his voice hoarse as he again pleaded for assurance from his employer. The monk had his prayer beads in hand.

They were already slipping through his fingers, even though Edmund hadn't yet knelt to chant out the words that accompanied them.

"I'm not certain I can fault her," Faucon offered quietly, so the lad across the glade didn't hear him. "So oft had life beaten her and so much had been stolen from her, that it left her weakened and without purpose. To live on after her precious daughter was gone, only to die from the disease that Odger had ultimately forced upon her, must have been more than she could bear."

Edmund's face paled. Moisture filled his eyes. "So it must have been for my mother. I was wrong to think ill of her," he breathed.

Surprise shot through Faucon. He stood still, waiting for the monk to say more. Instead, his clerk turned and knelt next to Amelyn, then bowed his head as he began to pray.

Still pondering his glimpse into Edmund's past, Faucon crossed to where Gawne lay on the ground and crouched next to the boy. Although the lad yet had his face pressed into the leaves, Gawne's grief was almost spent. When Faucon stroked his back, the boy shuddered at his touch and sought to catch his breath. Turning his head to the side, resting his cheek on his arm, he looked at his Crowner. This hadn't been his first spate of tears. This second shower had laid new tracks through the dirty remains of that previous storm.

"I didn't know what she intended," Gawne managed, his voice wispy. "I wrapped Jes for her because she didn't want anyone to be afraid of touching Jes because of her disease when the time for burial came. Then she asked me to bring her some water. By the time I returned with her cup, she'd started it." He paused to gag, then continued at a raw whisper. "I had to watch her as she finished the task, then stay by her as she died."

"This is my fault," Faucon offered. "Hew suggested last night that Amelyn might not recover from Jessimond's death. I heard him, but did not comprehend how dire his warning. Your guilt is mine. Thus, will it be our duty to pray for Amelyn's soul, doing so until we die. Perhaps if we explain to our Lord often enough how deeply she grieved for her child, He will take pity on her and spare her eternal damnation."

That drew yet another trembling sigh from the lad. Gawne nodded as if the movement of his head was all he could manage. Faucon gave him another moment, then asked, "Are you settled enough that you can answer my questions?"

The boy closed his eyes for a moment, then struggled to sitting with a sigh. He wiped grief from his face with his sleeves, taking much of the dirt with it. Beneath the smut, his face was wan.

"Meg accused me of killing Jes. I didn't do it," he offered on a shuddering gasp. "I would never have hurt Jes!"

"As I said, I know you didn't kill the girl," Faucon assured him.

"But what will happen to me?" Gawne asked, his voice hoarse and his words broken. "What if I return home and she again names me murderer in front of everyone?"

"Rest easy on that accord," Faucon said. "Once I accuse Jessimond's killer—and you may trust that I will name the one who did this—the matter will be resolved in your favor. Now, tell me your tale."

Words spewed from the boy. "It was Meg who killed Jes! That's why she accused me!"

"You saw her commit the act?" Faucon asked swiftly, wishing Gawne had witnessed Jessimond's death but certain that he hadn't.

"Nay," the boy moaned, tears again sparkling in his

eyes, "but I should have. I was to have been here with Jes that night. She asked me to meet with her, saying she needed my help. I was going to leave once Da and my brothers slept, but Da had brought out his first cask of plum wine. Fearing it might explode, he opened it in the doorway. Once it was tapped, that's where he chose to sit, right there in the doorway, with me trapped inside. There was no way for me to leave save to push past him and, if I had tried, he would have stopped me. He'd never have let me go. I waited, but he was still sitting there when it was time for Rauf and me to take to our pallet for the night. I meant to stay awake until he retired—" here, Gawne paused for another shuddering breath. A single tear trailed down one cheek. "Instead, I fell asleep when I should have been here," he repeated at a whisper.

Faucon eyed the boy in pity and wondered how the outcome of that night might have differed if Gawne had managed to escape his sire. Moreover, if Gawne had indeed told Hew that Jessimond had come into the woods to meet someone, he'd lied, doing so to shield himself from the pain of failing his friend. "Can you show me where you found Jessimond's body when you arrived here the next morning?"

Nodding, the boy came to his feet, once again swabbing his face with a soggy sleeve. Together, they crossed to a spot not far from where Amelyn had finished her life. Alf followed, maintaining a respectful distance as he watched what went forward between the boy and his Crowner.

Faucon crouched, scanning the area. Despite the rain two nights ago, much of the tale told by the crushed leaves and grasses, and broken ferns could yet be read. Once he had a sense of what had happened, he sifted his hands through the litter. There were indentations in the mossy layer beneath the leaves.

Clearing away the debris, he looked at what he'd found. The one who had knelt here had been heavy enough to break through that soft emerald layer. During the struggle as Jessimond's life ended, bits of green moss had been driven into the even softer soil hidden beneath it.

Shifting, he eased into position, putting his knees into the dips. Alf stepped around him to crouch just beyond Faucon's reach from where he knelt. "About here?" the commoner asked, touching his finger to an area of crushed grass.

"I think," Faucon replied with a nod.

He shifted to look over his shoulder at Gawne. "Where my man points, is this where her head rested when you found her?"

Gawne blinked at him in astonishment and nodded mutely.

"What of her clothing? Did you find her garments?" he asked.

This time, the boy shook his head to the negative. His eyes closed and he swallowed. "I looked every-where. Why would her clothing have been taken?"

Not for the reason Faucon had originally believed. At last, the bits and pieces in his head were beginning to arrange themselves into something that made sense.

"Think back over the last few days of Jessimond's life. Did she tell you anything that surprised you? Anything unexpected. Not just about her. Perhaps about wishing to meet her father? Or it could have been about Meg or the kitchen."

Gawne frowned at that. "Nay, nothing. Jes didn't know who her father was. She only once talked about her sire. Before Martha died, she told Jes why Amelyn didn't know who had sired her, that—" he broke off mid-word, the sudden uneasiness in his gaze suggesting he didn't wish to breach a confidence.

189

Faucon completed the lad's sentence for him. "That Jessimond had been conceived in rape. Amelyn told me."

Gawne gave a relieved sigh. "Jes made me swear a blood oath that I'd never reveal that. As for Meg, all Jes ever said about her was how much she hated her," the boy said.

Then he paused to chew on his lip for a moment. "What about something strange that Meg did?"

"If it strikes you as odd, I'd like to hear it," Faucon replied, nodding his encouragement.

"Meg went to Alcester three days in a row just before Jes died. Each time she went she was gone for the whole day and didn't return until so late that none of us knew she was returned until the next morn." Gawne said. "One of those days was a baking day. Meg left before her own loaves were finished. That's something she's never before done. Why would she go to Alcester without her loaves to sell?"

Yet frowning in confusion, Gawne continued. "Instead, on the baking day, Meg left Jes to finish the loaves, again something she'd never done. Jes told me that after she took all the loaves from the oven, she put them on the kitchen table to cool, the way Meg always did. But while Jes went to the well to fetch water for cleaning, someone entered the kitchen and stole every loaf."

"All of them?" Faucon replied in surprise. "What did the good wives of Wike have to say about that?"

Gawne shrugged. "Nothing at all. Nor was anyone in Wike without bread that night. Save for Meg."

That made Faucon grin. Thus had the women of Wike taken what little vengeance they could on the one who'd stolen from them for years.

"Jes said Meg was very angry when she finally returned, that being after it was full dark, as I said, sir,"

Gawne went on. "When Meg learned what had happened to her loaves, she took her fists and a switch to Jes, beating her to drawing blood."

Alf's brows rose at that. Faucon released a breath of sour amusement. It didn't surprise him that the bakestress had lied about the reason she'd beaten her ward. No thief wanted to admit that another thief had stolen from her.

"Well done. That helps me greatly," he told the boy. "Now with that same inner eye trained on the unusual, think of this place. Was there anything here that stands out to you when you came upon Jes that morning?"

The boy frowned in thought. After a moment, he gave a helpless shake of his head. "I saw nothing but Jes, dead." Moisture again filled his eyes.

It was what Faucon expected to hear. Sitting back on his heels, he again scanned the area where Jessimond had breathed her last, gauging how far her fingertips might have reached and all the possible positions in which her arms might have come to rest. With that in mind, he began to gently and carefully scour the grasses.

"What do you seek?" Alf asked.

"Threads, scraps of clothing, hair," Faucon replied without moving his gaze from the ground he explored. "Something the child might have torn from the one who killed her as she struggled to preserve her life."

Nodding, Alf leaned to the opposite side and did the same. Gawne watched. In that moment the only sounds were the continuing raucous call of departing swans and geese, Johnnie's quiet huffs as he rocked his sister and the sibilant sound of Edmund whispering his prayers.

Just as Faucon was ready to admit defeat, he found what he sought. A tiny knot of white threads clung to the frond of a fern. But when he leaned forward to retrieve them, he stretched farther than he expected. With the threads pinched between his fingers, he sat back on his heels, staring at them in disappointment.

Alf sat back as well and watched him. "They don't help?" the soldier asked.

"They do, but not the way I'd hoped," Faucon replied, still shuffling the last of his loose pieces only to discover there was no space for them. That brought his attention back on Gawne. "Lad, your father says he offered to take Jessimond into your home."

"Too late," Gawne cried softly. "Jes was already dead when Da said those words."

"Had you spoken to him about Jessimond before that time?"

"Aye, only always," the boy retorted in frustration. "I'd asked and asked, telling him how cruel Meg was to her and to Johnnie. And I'm not the only one who asked. Last month, some of our neighbors came to Da. They demanded that he to take me to the forge, to keep them from having to tend me. They told Da it wasn't fair that he was shirking his duty to me. Then they warned him that if Odger fined them because of me and Jes, they'd see to it that Da paid the whole amount. Then my older brother said that he should marry Jes and settle the issue."

He paused to draw a breath and scrub at his face again with his sleeve as his lips curved into a ghost of a smile. "I think Dob liked Jes and I know she thought him handsome. Even though Da said that their union would surely resolve the issue, he never spoke to our bailiff." The boy shook his head and gave a sad hiccough. "He still misses Ma and I don't think he can bear the thought of another woman in our house."

Nodding to acknowledge the lad's words, Faucon pried open his purse. As he stored the bits of thread into the leather pouch, his thoughts wove and knotted until they were as tangled as the threads.

Pulling the drawstrings to close his purse, he again looked at Gawne. "Did you tell Amelyn any of what Dob and your father planned?" he asked gently.

The boy offered a tiny shrug. "She was grieving so. I thought it would make her heart easier to know that Dob would have taken Jessimond even if she had no dowry and was a bastard."

"You are a kind and honest lad, Gawne," Faucon said with a slow smile. "I pray you carry those traits into your manhood. Now, I must ask you to remain here with Jessimond and Amelyn for a while longer."

The boy's gaze shifted uneasily to Johnnie and the leper's corpse. What little color had returned to his face began to fade. "By myself?" he whispered.

"Nay, not at all," Faucon laughed. "This is my man-at-arms, Alf," he continued, presenting the soldier to the boy. "He'll stay with you. When the time comes for the inquest, I'll fetch you or send Hew to you in my stead. Only then will you return to Wike, with Alf to carry Jessimond's body for you this time," he offered with a smile.

Alf heard his cue. "We'll do well enough here, lad," the soldier said. "I wager you've got a trap or two, haven't you? I know I did as a child. Do you think there'd be anything in them? I have flint and tinder," he coaxed, touching the purse that hung from his belt as he smiled at Gawne. "I'm not from this area. Are there many stones around here? Perhaps we can begin building a cairn over the leper while we wait for your Crowner's call to return. Do you think we can get her brother to help us?"

It was more than a distraction the Englishman offered the boy, but a kindness as well. There was no point in taking Amelyn elsewhere for burial. No church in the world would have her, not when she was a leper who'd taken her own life.

"Maybe you can find enough stones for two cairns," Faucon said, sending a grateful smile Alf's way. "I think mother and daughter should stay here together."

Gawne shot a startled look at his Crowner, then released his breath in a slow, pleased stream. Although his smile was tenuous, it was filled with gratitude. "Aye, that would please them both, I think."

Then the boy looked at Alf. "I do have traps, and I'd very much like to eat," he said shyly.

Chapter Fourteen

To Faucon's complete astonishment, when he told his clerk he was leaving the glade to seek out Hew, Edmund announced that he would stay to help the boy and soldier gather stones for Amelyn's cairn. Faucon couldn't have been more pleased. He needed quiet time with his thoughts, to sift through what he knew and pluck out what was yet missing. And time to ease his soul over what Amelyn had done.

There was no better way to achieve what he needed than a solitary walk in the woods, especially on a beautiful autumn morning. As he strode along, following Gawne's thorough instructions on how to reach the monks' hogscotes, his passage scared up partridges. Overhead, what had been but the occasional flock of geese or swans earlier this morning had become an exodus. The birds filled the air, arrow-shaped flock after flock. Their harsh and constant chatter drowned out the gentler sounds of field and forest.

Of a sudden, the yearling roebuck Faucon had been eying raised his head. The little creature's ears shifted as he looked behind him, away from the oncoming man. Then the buck sprang into motion, leaping out of the grassy area by hasty bounds. Only then did Faucon hear the grunting and shuffling of the hogs over the noise from above him. That had him grinning. Gawne did, indeed, know these woods well.

"Brothers! Watch your hogs. I'm coming to you," Faucon called out, even though he hadn't yet caught a glimpse of the monks or the vicious creatures they herded. The last thing he wanted was to startle the unpredictable beasts when he had no spear or bow to defend against them.

"Hold a moment," a man called in return, then three sets of sharp whistles pierced the air. Hogs squealed and grunted as they were driven back from the path. As the porcine complaints died into something less displeased, the same man shouted, "Come now. It's safe."

Faucon pressed forward on the path, his hand still on his sword, just in case. There was no need. Three monks stood far off the path, their crooks lowered crosswise at their knees. That created a makeshift barrier meant to deter any of the long, lean and deadly creatures they tended from charging a stranger. Their barrier appeared unnecessary at the moment. The hogs, only the sows the monks had kept to provide next year's meat, had their backs to Faucon and the path, their snouts deep in the earth. That soil flew suggested they'd given up nuts for grubs or mushrooms.

"Sir Faucon!" It was the shortest of the monks who greeted him, the novice who had carried his message to the anchorite this morning. "What are you doing here in this wild place?"

"Looking for Hew of Wike," Faucon replied.

That made all three monks eye him in surprise. One of the two taller brothers replied. "So it's you he waits for, not the leper. Walk on another quarter mile or so and you'll find our cotes and Hew."

Faucon nodded his thanks and started forward only to pause. "Tell me, have you seen anything or anyone here in the woods that struck you as odd over this past week?"

"Nay, nothing, not since the headman of Wike came out to rail at us for letting Hew sleep in our shelter near the cotes," the tall monk called back, shaking his head in disgust over Odger.

"What about that woman the other morning, the one who'd lost her way in the woods? She was bruised and dirty," the novice asked, looking at his brother as the third monk turned his back to the knight to keep his eye on the hogs.

"That vile woman? She lost her way long before last week," the tall brother scoffed. "I don't think our new Coronarius is asking about Alcester's procuress returning home from here, looking the worse for wear. He's not interested in whores and their sins," he replied.

With that, another of the few loose pieces yet Faucon held within him found its home. It hadn't been Gawne who told Hew that Jessimond had fled to meet a stranger. He grinned and lifted a hand. "On the contrary, that's exactly what I meant. Thank you, brothers. Enjoy this glorious day!"

It just a bit longer before he entered a wide clearing. Most of it was caught inside a fence made of branches woven around upright posts. The earth within that enclosure was naught but a sea of reddish mud, nary a blade of grass to be seen. Such was the destruction hogs wreaked, and the reason Odger feared for Wike's fields.

Basking in the sun was the boar who serviced the monks' sows. The brute had already eaten what he liked from the pile of kitchen leavings, no doubt brought by the monks from their abbey kitchen. The boar lazed in front of the larger of the three cotes within the enclosure. The structures that housed the hogs were triangular in shape and made of lashed wooden walls with thatched roofs that extended all the way to the torn earth. A single large hatch, leather straps serving for hinges and clasp, in the front of each structure offered the hogs access into their shelters.

As Faucon rounded the corner of the enclosure he found Hew. The old man sat with his back to the fence, a wooden mallet in one hand and a freshly crushed nut before him. In the basket at his left was a diminishing pile of whole walnuts while the basket to his right held a growing pile of shelled nut meat.

The old man looked up and offered an almost toothless grin. "Sir! Good morrow to you."

"And to you," Faucon replied, halting beside the rustic and offering a hand to aid Hew in rising. "Although I fear this morning is not a good one. We found Amelyn with Jessimond in the woods."

"So I know," Hew replied quickly as he regained his feet and then his balance. "After you departed, she insisted on taking Jessimond back to their hidden spot. She had me find her something to use as Jessimond's winding sheet, then schooled Johnnie carefully so he would bring you to her when you arrived in Wike this morning."

"Then you didn't realize what she intended," Faucon said gently.

"What did she—" the old man started, then his wild brows rose high upon his creased forehead. His mouth opened but no word issued. His expression sagged.

"Nay," the rustic pleaded at a whisper.

"I fear so," Faucon replied, once more mourning for Amelyn.

As swiftly as guilt bent the rustic's shoulders, anger followed. "May God take Odger! He is the cause of this," Hew shouted. "Call him to the inquest, sir! Let me tell the folk of Wike that they keep a rapist as their head-man, even if he doesn't prove to be the man who sired Jessimond. Then I'll accuse him of Amelyn's death, for if Odger had not taken vengeance against her on that long ago day, she would yet live, whole and healthy!" he raged, beating at his breast with his palm since his stiff, misshapen fingers wouldn't close to make a fist.

Fearing the old man might break frail bones if he

continued, Faucon caught his wrist. "So it shall be done," he promised Hew, "but in doing so I must break my promise to you. I can no longer guarantee you the murdrum fine."

"What care I for that?" Hew cried out, straining at his Crowner's hold. Tears filled his eyes. "Just know that if you leave and Odger has not paid for what he's done, I will find a way to end his life, this I vow. When he's cold, bring the hangman for me if you dare!"

That had Faucon grinning. He released the old man's arm. "There'll be no need for your sacrifice, Hew. You have my word on it," he told the man and meant it. That part of this sordid tale was clear enough.

"As for Amelyn and her daughter, my clerk and my new man-at-arms are in the glade with Gawne and Johnnie. The four gather stones to build a cairn for Amelyn. It's my thought that after the inquest is complete, Jessimond should be returned to her mother's side to take her final rest."

Hew released a breath at that, yet struggling to tame his emotions. At last, he nodded. "Aye, Amelyn would like that very much, sir. Indeed, I think it's what must be done if we're to keep her from joining those haunts who already walk within these woods. So great was her love that I doubt even death is enough to stop her from seeking out her precious babe if we try to part them."

"Just so," Faucon agreed with a nod. "Now, if you're calm, I need you to think back over the week just past. You said yesterday that Jessimond had fled the kitchen to meet with a stranger. Now, the monks tell me they saw a whore, the mistress of a stew in Alcester, enter the woods a few days ago."

This shift of subject had the old man blinking in surprise. "There's only one brothel in Alcester. Was this bawd big for a woman and broad?"

"That I cannot say. The monks didn't describe her,"

Faucon replied with a shrug.

"But I do know what she looks like," Hew shot back, his voice rising in excitement, "and I did see such a form moving through the woods on the night Jes died! I never would have thought it was the bawd. I'd been delayed in Wike until well past dark that night. My family was celebrating my older son's saint day. After passing through the hatch to enter the forest, I heard movement. When I glanced toward the sound I gave thanks because the one who moved away from me on that path was very much alive. No haunt carries living flame."

Here, Hew paused to release a harsh breath. "Would that I'd known then that Jes had fled the kitchen. I would have followed instead of hurrying off in the opposite direction, fearing for my own safety."

"How could you have known it was this bawd in the dark?" Faucon asked.

"You are right to ask that question," Hew replied, "but I am certain even though the night was dim, what with the moon but a sliver. This one held the lamp in front of her whilst her back was to me, but hadn't I seen this exact form before and only recently, one not so tall but broad? It's you telling me that the monks saw the bawd that convinces me. So too does this convince me of what Meg must have done. did this. She sold Jes to the bawd," the rustic insisted. "Didn't she tell us all the day after Jessimond left the kitchen that the lass had run to Alcester to whore? Sir, at last it makes sense," the old man almost pleaded.

"If Meg had sold the girl, then Jessimond would be whoring in Alcester, not dead," Faucon replied with a shake of his head. "Instead, tell me why you think the procuress would even know to seek out Amelyn's daughter."

"Because of what she said to Amelyn last month,"

the old man said swiftly. "I didn't think whores were even allowed in at the abbey, but when the woman walked past Amelyn along with all the other townsfolk who'd come for Prime service, she stared at us. I could see that even with Amelyn hooded and cloaked, the whore knew who she was. And I could tell that the two liked each other naught at all. If the bawd came for the service, she didn't stay until it was done. Instead, just a short while later she was again on the path, returning to the Street. This time, she stopped in front of Amelyn and said that she would finally receive full repayment for what she'd lent her."

Shock tore through Faucon. The pieces within him rearranged one more time, doing so at their will. When they came to rest, he couldn't bear to look upon the image they created.

Reeling as surprise gave way to all-consuming rage, Faucon turned to stare in the direction of Wike. Question piled atop question, but none of them would lead him to the certainty he craved, not now that Amelyn was gone. Yet, among them was one question that had a certain answer. Amelyn hadn't spent her life because of grief, but to shield another from the ultimate hurt.

To Hew, he said, "Odger has taken all of Wike into the forest to collect wood."

"Aye, so I know, sir," the old man replied, his voice muted and his head bowed. "They're a mile or so from here. My grandson came earlier this morn to bring me these nuts, something to occupy my hands while I awaited you."

"Will you carry a message to them for me?"

"Aye, that I can do, sir," the rustic replied, his voice still subdued and his neck bent in a position of humility, one that ill fit him. "What would you have me say to Odger when I find them, sir?"

Only then did Faucon realize that his rage had

driven him for his sword. His fingers were clenched around the pommel as if he meant to draw it. Releasing his weapon, he brought his arm back to his side, battling for calm. Overhead, the sun said it was yet an hour or so before midday.

"You'll tell Odger that I will hold the inquest at the hour of None. Make sure he knows how enraged I am by his defiance. Tell him that I will see him fined for what he's dared, then say that the amount of my fine will increase should he delay the return of your folk to Wike. If he asks about Jessimond, you'll say that I have her body and no more. Nor will you mention that Amelyn is dead."

"As you will, sir," Hew agreed, still not daring to raise his head to look directly at his Crowner.

"Many thanks," Faucon said brusquely, then whirled, returning to the path that led to Alcester, all the joy gone from his day.

"Brother Henricus, I am Sir Faucon de Ramis, newly appointed Coronarius and Keeper of the Pleas for this shire. As is my duty, I am investigating the death of Jessimond, daughter of Amelyn the Leper," Faucon said in introduction to the island abbey's diseased anchorite.

The sub-abbot had been walled into a cell built into the cellar of the abbot's house. Two small rectangular openings, screened to prevent a wayward touch, allowed the monk bare glimpses of the world he'd forsaken. Air and light came to him through the opening in the exterior wall, while the inner one permitted him to communicate with his brothers. Or his Crowner. Faucon sat upon a stool that brought his face to the level of that small, screened rectangle. At his feet was the hatch that allowed food and drink to be pushed into the cell and the monk's wastes to be removed. If a door existed in the cell, it was hidden, covered by a coat of plaster.

It had taken Faucon the full length of his walk between the hogscotes and the abbey to tame his rage. Time well spent. Arriving in control of his emotions had prevented him from overstepping with the abbot, and that had resulted in the churchman's invitation to share lunch. The rich meal would have enraged Edmund, but it hadn't been food that Faucon craved. After entertaining the abbot with tales of his own more august relatives, he'd pleaded ignorance about local history. The abbot had proved Faucon's sire right and offered up every bit of gossip he had in store. That left the man so sated and expansive that when Faucon asked to speak with his former sub-abbot, the churchman agreed without hesitation and despite the anchorite's earlier refusal.

"I can tell you nothing in that regard. I have no knowledge of the child's death," Brother Henricus replied, his voice hoarse and weak as he sat upon his stool on the other side of the opening. Between the dimness of his chamber and his cowl, Faucon could seen nothing of the ravages of his disease.

"But you can tell me about the child's mother. Amelyn was your leman."

The monk sighed, the sound fraught with regret. "I sinned. My confinement to this cell is part of my penance."

"This is no penance, it is a kindness," Faucon retorted, now speaking with the authority that had had Oswald bowing to his wishes, "a greater kindness than was ever shown to Amelyn of Wike. You have much to answer for in regard to her, especially now that both she and her daughter are dead."

As the monk heard these words, his shoulders bent

and he buried his face in his hands. "May God forgive me," he muttered into his palms, rocking on his stool.

"Pray as you will, but know that as you do, I shall be praying that our heavenly Father dooms you to the eternal fires. You're no monk," he spat out in disgust. "You only took your vows because your family willed it. You never had any intention of honoring your vow to our Lord."

Like Faucon, Henry of Kinwarton was a second son, in this case the cousin of the abbey's founder. He had been given to the Church with the expectation that he would rise in rank until he could use the power of his position for the benefit of his family, just as William of Hereford did for his kin. Instead, the man had squandered the opportunity, concentrating instead on pleasing himself.

"Pity poor Amelyn," Faucon continued harshly. "She came to Alcester an innocent in all ways. She knew nothing of whoring, nothing of this place and nothing of you. And weren't you and the procuress waiting for one just such as she? The bawd didn't want you using her girls, not when she knew you were diseased. So when she told you about a beautiful woman newly come to Alcester to whore, you lent the bawd funds to give to Amelyn, then used that loan to force Amelyn to serve you. You doomed Amelyn to death to feed your sinful appetites!"

The man within the cell but rocked, his face yet buried in his palms.

Faucon's eyes narrowed. "I know the bawd came to see you last month. Tell me what she asked you. Best you speak the truth, for I will know if you lie."

The man on the other side of the grate at last lowered his hands. There was no seeing his face in the shadowed cell. "Lina asked what Amelyn had told me of Wike and its folk," he said, his voice thick with tears. "I told her the truth, the same thing I now tell you. Amelyn never spoke to me of Wike. The only thing she ever shared about her life before whoring was that her daughter was precious to her beyond all else and made in her image."

It was a dragon's breath Faucon released. The monk had done worse than doom Amelyn to death. His words had convinced the procuress that it was worth her time to negotiate with Meg, who had no doubt set a steep price for the purchase of Jessimond.

"You selfish coward," he spat out in disgust. Where was the justice in this unholy monk holding tight to the comforts of his house, when Edmund, who had more courage than a lion despite his peculiarities, had lost all he held dear?

"I suspect your cousin pays a steep price to keep you walled in here rather than walking the byways in a leper's cloak, bringing shame upon your family name. After I leave, you'll request that your abbot draw from that sum to secure a place here for a new servant, Amelyn's mute and crippled half-brother. If you're asked why you wish to do this, say that our Lord has given it to you to see this youth gently cared for until his death, even if it means you go hungry to do it. If the brothers try to make him a beggar, you will refuse, telling them that you know the youth and he is capable of working in the kitchen. Betray me, and I will seek every avenue to have you accused of abetting the murder of the leper's daughter. Should I fail at that, I'll instead inform my uncle, Bishop William of Hereford, what you've done. Unlike you, my uncle is a man who honors his vows and expects the same integrity from those in his order. I guarantee you'll live out your last years begging for bread like the woman you used."

With that, Faucon came to his feet, kicked his stool to the side and departed.

Chapter Fifteen

He, Edmund, and Alf, who bore Jessimond in his arms, stopped before Meg's kitchen. Johnnie had remained in the glade after their attempts to remove him resulted in high-pitched squeals and thrashing limbs. Once released, the simpleton went back to gathering rocks for Amelyn's cairn. That's when Gawne insisted on staying behind to watch over him. Although Gawne freed no squeals and hadn't thrashed, it was clear the lad didn't trust his neighbors not to accuse him of Jessimond's murder.

"Is this where you intend to hold the inquest, sir?" Edmund asked, his breathing once more steady after his second perilous journey over the plank bridge. This time he'd rearranged his basket on his back before stepping out over the gap. With the strap crossing his chest, both of his arms had been free to extend for balance, and he'd moved at a snail's pace.

"Can you think of a better place than here, where that poor child was forced to live out her last miserable years?" Faucon asked bitterly.

Edmund had no answer for that. Instead he said, "We'll need a table for the corpse."

"There'll be one inside," Faucon replied, and started toward the kitchen door.

It was a baking day, and the oven radiated warmth along with a sweet, yeasty scent. The door to Meg's realm was ajar. He pushed it wide, only to have it bounce back at him as it collided with something behind it.

Stepping inside, he looked for the bakestress, but she wasn't within. The interior of the chamber looked much like the interior of any rural commoner's home except for the great maw of a fire pit to one side of the door, one big enough to have once provided meals for a knight's household. And one that hadn't been used at its full capacity since Wike Manor had been abandoned. Meg did her cooking on a much smaller hearth stone at the other side of the doorway. It was that stone that had stopped the door.

At the forward center of the space was a narrow table, naught but four loose planks set atop a pair of braces and covered in flour. Bits of stolen dough were piled in one corner. Overhead, bunches of herbs and smoked meats hung from the beams that held the roof aloft. So did two small, well- made iron pots and an array of wooden cooking implements.

Stacked high against the wall to his left were hempen bags filled with Meg's winter provisions, be that unshelled nuts, whole grain or dried fruits. The right wall was lined with barrels and casks of all sizes, set one atop the other. They would contain brines, vinegar and fermented drink. Filling the floor space under the table were an array of clay pots. That they held milled grain was proved by the powdery stuff that caked their exteriors.

All that clutter left only a thread of a path on either side of the table for access to the sleeping area at the rear of the chamber. A pair of straw-stuffed pallets was stacked against the back wall. Fastened to the wall above them were two shelves. One held bowls and spoons, the other a fine wooden coffer.

The box was as long and high as Faucon's forearm, and of startling quality for a place as impoverished as Wike. Bossed in brass, it had been polished to a glossy sheen where it wasn't decorated with a colorful painted design. Although it had a hasp with a loop, the lock that should have held it shut lay on the shelf next to the chest, its pin yet inserted into it.

Faucon gave vent to a harsh breath. Meg had taken his threat to heart this morn. She'd fled with her treasure.

Easing his way along the narrow route, he took the box from the shelf. When he turned to place it on the end of the dusty table, he found Edmund standing at its opposite end. Alf, yet bearing Jessimond's wrapped corpse in his arms, remained just outside the shed, watching his employer through the doorway.

Faucon opened the coffer and answered one of his remaining questions. He removed the carefully folded garments. Rich they were not, being nothing but a clumsily made and plain green gown and an undyed linen shift. But they were hardly worn and, despite their poor construction, still worth whatever coin Meg had originally paid for them.

Holding them up, he displayed them to the soldier and the monk. "Brother, when you put pen to parchment, note that we found Jessimond's garments in the kitchen of Wike's bakestress."

"It doesn't surprise me that such a woman might have killed a child," the monk said in disgust while in the doorway Alf shot a startled glance to the side.

"'Ware Brother!" the soldier shouted as he darted out of Faucon's view.

Edmund started to look over his shoulder, only to scream and arch backward. His hips jammed into the edge of the table. The resting planks shot toward Faucon, bringing flour and dough with them and sending the coffer flying. Holding tight to Jessimond's gowns, he reared backward into the pallets. They slid and he careened to the side. Planks crashed into the wall, then clattered to the floor. The braces toppled. He fell onto the nearest pile of sacks. A cat screeched.

"Get out of my home!" Meg shrieked at the same time.

She stood inside the door, holding a shovel high, ready for the next blow. Then the shovel was torn from the old woman's hands. Roaring in rage, Meg whirled, fists closed and raised. Alf was the quicker. The woman's head snapped back as he struck. Stunned, she reeled, then dropped to sprawl into the cold fire pit.

Stuffing the gowns beneath his arm, Faucon scrambled toward Edmund, who lay face-first on the earthen floor. Whatever semblance of order there had been in here before Meg's attack was gone. Bags lay helter-skelter, jars were tipped, their contents spilling out onto the floor. His feet slipped on balls of dough, the ooze from barrels, and the nuts that rolled out of toppled bags.

As Alf stepped closer to the prone clerk, shaking his hand, Faucon crouched alongside the monk. Edmund hadn't yet stirred. The clerk's precious writing implements were strewn about him in the grain dust. If his basket was no more, the piece of wood he used as a desk yet rested across his back, whole and solid. Faucon lifted it. And now marked. With a finger, he traced the new shovel-shaped dent on its surface. Only his clerk could have been saved by a desk.

Setting aside the wood, he put his hand between the remains of the basket and Edmund's back. There was no obvious break. Still the monk lay still and silent.

"Brother, are you awake?" he demanded.

"I'm not certain," came Edmund's weak and shaken reply.

Faucon grinned, so great was his relief. "Are you hurt? Did your head hit as you fell?"

"Nay," the monk breathed, still not moving.

Looking at Alf, Faucon said, "Together."

They both took an arm and brought Edmund to his feet. The monk swayed for an instant then caught his balance. Drawing a deep breath, thus proving he had no broken ribs, he squeamishly tightened his shoulders and his arms.

"You can release me," he told soldier and knight.

When they didn't instantly comply, he raised his hands in protest. "I'm whole and unbloodied. Let go." This was a command.

Alf did as he was bid, backing into the doorway to block the opening despite that Meg yet lay stunned in the pit. Faucon wasn't so quick to comply. "You're certain?"

"Aye, it's only my pride that's damaged," Edmund admitted as he wrenched his arm from his Crowner's grasp.

His movement sent bits of his ruined basket raining from his back. The monk gasped and reached behind him. When there was nothing for him to feel, his eyes flew wide.

"My supplies!" he cried, dropping to his knees to scrabble through the wreckage, seeking his precious bits and pieces.

Faucon crouched with him and found the monk's quill knife. "Best you take time to give thanks to our Lord for that piece of wood of yours. The old woman meant her blow to break bones," he said as he handed it to Edmund.

His clerk paused in his search, his gaze yet fixed on the floor before him. He drew a shaken breath, then closed his hand about the stoppered horn in which he stored his powdered ink. As he lifted it, his hand trembled, the aftereffect of Meg's attack. He drew the horn to his chest as if he meant to disguise his reaction.

"So I shall," Edmund said, yet refusing to meet

Faucon's gaze, "but I think we're better praying that I have what I need to complete this inquest. Best you leave me to gather my things so I can get at assessing the damage."

The monk had peculiar courage, indeed. Faucon dared to lay a final touch on his clerk's arm, a comrade's acknowledgment of bravery. As he expected, Edmund flinched away from him. That made him smile.

"I'm glad you're unharmed, Edmund," he said, then retreated to stand with Alf so his clerk could collect himself under the pretense of gathering his supplies. "That's no measly monk I have scribing for me. That's a soldier, albeit one in Christ," he told the commoner, still smiling.

"So he is," Alf agreed with a nod, then gave a jerk of his head toward Meg. She whimpered as she began to stir. "And that is a woman who needs more than her tongue torn from her mouth."

"Such is the arrogance of one who finds value only in coins. To achieve her riches, such as they are, she has traded all that is good and right for unfettered control over her body and her piece of our world," Faucon replied.

As if she heard him, Meg groaned and came upright with a start. Her lip bled where Alf had split it. Hidden behind the fall of her plait, the side of her face was bright red. Yet, despite the pain Alf's blow had surely caused, not a single tear moistened her eyes.

An instant later, her senses steadied and her panicked gaze shot straight to the empty shelf at the back of the room. "Thief!" she trumpeted weakly as she looked to her Crowner. "You've taken my box."

"Your box is on the floor, right where you sent it when you attacked my clerk," Faucon said flatly.

Then, taking Jessimond's clothing out from beneath his arm, he displayed the garments to the woman. "It's not the box you seek, but what was in it. You removed these from Jessimond's corpse on the night she died."

The old woman's face whitened at his charge. Then her eyes narrowed as she again raised that shield of hers, ready to once again engage him in battle. "She was dead when I found her. I wasn't going to let new garments rot on her, not when I'd just spent good coin for them."

Faucon cocked a brow. "Ah, I see. But why would a miser and a thief like you ever open your purse to buy these garments in the first place, especially to clothe one you despised? Let me guess. Could it be because you didn't want Lina the Bawd to see the child she intended to buy dressed in rags? You didn't want the procuress to think you desperate. That might have encouraged the whore to short you on the price you two had finally agreed upon after almost a month of haggling."

Shaking his head, he said, "I fear you overreached yourself this time, and it will cost you far more than just the loaves you lost when Jessimond finished your baking. Your downfall already begins. Until today, no one has dared raise a hand to you. Look at you now, sitting in this pit with a bleeding lip and bruised face."

Meg wiped the blood from her mouth, still glaring at him.

"What a shame you've just buried that fat purse of yours," Faucon continued, speaking as if he commiserated with her. "Now, who among your neighbors will you trust to retrieve it after you're charged with Jessimond's murder? Without that purse, how will you buy your freedom from whatever gaol holds you?"

That sent panic again darting through her gaze. She began to strain and push, trying to herself out of the pit. All the while, she kept her gaze locked on her Crowner as if she feared he might attack her if she looked away.

"It wasn't me," Meg cried as she at last levered herself onto the earthen floor. Using her heels, she shoved herself backward until, panting, she collided with a barrel. "It was Gawne who killed her. It had to have been him. He took her to that hidden spot and killed her, then put her body in our well so it seemed that she had drowned."

"I fear not," Faucon replied. "Rauf and Dob will both swear Gawne spent the whole of that night sleeping inside their walls with their father in a drunken stupor and blocking their doorway."

"Nay!" she cried, her tone filled with new concern. "We didn't kill Jessimond!"

"We, is it?" he replied blandly. "And thus your late return on so many nights this last week, including the one on which Jessimond died. You weren't delayed in Alcester by a friend. You and Lina were waiting beyond the pale for the child to pass so you could snatch her as she escaped into the forest. That way, Lina could carry her off in secret while you tucked more coins into your purse and told your neighbors your ward had run away to whore like her mother." His words were as sharp-edged as his sword.

Jessimond had wanted to meet with Gawne that night to tell him she'd divined Meg's intention, if not the whole of the bakestress's plan. Meg's final beating hadn't been about the bread or the girl's defiance. It had been meant to drive the lass into fleeing to the forest, just as she had eventually done to seek comfort from a friend.

If only. Again, that refrain sang within him.

If only Amelyn had come to Wike early. If only the girl had but held tight to the kitchen for two more short days until her mother's arrival. Amelyn would have instantly understood what Jessimond could not. Faucon wanted to think that mother and daughter would then have run, even if all that lay ahead of them was starvation and death.

From a distance he caught the faint sounds of men and women shouting and singing. The folk of Wike were returning. He glanced behind him to see how far his clerk and Alf were in preparing for the inquest.

Not far. Edmund sat in the wreckage, some of his bits and pieces in his lap as he listened to his employer and the bakestress. Alf stood in the doorway, arms crossed, still as stone, watching with too much interest in what went forward. This, when Faucon needed no witnesses to what he intended.

"They come for the inquest," he said. "Alf, we need that table outside, plus whatever Brother Edmund requires for his use. Brother, best you ready ink and quill," he added as a prod to Edmund.

As both monk and soldier instantly turned to their tasks, Faucon leaned closer to Meg. "But you were doomed to fail from the start. Although Jessimond might not have known the fate you intended for her, she knew you were waiting for her near the hatch. When she finally left Wike, I wager she did it through the holly. How frustrated that bawd must have been by the third night. She must have been demanding that you bring the girl to her in Alcester. But you knew that was impossible. Jessimond would have resisted and John-nie was devoted to her. I've heard his cries. They're ear-piercing. Nay, the only way to wring the profit you wanted from Jessimond was for the child to flee this place on her own, having convinced her uncle to abet her escape as she'd done in the past."

Meg was pressed as flat as possible against the barrel. As her Crowner spoke, she steadily and slowly shook her head side to side, negating his every word. Faucon dipped his fingers into his purse and brought out the bits of thread he'd found in the glade.

"If the bawd was angry at the pale, she must have been furious when the two of you entered that glade to discover her prize was dead. I'm guessing she was so enraged that she tore your apron when she attacked you." As he spoke, he pressed the threads to the breast of Meg's worn apron, right over the new patch.

The woman drew a sharp breath. Her hands began to shake. To hide that, she closed her fists then raised them to her heart. He drew back his hand, returning the threads to his purse.

"These tiny bits are all I need to show the folk of Wike. When I tell them where I found them, and my suppositions about how they came to be there, I'll share my speculations about the fate you intended for Jessimond. I don't even need to mention that your motive was coin. Everyone here will know that," he added, then cocked his head.

"What think you, Meg? If, after I speak my piece, I then call out some other name for them to confirm as Jessimond's killer, someone who doesn't steal food from their hungry babes, what do you think they'll do? Do you think they'll protest that they've heard you more than once threaten to kill the innocents you were meant to protect? And there Jessimond's corpse will be, stretched out upon your table in front of your door. Do you think they'll argue, telling me I'm wrong about who I name? Might they insist that it was you and no other who killed that poor beaten lass? They might even do that in full knowledge that you are truly innocent, instead seizing the moment to rid themselves of the woman who steals from them but is protected by their lady."

Meg swallowed, but she still refused to yield. Instead, she held that shield of hers high even as his blows began to crush it. Outside her kitchen, her neighbors whistled and sang, laughed and chattered as they gathered in her yard.

"But I didn't kill her," she whispered, haggling now, bartering for her life.

Faucon waited to hear what she brought to the table, already certain there was nothing of value in it for him.

"Aye, Lina and I waited in the ditch for Jessimond to pass over us," Meg started. "But as you say, night after night, she didn't come. Then, on the night she died, Hew crossed the ditch right atop us not knowing we were below him. When he reached the other side, he cried out.

"Praying it was Jessimond he saw, I crawled up the ladder once he walked on. That's when I saw the light flickering in the shrubbery and knew it was someone in the woods. I was sure it was the girl!

"Damn Lina!" the old woman snarled then. "It's all her fault we didn't catch the little brat. That bawd is a plodding cow and so afeared of the dark that she wouldn't let me go ahead, nor would she walk any faster for fear of falling. The best I could do was keep my gaze fastened on the light as we trailed it, marking where it went.

"That's how I knew where Jessimond finally stopped. I kept my gaze on the place where the light disappeared, despite that Lina was in terrors once the dark was complete about us. She clutched at my arm and blubbered about the Devil coming for her each time the brambles caught her. Then Jessimond screamed, and at last the stupid bawd found some speed. But by then we were too late. When we entered that place, Jessimond was dead in the bracken. The rushlight was still burning, resting on a stump where the girl had left it."

Meg paused to draw breath, then made an impatient sound. "When Lina saw the girl in the ferns, she cursed me. She accused me of trying to get her charged with murder. As if I wasn't there alongside her?!"

Then the bakestress sneered again. "Aye, she tore my apron when she attacked me, but I was the stronger. I beat her until she cowered, then took my garments off the brat, grabbed the light and left the bawd to her terrors."

"Well now, all you need to prove your innocence is to call this Lina to confirm your story. Do you think she'll come?" Faucon asked, a grim smile upon his lips.

That sent Meg's eyes flying wide. Her mouth opened as if to speak. No word fell from her tongue.

"Since we're haggling," Faucon continued, "it's my turn to show you what I have to offer. In return for my saying nothing about your plot to sell Jessimond, you'll take my man Alf to where you buried your purse and let him retrieve it for you. Then the two of you will go to the abbey, and you'll give half of what your purse contains to the abbot to secure a pension for your nephew."

Her expression flattened in surprise at that. Then, despite that her Crowner would leave her half of what she'd stolen over the years, her fists opened and closed, as if she could not bear to release a penny. She had nothing left in her armory to throw at him save, "Odger will never allow Johnnie out of Wike."

"You may leave the matter of your bailiff to me," he replied in soft assurance as he blocked her last avenue of escape.

Even then, she refused to bow to him. Her jaw tightened in refusal. Resistance flared in her eyes.

Faucon shrugged. "As you will. I'm content to let your neighbors choose. You see, unlike you, I cannot lose. No matter which name the jury in Wike confirms, neither king nor court will be surprised when I add nothing to the royal treasure chests from a place such as this. But every soul in Wike knows about your purse.

And as long as you are locked away in some dungeon, I imagine their search for it will be frenzied and persistent. While they hunt, there you'll be, unable to buy your freedom and starving to death because you put profit over friendship. Perhaps you can find some comfort in the fact that you'll die before the hangman has a chance to stretch your neck," he added.

Meg gagged at that, as if she already felt the rough rope of the noose crushing her throat. She was beaten, her shield bent beyond use, her every weapon broken or discarded, yet her expression said she wanted to spit in his face. At last, moving as if every muscle ached, she came to her feet. There she stood, her chin lifted, hands on her hips, defiant to the end.

"Call your man," was all she said.

Chapter Sixteen

"Well chosen," Faucon said as he rose, Jessimond's clothing yet tucked beneath his arm.

"My garments," Meg said in harsh reminder.

"Jessimond's garments," he replied with a shake of his head. "You gave them to her and she will take them with her into eternity."

Turning, he moved to the doorway, blocking it with his body. Now that his goal was almost in hand, he was unwilling to risk losing her.

Outside, Alf had laid the child's bound corpse on top of the reassembled table that stood before the oven. Given the girl's small size, he'd needed only three of the planks to support her. Abutting the makeshift catafalque was the fourth plank, stretched across two barrels. Arranged in a precise line along one end of this temporary desk were Edmund's writing tools. The monk had pulled another barrel toward the center of this plank to use as a stool, and was mixing his ink in a small wooden bowl. The piece of wood that had saved him from Meg's shovel rested atop one end of their parchment roll, a weight to hold the skin in place against the day's light breeze. From where Faucon stood he could see that board now owned a bit of a curve, rendering it unusable as a desk.

As Alf noticed his new master, he returned to the kitchen door. "Sir?" the commoner asked as he came.

"Alf, Meg has decided to retrieve the purse she

buried. I need you to go with her. I suggest you carry the shovel and dig it up yourself," he said, his words laden with no small amount of sarcasm. "Once you have it, carry it for her to Alcester Abbey. She intends to donate half of its contents to the monks as a pension for Johnnie," he said carefully.

Edmund might be right about the monks and their lack of discipline bringing death to their house. But that day would arrive long after Johnnie had finished his life under the care of a congenial abbot who insisted on a rich kitchen.

Alf studied his new employer for a long moment. "And after that, sir? What would you have me do with her?" was all he asked.

"You may escort her to Hell's door for all I care," Faucon retorted without thought.

The commoner's brows and lips lifted. "Are you certain you want me to go that far afield?"

Faucon dragged his fingers through his hair, then freed a long slow breath. "My pardon. I vow I've had my fill of this end of the shire and all who reside in it. That includes the abbey." Or at least one who dwelt within its walls. "At the moment, I find I'd rather rent an alewife's bed than enter those gates again."

That teased a quiet laugh from the soldier. "Well, as much as I'll regret missing what happens here whilst I'm gone, what say you that once my task with the old woman is complete I go on to Haselor to arrange for your night's stay? Father Otto will happily play host to the monk, while I'm certain 'Wina's kin will be thrilled to offer you the best they have."

"My thanks," Faucon said, startled and pleased by his new man's offer. He stepped outside the door so Alf could enter the kitchen. "That will do very well, Alf."

"Then, until I return, sir," the commoner replied. He picked up Meg's shovel from where he'd leaned it against the outside wall, then paused in the doorway to offer a quick wink. "By the bye, if this is a Crowner's day, then I think we'll do well together, you and I."

That made Faucon laugh. "I fear you'll be disappointed, or so I hope."

Then, having placed the matter of the bakestress into his man's capable hands, Faucon turned to face the yard. Bound with hempen rope, great bundles of branches—faggots for Wike's winter fires— were piled near the decaying manor house. There they would stay until reclaimed at the end of the inquest.

By habit and tradition, the men and boys older than twelve—Faucon gauged that number as no more than sixty of the two hundred or so souls that dwelt in Wike—had drawn close to where Jessimond's corpse was displayed. Faucon found Hew among them, near the back of the group. The rustic leaned heavily on a young man who very much resembled him. As their gazes met, the oldster offered his Crowner a confident nod and a smile. Whatever else, that motion said Hew meant to cause his bailiff grief at this inquest.

As for that bailiff, Odger stood at the forefront of Wike's menfolk, near the foot of the catafalque. His crossed arms and narrowed eyes said he hadn't much like being called like a dog to his Crowner's heel.

Although it wasn't customary for women or children to attend such an event, the wives of Wike hadn't gone on to their homes after their jaunt in the woods. Instead, the mothers, daughters, wives, and sisters of the jurors stood in a nervous but curious group at the back of the jury. Like their menfolk, they carried pruning hooks and shepherds' crooks, for only with these tools could they take wood from the living trees within the king's forest.

As Alf led Meg out of the kitchen, his hand firmly grasping the old woman's upper arm, Odger's arms opened. He stared at the pair in surprise. "Who is this man? Where does he take our bakestress?" he demanded of his Crowner.

"My man-at-arms has agreed to escort Meg as she tends to some private business," Faucon replied, then raised his voice to address Wike's housewives. "As you can see, goodwives, Meg is leaving for the next while but your bread yet bakes in her oven. Who among you will tend it in her stead? I'd not have it said that I allowed your bread to burn."

"I will," replied a young woman, plain but fresh-faced. The clean white cloth she wore upon her head named her married. As she made her way to the oven he saw it in the curve of her lips and the jaunty sway of her hips, and in the way the other women eyed her. This was the one who had dared to defy Meg and steal from the thief.

He looked at Edmund. "What of you, Brother? Did you find everything you need to complete our task today?"

"Aye, I'm ready," the monk replied with a nod, "but you aren't. You've not yet unwrapped the corpse so these men may see how the child's life was ended," he warned in unnecessary instruction to his Crowner. "And your jury is short by three."

Startled, Faucon stared at his clerk in amazement. "You've already tallied and named the jurors?"

Edmund shot him a disbelieving look. "Hardly so. Even *I* am not so swift in my notation," he replied, "but I can see what's in front of me well enough. The smiths are missing when they are required to come, just like the others, and to confirm their earlier oaths regarding the girl's parentage."

Only then did Faucon hear what he'd missed in the continuing raucous noise of migrating waterfowl. There was no clang of hammers from the smithy. That brought him around to Odger. "Bailiff, your jury is not yet assembled. The smiths are missing."

Subtle surprise darted through the bailiff's gaze as he, too, recognized what his Crowner had just noted. He looked at the man standing next to him. It was one of the farmers who'd aided in Jessimond's removal from the well. "Run to Ivo's home and fetch him and his sons."

"Are they there?" the farmer asked, already moving.

"They'd better be," the bailiff retorted to the man's back.

While they waited, Faucon unwound Jessimond's bindings, exposing her head and neck. Death was already ravaging her, expanding her even as she was being consumed from within. Her skin was now green and her neck swollen, thankfully not so much that the bruises on her throat couldn't be distinguished.

It wasn't but a few moments later that the smiths and the farmer jogged into the manor's demesne. Much to Faucon's surprise, Ivo and his sons wore shirts, albeit with no tunics atop them. The linen garments were clean and white, and unblemished by any burn marks.

As they drew near the yard, Odger's chin lifted sharply. "Why did you leave the smithy?" he demanded of Ivo.

"We've repaired or replaced as many axe blades as we can with the supplies at hand. Until you bring us more iron, there's nothing to be done. So we banked the coals and returned home to do our own work," Ivo called back, as he came to a halt behind Edmund's desk. His elder sons started past him, intending to join the other jurors. When their father stayed where he was, they hesitated, then retreated to stand with him.

The smith glanced across the crowd in the yard. "Where is Gawne?" he asked Faucon.

"Yet outlaw, soon to be named murderer," Odger

retorted, then faced the folk he ruled. "We gather here this day to confirm that Gawne, son of Ivo, did murder Jessimond the Whore's Daughter."

Instantly, Edmund thrust up from his barrel to shout, "That is not how this is done, nor is it yours to do! Usurp your place on pain of fine, commoner!" So said the mere clerk as he usurped his Crowner's place to rebuke one he had no right to chide.

If the monk's rebuke didn't surprise Faucon, it caused Odger's mouth to gape and his eyes to widen. Between the monk's scold and their bailiff's reaction, muted laughter rumbled across the jury. It sounded much like distant thunder.

Satisfied at having quelled so unruly a disruption, Edmund seated himself again, then shifted into his native tongue to speak to his employer. "Sir Faucon, your jury is in attendance. You may call for them to swear when you're ready."

Hiding his grin, Faucon called in English, "Men of Wike, you come this day to view your deceased neighbor, Jessimond the Leper's Daughter. Swear you all before God and these men that you will speak the truth if asked to give any information about her death, or about any appraisals or assessments regarding her property and estate."

The idea of anyone in Wike having property or an estate worth valuing teased another amused sound from the watching men. Nonetheless, each of them raised his voice and called, "I so swear!"

From the corner of his eye Faucon watched Ivo and his sons. The younger smiths raised their voices, but not so their sire. Instead, Ivo stared at Edmund's moving quill as if he were enchanted, or perhaps just found the scribing of words upon skin as magical as a player who ate fire.

"Give me a moment," Edmund warned his employer, unaware of Ivo's interest and yet speaking French. His quill scratched, then he nodded and lifted its tip from the parchment. When he looked up at his Crowner, he said, "Sir, before you call them to the corpse, I think we must address the matter of Englishry and the murdrum fine with them."

Faucon blinked. He'd forgotten to tell Edmund that he'd released any hope of collecting that fine. But with the monk's words, the pieces he held within him shifted one last time. Although the change was infinitesimal, he saw how he could wring everything he wanted from this inquest. But only if Edmund complied.

"You're right, we must address the child's birth and the possibility of collecting that fine," he agreed. "But to do so in the way that will best serve our king, I must beg your indulgence, for I will need to breach the usual form of the inquest."

The monk's brow creased at that. He eyed his employer for a quiet moment. "Will what you do win justice for the leper?" he asked softly.

Startled, Faucon eyed his usually rigid clerk, wondering what it was about Amelyn's story that had so touched the monk. "I believe it will."

"But you cannot break the law or all will be for naught," Edmund warned.

"If I tread amiss, warn me," Faucon replied.

The monk freed a long, slow breath. "So I shall. Proceed," he said and turned his gaze back to his parchment.

Faucon took a moment to formulate his words. "Men of Wike, in the matter of Englishry, four of your neighbors have spoken as the law requires," he called out, his voice raised so all could hear. "These four have sworn that the name of the man who fathered Jessimond was unknown at the time of her birth and remains unknown until this day. So too, have I learned from the mouth of Amelyn the Leper that she came with Jessimond after being taken by force in the dark of night by a man whose face she did not see, nor did she recognize him by any other means. Against that, the law requires I declare Jessimond the Leper's Daughter Norman born."

On the other side of the corpse, Odger blanched. The man's reaction told the tale. Wike's lady did not wish to keep her troublesome bailiff at all, and Odger knew that well indeed.

As the bailiff's shock gave way to a desperate need to save his position, he whirled to face those he ruled. "Neighbors!" he bellowed, "I will not let this knight press the murdrum fine on all of us, not when that sum will steal food from the mouths of our children!"

Instantly, everyone in the yard raised their voices, shouting that they would swear the child was English, born and bred. Faucon was about to demand that they quiet when he caught movement at the back of the crowd. It was Hew, supported by that younger version of himself. The two were making their way toward the front of the crowd. As Hew went, he leaned close to each man he passed and spoke. Those men then turned and did the same with the others around them. Within but a few breaths, quiet began to overtake the jurors. Where their menfolk went, the women of Wike followed. Outrage died into a tense silence, fraught with curiosity.

Startled, Odger scanned those he ruled. "Who among you told this knight that the name of Jessimond's sire is unknown? Who among you wishes to see every soul in Wike driven into starvation and penury by such a fine?!" His voice rose steadily until it seemed he raged.

Now at the front of the jurors, Hew turned to face his neighbors, using his grandson as a brace. "I am one of those four," he called out. "As you well know, I am an honest man. But how could I do other than speak the truth to our Crowner? Was I not there, just as you were, the day Amelyn took her punishment for fornication on yon porch?" He waved his twisted fingers in the direction of the manor house. "And on that day did we not all witness how she could not name the man who fathered her child?"

Then the rustic looked around him. "Where are the other three honest men of Wike who spoke these same words?" he demanded.

Yet standing behind Edmund with his father and his brother, Dob took a step forward. His younger brother stood with his head shyly bent. Ivo did the same, but the elder smith's hands were folded as if in prayer.

"Rauf and I did the same, as did my sire. Odger," Dob pleaded to the bailiff, "we didn't know what the knight intended when he asked about Jessimond. But I think even if we had, we could not have lied. How, when it's common knowledge that the name of Jessimond's sire has never been spoken? Aye, even Jessimond doesn't...didn't know the name of the man who sired her, or so Gawne has told us."

"Who can believe testimony given by the one who killed this girl!" Odger shot back, a new edge to his voice.

That gave Faucon the opening he needed. "The boy didn't kill the leper's daughter," he said, then called to the smith's middle lad. "Rauf, will you confirm what Gawne told me, that on the night Jessimond died, your younger brother never left your shared pallet?"

"I will," the boy replied. Although his voice was quiet, the yard was so still his words rang out like a bell.

As a murmur rolled over the watching folk Faucon moved on, his gaze connecting jurors standing closest to the corpse as he pointed to the bruises that marked the girl's neck. "Moreover, see here. The one who laid these marks upon her neck has the hands of a man not a boy."

He positioned his hands above the marks, not quite touching the girl's flesh, then slowly closed his fingers as if squeezing. That set a few of those closest to Jessimond looking at their own hands, then eying the marks on the dead girl's neck.

"Aye," Faucon encouraged them, "now you see what I do. A small lad like Gawne couldn't have done this." He scanned the crowd before him. "Instead, she was not only killed by a man full grown, but by the man who fathered her."

That sent an excited ripple across the watchers. They watched him eagerly, but Faucon didn't give them what they wanted. Instead, he shifted to look at Odger.

"So bailiff, if you wish to avoid the murdrum fine, call now to the men of Wike. Demand that the one who sired this girl step forward at this late date and claim his daughter. Demand that this man admit he took Amelyn against her will, setting fertile seed into the womb of a woman he believed to be barren. Make this man confess that on the day you laid an unfair and deadly punishment upon an innocent woman, he held his tongue like the coward he is to protect himself. Then, when this man has confessed, let his neighbors confirm him as Jessimond's killer."

Faucon again sent his gaze across his jurors. "Or perhaps none of you believe that one of your own might have done such a heinous thing to a woman who was a neighbor and a friend. In that case, which of you is willing to let the hangman take you so your bailiff might retain his position? For if no man speaks, I fear your lady will dismiss him, doing so because he overstepped your traditions when he forced Amelyn to whore. How can your lady do any less when she learns that it's because of her bailiff that she must open her purse?"

This time the sound that made its way across the yard was stronger and darker. Some jurors eyed each other, heads shaking in worry or, mayhap, disbelief. Others locked their gazes on Odger, brows lowering. But still they held their tongues.

Their wives and mothers weren't so subtle. The women whispered as they moved and shifted between each other. The sound of their voices rose and fell like gentle waves upon the ocean.

"What nonsense is this?" Odger demanded, his expression a disdainful mask. "Our lady has no cause to dismiss me, because there will be no murdrum fine for Wike. If you know the name of the man who both fathered and killed Jessimond, raise your voice, Crowner. Tell us who it is."

"So I shall, Odger of Wike, but only when the others tell me they're ready to move on."

"I have told you," Odger shot back in command. "Speak the name."

"This is an inquest, not a field of wheat. Here, you are but an equal to the others and one among many. Be patient and wait until they've had their say," Faucon said in calm reply.

That sent Odger around to face those under his command. "Raise your voices! Demand that this new Crowner reveal the murderer's name so we may confirm it, bury the leper's daughter, and get on with our day!"

But those men he had controlled until this moment now held their tongues. There was no sound in the yard save that continuing hiss of whispers from the women. Faucon waited another moment, then raised his voice to fill the fragrant air around the kitchen. "I have waited long enough for your reply," he said, then shifted to look at the smiths.

Like the others in the yard, Dob and Rauf stood

with arms crossed and mouths tight, their gazes fixed on Odger. Not so Ivo. He still watched Edmund's parchment. His clasped hands were pressed to his heart now. That had sent his shirt sleeves back, sliding down to the middle of his forearms, revealing the ring of small bruises around his left wrist, the marks Jessimond had left as she tried to keep her sire from ending her life.

"Ivo the Smith, I name you murderer of Jessimond the Leper's Daughter," Faucon called out. "I also charge you with the rape of Amelyn of Wike thirteen years ago."

A sharp sound of astonishment rattled both the men and women in the yard. Ivo swayed, but he didn't lift his head. Instead, he opened his hands and buried his face into his palms.

Rauf stared at his father, his face white and his eyes wide. Dob's mouth moved. It took him two tries before he managed to expel his words.

"Da! Tell the knight he's wrong. Tell him. Tell me!" he shouted, anger overtaking shock.

Ivo's shoulders began to shake. His head remained bowed, his face yet hidden in his hands.

"Nay, Da!" Dob sobbed, then turned to look at his neighbors. "You all know my father! He's kind and gentle, almost too much so. He couldn't have hurt Jessimond."

As he pleaded, Faucon shifted to look at Hew. The rustic met his gaze, frowning and shaking his head. Faucon raised his brows in prodding encouragement. The old man's eyes widened in surprise. Then understanding dawned in the man's eyes.

"This I cannot believe," Hew called out an instant later. "I say our new Crowner is mistaken."

There was a swift rustling as every soul within the yard turned to watch the rustic.

"There is no mistake," the bailiff bellowed as he looked at Faucon. "Call for us to confirm the verdict, so we can put this sorry affair behind us."

"In a moment," Faucon replied with a careless shrug. "I'd like to hear why the rustic believes I'm wrong. Speak on, old man," he said.

Hew shifted to face the jury. "Hear me now, neighbors. I was with Amelyn and Sir Faucon at the well yesterday when she told her tale of rape. Aye, she said that the one who'd taken her held her face-down so she couldn't see him, and that he said not a word as he did the deed. But when our Crowner asked Amelyn who she thought had done this awful deed, it was Odger she named, not the smith," he called, shifting to point his twisted hand at the bailiff. "She said that the only man who could have done this to her was the same man who had tried and failed to take her two months before."

Gasps and cries rose from the watching women. One old woman sat hard upon the ground and began to rock, head bowed and arms tight across her mid-section. Another woman stared straight ahead, her gaze glazed as silent tears flowed unnoticed down her cheeks. More than a few threw arms around each other, as if they needed support to remain afoot.

Odger's face darkened. He took a step toward Hew, his fists closed in threat. "Slander me at your peril, old man. I did not take Amelyn, not on that day. Not ever."

A raging shout exploded from the old woman seated on the ground. She came to her knees. Her fists were pressed to her temples as she screamed, "Liar! Liar! I know you took Amelyn. You must have. Why not her, when you took me against my will?!"

"Are you mad?!" Odger shouted at her. "I never touched you, Bet."

Then he shifted to address the men he commanded. "I see what this is. You all know how Hew hates me.

Now see how the useless ancient plots against me—" he jabbed his forefinger at Hew. "He has recruited Bet to lie for him as he seeks to dislodge me from my rightful place. Heed him on pain of your lives and that of your children. Without me to speak for us, our lady will soon forget that we exist. You heard Ivo. We need her coin to buy the iron for our tools. We need her to speak for us with the king's foresters so we can continue to gather wood and more from his forest." The wave of his hand indicated the faggots near the manor house. "Without me, Wike will die!"

Those he addressed stayed silent, frowning as they glanced from him to Hew to the kneeling woman.

"It wasn't just Bet and Amelyn that our bailiff took." It was the woman who cried the silent tears who spoke. Her face was white. She drew a ragged breath, then spewed, "He used me, too."

When the last word left her lips, her eyes rolled back in her head and she crumpled to lie senseless on the ground.

"They both lie! I did no such thing," Odger shouted again, but there was a new, panicked edge to his voice. As he spoke, he stepped backward only to collide with the planks supporting Jessimond, jostling her corpse.

Near the center of the jurors, a young man threw back his head. His bellow was wordless, the sound raw and feral. When he lowered his head, he raced toward his bailiff, the pruning hook in his hands raised for a killing blow.

"My mother doesn't lie! You used my mother!" he shouted as he came.

Chapter Seventeen

It was almost Vespers when Faucon returned to the headless cross that marked Coctune on the Street. Edmund waited there, atop his little donkey. Someone had given the monk a sack in which to carry his tools and he'd used the strap from his ruined basket to lash it to his saddle.

While Edmund had remained in Wike to record the names of the jurors after they confirmed Ivo as Jessimond's murderer, Faucon had torn the smith from the arms of his yet-disbelieving sons. Ivo had offered neither word nor resistance as he'd walked alongside the mounted knight to Studley. Once there, he had freely given himself into the custody of Sir Peter's steward.

Now, as Edmund urged his stubborn mount into the road, Faucon glanced into the hamlet of Coctune. Four men stood in front of the house in which Odger presently lay, broken and beaten, guarding the former bailiff from those he had once ruled. That he had not gone to Studley with Ivo was Edmund's doing. Although the men of Wike had insisted on confirming Odger as a rapist at the same time they confirmed the verdict of murder against Ivo, the monk warned his Crowner that Odger would never stand for his crime, not when the necessary proof was lacking. None of the women had been heard crying out during the bailiff's attack, nor had any of them called for her neighbors to aid her during Odger's attack, nor had any raised the hue and cry once the man had finished with them.

That left the men of Wike with nothing more than the hope that their former bailiff died of his injuries. As for Faucon, he found himself hoping no one took the matter of Odger's continued life into his own hand. Faucon didn't much want to return to this place for another inquest.

"Sir, despite the smith's confession, I still don't understand how you knew to accuse him," Edmund said breathlessly, when he finally got his mount aimed in the right direction.

"I wasn't certain until I spoke with Gawne in the glade," Faucon replied, stirring himself from his sour thoughts. "After what the lad told me, I was certain Amelyn hadn't ended her life because of grief, but to protect yet another innocent."

That only won him a stunned and disbelieving look from his gasping clerk. The sound of Edmund's choppy breathing almost made Faucon smile. He needed no more to tell him that the monk's back was bruised and the motion of his donkey was aggravating it. He'd won a similar bruise during a melee and suffered much the same.

"It's what the boy told Amelyn, about how Dob had offered to wed with Jessimond to save her from Meg but that Ivo hadn't agreed to the plan until the day after Jessimond was dead." Faucon sighed. "Instead of comfort, the boy's words broke her heart. You were there when I challenged Amelyn's memories of that night, questioning her certainty that Odger had done the deed. I think that from that moment on, Amelyn's years of denial began to crumble. By the time she heard Gawne's story, she could no longer avoid what she must have always known, that Ivo had been the one to rape her. After the lad told her his tale, she also knew that Ivo had killed their daughter to prevent his elder son from marrying his half-sister."

Mourning a woman he barely knew, Faucon trained his gaze between Legate's ears as he continued. "With that, everyone Amelyn loved was gone or destroyed in her memory, save for the cripple, and even he would be forever more denied her, while she faced a lingering and painful death. In that moment, she must have believed preventing her daughter's beloved friend from becoming an orphan gave some meaning to her life."

Faucon fell silent, dragged deep into his own guilt. If only. If only Amelyn had waited for him, or been willing to entrust him with what she'd learned. But so long had the poor woman suffered the betrayals of the men around her that she no longer believed any man worthy of her trust. Her ploy had almost succeeded. For a single instant after Hew had revealed Amelyn owed coin to Alcester's procuress, Faucon had believed her capable of killing Jessimond, if only to save her daughter from being made to whore. But then he remembered that Amelyn was Amelyn, a woman willing to take the lash to protect another.

"But how could the smith even find the girl to kill her, when he was drunk in his doorway?"

Edmund's question stirred him out of his dark thoughts. Faucon shot a surprised sidelong look at his clerk. "Ivo wasn't besotted that night, despite what his sons said. As for finding the girl, you heard the smith. He all but told us outright that he'd known from the beginning where his son and Jessimond were meeting."

"He did no such thing," Edmund retorted. "Nor can you say that he did! Remember, I was there with you. I heard what he said."

That teased a laugh from Faucon. "Brother, you need to listen with more than your ears. The smith said he and Amelyn had been to each other what Jessimond and Gawne were. Why do you think Amelyn chose that glade as the place to meet her daughter?"

He waited for Edmund's reply, but the monk only shook his head in confusion, so he answered his own question.

"Because it was the same place where she and her precious childhood playmate had shared their happiest hours. When Gawne escaped into the woods, his father kept watch but carefully. I cannot say when, but at some time Ivo must have come upon his son and Jessimond in that glade. Thus did Ivo turn his back on his neighbors when they complained about Gawne and Jessimond. He thought he was giving his grieving child the same happiness he'd known, and giving him the sister Gawne didn't know he had, just as he was giving his daughter the family he denied her. Remember how Ivo protested that Gawne and Jessimond were naught but innocent children sharing joy? How could he know that unless he'd seen it?

"Then everything went awry when Dob offered to wed Jessimond. Ivo is a coward. He could neither confess what he'd done nor was it in him to stand firm against his son's choice of wife. That left him no choice but to end his daughter's life, something I doubt he would have done if he'd known Amelyn was yet visiting Wike. It must have been easier to plan to murder the child when he thought he was sparing her a life of abuse and pain, one bereft of her mother's love," he added, thinking again on the smith's shock as the leper made her race for the well.

Here, Faucon fell silent, unwilling to share with Edmund the rest of the tale, the part that included Meg and how she and the bawd had appeared in that glade within minutes after Jessimond's death. As Ivo must have slunk back into hiding, avoiding discovery before he had removed Jessimond's body as he surely would have planned, the man's fate was sealed. Not because of what he'd done, but because the court had stripped away some of Sir Alain's duties. For if the sheriff had come to Wike it was a sure thing that Ivo would have held his tongue even as Gawne died in his place. Such was the depths of the man's cowardice.

Frustration streamed from the monk on a harsh breath. "I vow, I'll never be able to what you do, no matter how hard I try."

"Nor do you need to," Faucon said with a grin, "not as long as one of us can do it. Isn't that what you said to me yesterday? We both have our roles to play in this."

Nodding at that, Edmund glanced across the wastes to the edge of the forest. "Do you think they'll ever get the idiot to leave that glade?"

"Aye, I think he'll go once both Amelyn and Jessimond are laid to rest." Again, he withheld suppositions from his clerk. There was no point in sharing that he believed the idiot was Odger's bastard son, and likely not the only child the bailiff had fathered in Wike. Thus had Martha known to stay close to Amelyn on the day that Odger sought to take her. So too was that why Amelyn's stepmother had fought so hard to keep her damaged babe alive. Martha had wanted her bailiff to look upon what he'd created for each and every day of his life.

There was motion ahead of him on the Street. Lifting himself in his stirrups, Faucon eyed the riders coming toward him. One man was mounted atop a piebald, naming him Alf. The other rode a courser as white as Legate, save for black stockings the same color as the hair of his rider.

What little satisfaction Faucon had managed to retain over this day's resolution died. Holy Mother of God. What was his brother doing here at this end of Warwickshire? More importantly, was Will sane? Faucon's hand dropped to his sword. If not, blood would definitely be shed.

Martinmas

How could I have faltered when He not only led me to her, but fair placed her in my arms? Instead, I was careless.

The whip flies. The knotted cords bite into my back. My flesh tears. Blood flows.

A part of me whimpers, complaining that she was stronger than I expected. That she awakened without warning. That she flew from my arms before I was prepared. It was dark. The wind howled, hiding her from me as it tossed branches and bent grasses. The rain fell in sheets, making it impossible to see.

On and on the excuses flow when they are nothing but excuses. Again the cords tear into my back. Sinful! Weak!

I beg my Lord to answer, if not to give me the forgiveness I crave, then to reveal that He is yet with me, that I remain precious to Him. There is naught but silence and emptiness where once there was presence.

Lost in self-pity, I beg Saint Martin to bear a message to our heavenly Father. To no avail. I am no longer his comrade-in-arms, battling beside him to save souls.

All is lost. I am abandoned.

A Note From Denise

Thank you for reading this third book of my new mystery series. I hope you enjoyed Faucon and his third investigation as his shire's new Crowner. If you liked the book, or I suppose even if you didn't, consider leaving a review. If you've found any formatting or typographical errors, please let me know by email at denisedomning@gmail.com. I appreciate the chance to correct my mistakes!

I have to admit I absolutely enjoyed adding Alf to the team of sleuths I'm assembling. He stepped onto these page fully formed and wonderfully alive.

By the way, you'll find Oswald de Vere and Bishop William making appearances in my Seasons Series

Glossary

This book includes of number of Medieval terms. I've defined the ones I think might be unfamiliar to you. If you find others you'd like defined, let me know at denisedomning@gmail.com and I'll add them to the list.

Braies   A man's undergarment. Made from a single piece of linen that is tied around the waist with a cord. Worn more or less like a loin cloth but more voluminous so the garment can be arranged to cover the hips and thighs.

Chausses   Stockings made of cloth (not knitted). Each leg ties onto the waist cord of the braies.

Crowner   From the Latin *Coronarius,* meaning Servant of the Crown. The word eventually evolves into 'Coroner'

Dower   The bridegroom's offering to his bride. Generally dower should be one-third the value of the bride's dowry. Dower is an annuity for the wife, meant to support her after her husband's death. She holds her dower for her life time, and can accrue dower over the course of multiple marriages. Upon her death, her dower returns to the heirs of the original owner.

Dowry | What the bride brings to her husband upon marriage. Depending on her class, this can be a throne, estates, a skill (such as needlework), or in the case of peasant brides, pots and pans and other household goods.

Hauberk | A heavy leather or padded vest, sometimes sewn with steel rings. Usually worn in place of a chain mail tunic by common soldiers

Hemp | A soft, strong fiber plant with edible seeds. Hemp can be twisted into rope or woven for use in making everything from storage bags to mattress covers.

Pleas of the Crown
The list of pleas made to the king or his representative for justice. Not unlike the list of crimes and complaints filed at your local police station.

Shivaree | The serenading of the newly wedded and bedded couple by their guests to distract them from consummating their marriage

Toft and Croft A toft is the area of land on which a peasant's house sits. The croft, generally measuring seven hundred feet in length and forty in width. It was in the croft that a serf would grow their personal food staples, such as onions, garlic, turnips and other root crops, legumes and some grains.

Withe   A thin, supple willow (but also hazel or ash) branch

CPSIA information can be obtained
at www.ICGtesting.com
Printed in the USA
LVHW031111051220
673420LV00048B/1901